Posthumanist Readings in Dystopian Young Adult Fiction

Children and Youth in Popular Culture

Series Editor: Debbie Olson, Missouri Valley College

Children and Youth in Popular Culture features works that interrogate the various representations of children and youth in popular culture, as well as the reception of these representations. The series is international in scope, recognizing the transnational discourses about children and youth that have helped shape modern and postmodern childhoods and adolescence. The scope of the series ranges from such subjects as gender, race, class, and economic conditions and their global intersections with issues relevant to children and youth and their representation in global popular culture: children and youth at play, geographies and spaces (including the World Wide Web), material cultures, adultification, sexuality, children of/in war, religion, children of diaspora, youth and the law, and more.

Advisory Board

LuElla D'Amico, Whitworth University
Markus P. J. Bohlmann, Seneca College
Vibiana Bowman Cvetkovic, Rutgers University
Adrian Schober, Australian Catholic University, Melbourne

Titles in the Series

Posthumanist Readings in Dystopian Young Adult Fiction: Negotiating the Nature/Culture Divide, by Jennifer Harrison
The Sidekick Comes of Age: How Young Adult Literature is Shifting the Sidekick Paradigm, by Stephen M. Zimmerly
Female Adolescent Sexuality in the United States, 1850-1965, by Ann Kordas
Tweencom Girls: Gender and Adolescence in Disney and Nickelodeon Sitcoms, by Patrice A. Oppliger
Representing Agency in Popular Culture: Children and Youth on Page, Screen, and In Between, edited by Ingrid E. Castro and Jessica Clark
The Feeling Child: Affect and Politics in Latin American Literature and Film, edited by Philippa Page, Inela Selimović, and Camilla Sutherland
The Rhetorical Power of Children's Literature, edited by John H. Saunders
Children in the Films of Steven Spielberg, edited by Debbie Olson and Adrian Schober
The Child in World Cinema, edited by Debbie Olson
Girls' Series Fiction and American Popular Culture, edited by Luella D'Amico
Indians in Victorian Children's Narratives: Animalizing the Native, 1830–1930, by Shilpa Bhat Daithota
The Rhetorical Power of Children's Literature, edited by John Saunders
Misfit Children: An Inquiry into Childhood Belongings, edited by Markus P. J. Bohlmann
The Américas Award: Honoring Latino/a Children's and Young Adult Literature of the Americas, edited by Laretta Henderson
Critical Childhood Studies and the Practice of Interdisciplinarity: Disciplining the Child, edited by Magdalena Zolkos and Joanna Faulkner

Posthumanist Readings in Dystopian Young Adult Fiction

Negotiating the Nature/Culture Divide

Jennifer Harrison

LEXINGTON BOOKS
Lanham • Boulder • New York • London

Published by Lexington Books
An imprint of The Rowman & Littlefield Publishing Group, Inc.
4501 Forbes Boulevard, Suite 200, Lanham, Maryland 20706
www.rowman.com

6 Tinworth Street, London SE11 5AL

Copyright © 2019 by The Rowman & Littlefield Publishing Group, Inc.

All rights reserved. No part of this book may be reproduced in any form or by any electronic or mechanical means, including information storage and retrieval systems, without written permission from the publisher, except by a reviewer who may quote passages in a review.

British Library Cataloguing in Publication Information Available

Library of Congress Cataloging-in-Publication Data

Names: Harrison, Jennifer, 1983– author.
Title: Posthumanist readings in dystopian young adult fiction : negotiating the nature/culture divide / Jennifer Harrison.
Description: Lanham : Lexington Books, 2019. | Series: Children and youth in popular culture | Includes bibliographical references and index.
Identifiers: LCCN 2019004924 (print) | LCCN 2019012971 (ebook) | ISBN 9781498573368 (Electronic) | ISBN 9781498573351 (cloth) | ISBN 9781498573375 (pbk.)
Subjects: LCSH: Young adult fiction, American—21st century—History and criticism. | Dystopias in literature.
Classification: LCC PS374.Y57 (ebook) | LCC PS374.Y57 H37 2019 (print) | DDC 813/.6099283—dc23
LC record available at https://lccn.loc.gov/2019004924

Contents

Introduction: Young Adult Dystopia and the Posthuman Perspective   1

1   Carrie Ryan's Forest of Hands and Teeth: Sex, Infection, and Hopelessness   19
2   Lois Lowry's The Giver: Biotechnology, Wilderness, and Government   35
3   Patrick Ness's Chaos Walking Trilogy: Language and the Nonhuman Other   51
4   Neal Shusterman's Unwind: Posthuman Recycling and the Death of the Hero   67
5   Philip Reeve's Mortal Engines Series: Posthumanism, Evolution, Apocalypse, and Time   83
6   Adam Rapp and Mike Cavallaro's *Decelerate Blue*: Solarpunk, Consumerism, and the Posthumanist Future   103

Conclusion: Young Adult Dystopia and the Posthuman Perspective   119

Bibliography   127

Index   137

About the Author   139

Introduction

Young Adult Dystopia and the Posthuman Perspective

Going back at least as far as Lois Lowry's *The Giver*, and perhaps even further back to sci-fi classics such as *Z for Zachariah*, *Day of the Triffids*, and *The Handmaid's Tale*, dystopia has proven enduringly popular with young adult (YA) audiences, and has enjoyed a boom in popularity following the publication (and subsequent translation into blockbuster films) of series such as Veronica Roth's Divergent and Suzanne Collins' Hunger Games. The YA dystopian genre continues to develop in new and exciting directions, expanding into comics and graphic novels, as well as film and television with texts such as Adam Rapp and Mike Cavallaro's *Decelerate Blue*, Columbia Pictures' *The 5th Wave*, and HBO's *The 100*.

With greater popularity, however, has come greater scrutiny. Media critics have delighted in condescending remarks about the trend of "adults" succumbing to the pleasures of the "childish" YA genre; some have even suggested that readers "set aside the transparently trashy stuff like *Divergent* and *Twilight*, which no one defends as serious literature" (Graham, 2014). Of course, what such condescension ignores is the tremendous influence these immensely popular "trashy" books and series have on large numbers of young and adult readers alike. Professor of English Lisa Rowe Fraustino (2011) offers the following explanation for the growing fascination with YA dystopia in the popular imagination:

> We want to hold on to our individuality, our humanity, our ability to love and connect to others. We have always wanted to hold on, but in today's global communications network we can't avoid facing overwhelming obstacles. The

more we understand how small and powerless we really are against the immense forces that control our existence, the more we yearn to feel meaningful.

Part of a wider *New York Times* debate on the importance and relevance of the YA dystopian genre, Fraustino's remarks situate the genre firmly within a sociopolitical context specific to the conditions of a global technological era. As such, it brings into focus the urgent need for a defense of YA fiction as a genre that is not only popular, but also socially and politically relevant.

Fraustino's comments are interesting not only because they set out to defend the relevance of the YA dystopia genre, but also because they highlight a fundamental tension in the global technological era between humanist values and ideologies ("our individuality" and "our ability to love" for example) and lived experiences which have increasingly come to be understood as posthuman. Posthumanism can be broadly understood as any representation or critical discourse that speculates about radical changes in what it means to be human. Some of these are bodily changes, which speculate about the effects of technologies such as artificial intelligence, IVF and designer babies, or mind-altering pharmaceuticals. Other changes are social and political, and include expanding understanding of alternative sexualities, the differently abled, animals, and so on. Still more speculative changes are philosophical in nature and question the assumption that human beings are separate and distinct from nonhuman other and their environment. As we will see shortly, all iterations of the posthuman problematize humanist notions of a universal human nature ("all humans are autonomous individuals" or "all humans love") upon which the desires identified by Fraustino are based. As Fraustino's comments suggest, these desires are increasingly untenable and unrealistic in a world that is increasingly posthuman. Dystopia, therefore, can be understood as a literal depiction of this tension—a portrayal of the failure of humanist ideologies. Despite the apocalyptic nature of many dystopian narratives, dystopia is not the threat of the end of the human (who always seems to keep going) but the threat of the end of humanism.

More specifically, most dystopias (including YA dystopias) primarily engage with a single, overarching humanist assumption: that human beings can be defined in their difference to and separation from an environment[1] of nonhuman others (with "nonhuman" defined both loosely and subjectively most of the time). Anthropologist Layla AbdelRahim (2015) argues convincingly in her introduction to *Children's Literature, Domestication, and Social Foundation* that much of human civilization has been premised on this notion, and that the values and practices of many human societies take protection from a dangerous and hostile environment as a starting point. She argues that this assumption provides justification for societies structured around notions of control, eventually culminating in the social philosophies of

Hobbes and Locke, which were themselves foundational to humanism as we know it today.

In many YA dystopias, however, humanist control—and therefore humanist society—is violently disrupted by the dissolution of the barrier between human and environment. Whether that disruption is the result of zombies, nuclear holocaust, warfare, or natural disaster, these dystopias' apocalyptic starting points break down the barrier between society and environment, exposing human bodies and minds to the hostile "outside." Human beings in these narratives return to a state of vulnerability, at the mercy of sickness, the climate, predators, and inter-human exploitation and violence. However, as they depict human beings attempting to adapt and survive in these new conditions, it is often the original (humanist) society and philosophies that are called into question: that which led to apocalypse in the first place. Many YA dystopias, therefore, now flirt with the idea that it may not be the human *loss of* control, but the human *need or desire for* control that is dystopian.

The purpose of this book is argue that in YA dystopian fiction, YA authors are in fact adopting didactic modes ideally suited to a social ethics of the Anthropocene. They do so by exploring posthumanist possibilities alongside their attack on humanist ideologies: YA dystopian texts provide models for how young people can positively negotiate between the development of individual subjectivity and collective identity; they offer new ways of considering concepts such as time, progress, evolution, and development; they reconsider binary constructions and hierarchies; they renegotiate and reconsider social structures such as the family and the community; and finally, they depict identity and bodies as fluid, fractured, and mutable. Furthermore, what is of fundamental importance is the way in which each of these functions ties into a larger reconsideration of the relationship of human individuals to an environment that has traditionally been construed in humanist society as hostile, threatening, and separate. Whether these authors and texts are accepting, ambivalent, or hostile to the posthuman societies and values they depict, they all explore the end of humanism as a real and immanent threat.

HUMANISM AND THE ANTHROPOCENE: WHERE WE ARE NOW

If one wishes to understand the ways in which humanist ideology might contribute to many of the issues we face today, then dystopian literature is an ideal starting place. The very definition of a "utopia"—and by extension of dystopia also—is based on humanist assumptions about the binary separation of the human from the environment, which posits the carefully planned societies of Thomas Moore and other utopian writers as the height of human civilization, as distinct from "uncivilized" nature. As AbdelRahim (2015) explains: "Civilization is the sum of domesticated relationships with everything material and symbolic that issues from the labour and consumption of those categorized as resources and the (necessarily) unequal value for that labour, victimhood, and lives" (8), and "this awareness of difference and separatedness, coupled with a narrative that legitimates hierarchy, gave birth to humanism" (9).

AbdelRahim's concept of control can be seen clearly at play in a central concept of posthumanist thought: that of the Anthropocene. The Anthropocene is a term referring to what has been proposed as a new geological epoch, dating from the point at which humans began to have a significant impact on the earth's geology and ecosystems (Ellis, 2018). As such, it is fundamentally humanist, concerning itself with the power and centrality of human beings. The Anthropocene is all about control of a hostile environment; impacts such as climate change, deforestation, mass extinction, and even war and genocide can be understood as results of the perceived need of societies to control their environments through technology and violence. Human societies battle constantly against each other and their environments for comfort and security: we seek to control the weather, manage resources, remove threats such as predators and competitors, and even cheat death. Humanism as a philosophy and, as a social framework, provides both the tools and the ideologies for this control, justifying environmental exploitation and destruction, social inequality, war and genocide, and the scientific manipulation of the basic building blocks of life itself, all in the name of human progress, which, at heart, means progress away from the chaos and unpredictability of nature, toward total human domination of the planet and everything (and everyone) on it. Utopia exists only when this total domination has been achieved, allowing human civilization to thrive unchecked by threat or opposition. In contrast, when control fails and civilization succumbs to opposition and threat, the dystopia is born.

Of course, this dream of domination rests on a crucial tension: that which exists between the universal "human," and the distinct and varied individuals who drift into and out of that category. "Civilization," therefore, has made demands as varied as the demonization and extinction of wolves, the designation of dark-sinned individuals as subhuman slaves, and the destruction of vast tracks of rainforest to make way for bio-fuel crops. Such demands achieve the control of "humans" (as a universal category) over their environment by explicitly designating (specific) Others as "nonhuman." John Stephens (1992) defines humanist philosophy as the conviction that "there is an essential human nature which underlies all changing surface appearances; important human qualities, such as Reason, Love, Honour, Loyalty, Courage, etc., are transhistorical; [and] human desires are reasonably constant, unchanging truths" (203). Such an assumption, however, demands that essentially subjective concepts such as "reason" or "love" be defined explicitly (and exclusively) so that they can be used to categorize those who do or do not possess them as either human or nonhuman. The wolf, for example, was not only a threat to human lives and livelihoods, but was a justifiable target for violence because it lacked "human" abilities such as love, reason, and honor; the same argument has at different times been applied to Jews (a threat to Aryan "civilization") and Native Americans (a threat to American "civilization"). In a similar manner the destruction of rainforests or the manipulation of human, plant, and animal genes have been justified as the exercise of human "reason" over a chaotic, unreasoning environment.

Humanism, in other words, establishes constantly changing and evolving binary oppositions: human/primate, human/negro, human/madman, human/ wilderness, human/livestock, and human/microbe to name but a few. While humanism holds the first part of these binaries as steady and constant, that which occupies the second half, or "outside" of the binary, evolves constantly according to sociopolitical contexts: the negro and the madman have been shifted firmly into the "inside," for example, as a result of expanding concepts about "human rights," while the primate hovers on the verge of inclusion as anthropologists and zoologists learn more about the origins and DNA of the *homo* genus. That which is categorized as "human" has the right to control; that which is not needs to be controlled for civilization to thrive and utopia to be achieved. The Anthropocene, therefore, is fundamentally about control: control that is achieved through clear distinctions between outside and inside: the binary oppositions of human/nonhuman, civilization/wilderness, and order/chaos are the foundations of modern society.

YA DYSTOPIA AND THE END OF HUMANISM: WHERE WE ARE GOING

If humanism preaches the ascendancy of the human over the environment and nonhuman others, then the achievement of this perfect control must be humanist utopia, and its loss humanist dystopia. As David Sisk (1997) explains, utopian vision can be understood as predicated upon the assumption that "men can perfect themselves by creating the right environment" while dystopian thought doubts "our race's capability consciously to subordinate individual drives and desires to the needs of the greater social whole" (4). It is therefore no surprise that, as we move into a modern, global information era, dystopia seems to be in the ascendancy. Globalization and the democratization of information that has followed in its wake is characterized by a plurality of voices, identities, and modes of being: plurality that has increasingly placed pressure on humanist assumptions. While each member of a utopia lives in a state of carefully managed, orderly sameness (in More's utopia everything from emotions to items of clothing are regulated), dystopias often revel in the messiness, the randomness, and the chaotic freedom that attends the breakdown of humanist society—a breakdown that frequently makes space for those traditionally placed on the outside of humanist binary pairings. Marius De Geus (1999) states that "Utopias do not seem to suit a period which is characterized by pragmatism, postmodernism, and a lack of faith in all-encompassing ideologies and idealistic political visions" (19). All-encompassing is the key word here: dystopia is fundamentally about the fragmentation of humanism's unifying vision. Dystopias often achieve this by depicting either societies or bodies that have been breached from the outside: *The Handmaid's Tale*, for example, which depicts bodies rendered semi-sterile by environmental pollution and toxicity, or *Brave New World*'s depiction of genetically modified humans. In novels such as these, the category of "human" is challenged by intrusion, often resulting in extreme measures being taken to reestablish control over and clarity of boundaries. The women of *The Handmaid's Tale*, for example, are severely repressed in an attempt to reassert control over natural reproduction, while the genetic modifications in Huxley's World State are a result of attempts to control disease, aging, and death, but which also results in social stratification and inequality in the name of the humanist reason/unreason binary.

YA dystopias provide a further level of engagement with this inherent critique of humanism in that they often depict characters whose bodies and futures are in a "natural" state of constant flux: who embody, in other words, the nonessentialist and fluid human subject. The posthuman body—such as the cyborg, alien hybrid, or clone—has always been a key feature of dystopia, but a recent shift has occurred in a great deal of specifically YA dystopia from depicting posthuman bodies as the catalyst for dystopias that imagine the catastrophic destruction of the liberal humanist subject and humanist ideologies, to dystopias that depict the catastrophic results of liberal humanist subject positions and ideologies on the natural environment and human species as a whole. One reason for this shift is the observation of Kay Sambell (2004) that there is an inherent tension between the YA focus on individual development and a happy ending, and the dystopian genre's conventions of ambivalence and open-endedness. It is often in the attempt to resolve this tension that posthuman and posthumanist motifs emerge. Leif Sorensen (2014) identifies a tension in dystopian or postapocalyptic narratives "between depicting the apocalypse as an occasion for a humanist renaissance and as a traumatic break that initiates a period of becoming post-human" (566), but which either way forecloses the possibility of a complete and final ending. However, the YA genre's dependence on *bildungsroman* narratives of development demand a happy ending: compromise is therefore reached by depicting or at least hinting toward a future dependent not on resolution, but on change. Dystopias, therefore, may both reinforce humanist ideologies (they are the lost utopia) and at the same time—by insisting on the necessity of change—resist those same ideologies. In doing so, they gesture toward something other than utopia or dystopia: they gesture toward the posthuman.

POSTHUMANISM: WHERE WE MIGHT END UP

As a theoretical framework that allows for interrogation of the ontological boundaries of humanity, posthumanism is necessarily open to a multiplicity of interpretations. To understand many of the permutations of posthuman theory, it is first necessary to make a distinction between "the human" as an ontological state open to a variety of different cultural interpretations, and "humanism" as the most prevalent of those interpretations in current discourse. While the posthuman refers to an ontological state marked by its difference from "the human," "posthumanism" as a discourse refers both to critical engagements with what it means to be "posthuman," as well as a critique of the critical discourses of humanism as a social, political, and philosophical framework.[2] Halberstam and Livingston (1995) make this difference explicit when they write that "the posthuman does not necessitate the obsolescence of the human; it does not represent an evolution or devolution of the human. Rather it participates in redistributions of difference and identity" (10). In other words, the posthuman does not involve a departure from any particular quality of "the human," but instead involves a reevaluation of the assignation of qualities to that particular concept. It is in this sense that it often involves an explicit critique of humanist values. Posthumanism questions humanist assumptions such as the separation of humankind from nature, or that all human beings share universal qualities such as reason or emotion, and the injustices that have been built into Western society as a result of them. In the introduction to *Readers in Cultural Criticism*, Neil Badmington (2000) argues that most posthumanist thinkers share "a refusal to take humanism for granted" (10). While the posthuman condition may elicit responses of either elation or anxiety about the humanist subject, therefore, posthumanist discourse invites critical consideration of alternative ontological modes.

Two key recent explorations of the posthuman in children's literature in particular have examined the implications of this philosophical shift for young readers. Zoe Jaques (2015) defines posthumanism as "a late-twentieth-century reaction to the anthropocentric nature of humanism" focused upon exploration of the "boundaries between humans and those that might be broadly conceived as 'non-human others'" (2). In other words, children's literature in particular explicitly engages the posthuman through depictions of embodiment: both the unstable body of the adolescent and the hybrid bodies of monsters, cyborgs, and other "nonhumans"—both of which are key features of YA dystopia. In the more recently published *Posthumanism in Young Adult Fiction* (2018), Tarr and White argue that posthumanism is especially significant for the study of YA literature, because "adolescents are especially concerned with body issues" (xvi), adolescents "operate in our socially constructed stage of in-between-ness" (xvii), and adolescent characters are often motivated by "the power inequalities implicit in [YA] novels" to "question traditional social hierarchies and construct new moral values that reflect their personal experiences" (xvii–xviii). Bradford et al. (2008) also delve into the implications of posthumanism for YA audiences in their critical examination of dystopias in *New World Orders in Contemporary Children's Literature*. They argue that if humanism can be broadly understood as a theoretical framework that places emphasis on the primacy of human values, agency, and subjectivity, then posthumanism can be understood as the disruption of that framework through exposure of human subjectivity as "fragmented, decentered, tenuous, constructed, hybridized, and enacted or performed" (Bradford et al. 2008, 158). In other words, posthumanism suggests the nonexistence of "the human" as a clearly defined and contained ontological category. Their exploration of posthuman bodies in YA texts shows multiple, multifaceted responses in these texts to the fracturing of humanist societies such bodies catalyze. While the posthuman condition, therefore, is a key characteristic of many YA dystopias, posthumanist discourse offers different ways of interpreting that condition, which might or might not be considered dystopian after all.

Posthumanist discourse offers many intersections with humanist concepts of dystopia. The concept of the posthuman emerges through many different discourses of contemporary society, from the impacts of bioengineering and genetic science, to increasing human dependence on social media and information technology, to emerging understanding of human evolutionary history and processes. Often, these discourses elicit both excitement and anxiety about the unstable nature of the "human" body: how it can be defined, where it ends, and how it might change. Posthumanist discourse offers a variety of different ways of addressing these questions, but most of these interpretations rest on a challenge to fundamental humanist understandings of the body. For example, Alice Curry (2013), writing from a feminist ecocritical perspective, postulates a difference between what she views as the "posthuman" hybrid of human and machine, which she describes as "hybrid insofar as they enact a melding of man and machine but who do not necessarily signal a permanently re-envisaged earth-based interaction between humans and the natural world," and the "ecological hybrid," which she describes as "physiological embodiments of multiplicity [that] manifest dual or plural subject positions, identities and perspectives" (181). Like the recent scientific revelations have revealed—for example, the human dependence on the gut microbiome, or the high percentage of DNA we share with chimpanzees and mice—this second interpretation in particular challenges the traditional humanist view of human beings as separate to nature and nonhuman Others. Elaine Graham (2002) defines posthuman representation as a hybridization of the three categories of human, machine, and animal, "a dissolution of the 'ontological hygiene' by which for the past three hundred years Western culture has drawn the fault-lines that separate humans, nature and machines" (11). Her comprehensive exploration of "post/human" Others in popular culture concerns itself particularly with the relationship between perceptions of the posthuman condition of ontological uncertainty and discourses of monstrosity, whereby both demonstrate and destabilize "the demarcations by which creatures have separated nature from artifice, human from non-human, normal from pathological" (12). Her focus on monstrosity in particular indicates the ways in which bodies that breach the barrier between human and environment or human and nonhuman have been seen as threatening to humanist society, and have become the subjects of narratives that either celebrate or anathemize that threat.

Regardless of how the posthuman body is envisaged, however, the fact is that its manifestation is regarded with both anxiety and anticipation. For Francis Fukuyama (2002), for example, the possibility of entering a posthuman condition threatens the idea of "human nature" as a basis for "stable continuity to our experience as a species" (7); because he envisages "human nature" as fundamental to ethical considerations of human rights, the posthuman state for Fukuyama, writing primarily from the perspective of political science, represents an abandonment of human civilization as an effective regulating force. Writers of dystopian fiction often take these assumptions as their starting points, depicting posthuman bodies as indicative of or catalysts for the breakdown of "civilized" society. With its grim depictions of elite superhumans, genetically modified beings ruling over a slave class of those who could not afford modification, unfeeling zombified victims of mass-distributed, mind-altering pharmaceuticals, and nations full of aged and undying nonworking elders, Fukuyama's *Our Posthuman Future* reads like a confirmation of every dystopia's worst predictions.

However, with its focus on change the YA dystopia offers an alternative to such bleak dystopian outlooks. In his foreword to *Utopian and Dystopian Writing for Children and Young Adults*, Jack Zipes (2003) argues that both utopian and dystopian fiction "emanate from a critique of 'postmodern,' advanced technological societies gone awry—and from a strong impulse for social change" (ix), and that "[t]he utopian tendency of art is what propels us to reshape and reform our personal and social lives" (x). YA dystopia, because it takes for granted the unstable bodies of its adolescent protagonists and the bildungsroman insistence on personal and social change, offers a unique potential to challenge the humanist assumptions that underlie traditional dystopia. Sambell (2004) writes that children's dystopian texts "reveal a prevalent crisis in confidence in the human species itself" (248–49). Hintz, Basu, and Broad (2013) agree, writing that "[w]ith its capacity to frighten and warn, dystopian writing engages with pressing global concerns: liberty and self-determination, environmental destruction and looming catastrophe, questions of identity, and the increasingly fragile boundaries between technology and the self" (1). Marek Oziewicz (2015) points out that "[a] number of cognitive studies demonstrate that the human cognitive architecture is hard-wired for a script-based narrative understanding" (5); he argues that speculative fiction, by offering stories about alternative presents and futures, offers "one of the most important forges of justice consciousness for the globalized world of the twenty-first century" (4). Oziewicz describes speculative fictions as being "not about the actual, but about the desirable" (12), and makes a compelling case for YA speculative fiction as a means of helping young people formulate and reformulate "scripts" pertaining to all forms of personal and social justice. Engaging with Katherine Hayles' (1999) assertion that literary texts "actively shape what the technologies mean and what the scientific theories signify in cultural contexts" (21), Victoria Flanagan (2014) similarly argues that the didactic mode so prevalent in children's literature means that this genre in particular "actively seeks to intervene in children's perceptions of self and their relationship to the world around them" (6), making it an ideal site for posthuman and posthumanist explorations. Dystopian fiction, and particularly children's and YA dystopian fiction, therefore, stands in a unique position to bring problems to the attention of the generation that will either solve them or suffer from them, while simultaneously evoking strong emotions about those problems: emotions such as hope, fear, or anger.

YA dystopia can therefore be seen as more than mere sensational entertainment: it can be understood as providing young people with working models for how to negotiate a relationship with an increasingly indefinable world in an age of globalization; that is, how to deal with social issues such as racism, sexism, global environmental crisis, and so on, though the development of an enlarged and entangled subjectivity. Humanist subjectivity—particularly in relation to nonhuman others and the environment—has traditionally been the norm in children's and YA texts: as Bradford et al. (2008) point out "human-centered ('shallow') environmentalism" represents "a normative position for children's literature" (91). These are texts that bemoan the state of the environment and the human role in destroying it, and yet fall back on individual actions and agency by humanist subjects as the best and only means of addressing the problem: the single seed the child reader of *The Lorax* is encouraged to plant, for example. In contrast, more and more YA speculative fiction—and particularly dystopian fiction—is moving away from this model. Some, as will be explored in this volume, merely despair at the futility of such humanist solutions. Others explore alternatives to this model while still remaining invested in humanist ideologies such as individualism, rationalism, and progress. The most exciting texts encourage a focus not on the individual but on wider communities and biosystems, discouraging loan heroics as a solution to crisis.

While it may be easy to criticize YA speculative fiction as either frivolous or irrelevant, therefore, it is worth considering carefully the role these texts play in the spread of and/or challenging of the ideologies underpinning social and environmental issues. Lawrence Buell (2001), for example, makes a compelling case for the importance of both literature and popular culture for environmental ethics when he writes that "[t]he success of all environmentalist efforts finally hinges not on 'some highly developed technology, or some arcane new science' but on 'a state of mind': on attitudes, feelings, images, narratives" (1). YA dystopia is just one of the genres in which such states of mind are fostered, but in light of its growing popularity, it is an important one. Such texts have the potential to play an important role in challenging pervasive humanist myths and offering in their place a range of alternative perspectives for the construction of new myths of identity and purpose. Posthumanist YA dystopian narratives, in other words, offer specific and imaginable examples of ecocritical solutions for readers to consider and internalize.

As Hintz, Basu, and Broad (2013) argue in their keystone work on YA dystopia, "The dystopian worlds are bleak not because they are meant to stand as mere cautionary tales, but because they are designed to display—in sharp relief—the possibility of utopian change even in the darkest of circumstances" (3). Carrie Hintz and Elaine Ostry (2003) likewise outline a number of key characteristics of both utopian and dystopian fiction for young adults: these genres frequently place young adults in positions of responsibility for the future of society (1); they explore social structures and issues and encourage social activism and collective action (2, 3, 7), and "confront the tensions between individual freedom and the needs of society" (9). YA dystopia, therefore, offers the possibility not only of critiquing everything that has gone wrong with humanist society, but also that of providing a way forward—a potential utopian "ever after." That utopia would, by definition, be posthumanist in nature: not the end of humanism, but a revision or reimagining of it. These dystopias explore the failure of humanism for an audience uniquely situated to experience the consequences of that failure; they have a choice between presenting solutions and changes that reinstate humanist societies, or that overthrow them.

THIS VOLUME

The first part of this volume examines two dystopian series which, although they depict posthuman bodies, nevertheless remain firmly invested in humanist ideology. Chapter 1 explores ideas about death, infection, sex, and family in Carrie Ryan's Forest of Hands and Teeth series. Halberstam and Livingston (1995), have argued that the family—and the control over human sexual reproduction that it entails—has been a cornerstone of the development of humanist society: family, they argue, exists to control and contain human bodies, and thereby consolidate society against hostile nature through the inculcation of humanist values and norms. Family, in other words, can be seen as the justification for inequalities and injustices grounded in humanist values, as it becomes a characteristic through which humanity is defined in opposition to hostile and threatening nature. *The Forest of Hands and Teeth* is a zombie apocalypse narrative that imagines a postapocalyptic world in which most of human civilization has been wiped out by an infection that turns bitten human beings into the living dead; bodies in this text are fundamentally posthuman in their leakiness, porousness, and mutability. At the same time, however, in its refusal to relinquish the humanist romance narrative and bildungsroman format, as well as its embeddedness in a humanist alienation from an environment imagined as separate, hostile, and threatening, *The Forest of Hands and Teeth* remains fundamentally humanist in outlook, offering readers no viable alternative to the humanist dystopia it depicts. This series challenges the family as the foundation of humanist control but seeks to reinstate rather than to replace it.

In Lois Lowry's The Giver series, technology—and particularly biomedical and pharmaceutical technology—are the means by which posthuman bodies are created: individuals and societies in this series are defined in part by their relationship (or lack thereof) to technology. Technology mediates the essential "human" natures of individuals, and thereby the relationships of individuals to "nature." Like *The Forest of Hands and Teeth*, however, The Giver series pits both protagonists and societies against an environment that is depicted as both alien and hostile. Elaine L. Graham (2002) writes that "[f]antastic, utopian and speculative forms of fiction—epitomized by science fiction—shock our assumptions and incite our critical faculties" (13). This is significant particularly in light of her insistence on the constructed nature of scientific "truth" and "fact"; as she explains at length in the first chapter of *Representations of the Post/Human*, science depends for its credibility on the assumption of a normalized position of empirical neutrality and privileged objectivity, elevating itself in the popular imagination as the only valid "representative" and "mediator" or nature (34). YA dystopia challenges this assumption, and challenges the humanist notions of rationality, individuality, and progress upon which it is based. The Giver series poses this challenge as a depiction of limitations and abuses of science and rationality when they attempt to alter nature; by portraying the human relationship to technology as dehumanizing, Lowry asks the reader to critically question humanist assumptions about the control science and technology can exert over the human body and over the external environment. Although The Giver series takes steps toward questioning humanist assumptions about rationality, however, like The Forest of Hands and Teeth series it remains rooted in humanist concepts of self, environment, and progress and fails to offer a convincing alternative to the humanist dystopias it depicts. While Lowry's novels do challenge humanist values and ideals as they are seen taken to the extreme, they also reinstate humanist values in their insistence upon exceptional humanist heroes as the solution to extreme humanism. In The Giver series, humanist control over the human body fails, but this failure is lamented rather than celebrated.

The second part of this volume examines two dystopian series that go further than The Forest of Hands and Teeth and The Giver in depicting posthumanist possibilities as well as posthuman bodies; while both Patrick Ness's Chaos Walking series and Neal Shusterman's Unwind series problematize and challenge aspects of humanist ideology, both nevertheless fail to fully realize posthumanist alternatives to the problems they depict. Chapter 3 examines the role of language and rationality in Patrick Ness's award-winning Chaos Walking series. A departure from anthropocentric humanism is the foundation upon which environmental posthumanism is built: "Environmental theory stresses the link between the humanistic emphasis on Man as the measure of all things and the domination and exploitation of nature and condemns the abuses of science and technology" (Braidotti 2013, 48). For Lynn White Jr., writing as long ago as 1996 in *The Ecocriticism Reader*, the roots for anthropocentricism are deeply embedded in religion, and specifically the Judeo-Christian religion that has shaped Western thought and practice since antiquity (9), urging the transcendence of the mind and spirit over bodily existence. For Harold Fromm (1996), a key result of technology has been to distance man from nature (35); regardless of whether such belief results from religious or secular roots, the result is that Western culture remains largely predicated upon a dichotomous and hierarchical separation of the human mind and spirit from the physical "reality" of an environment that is seen as hostile: whether that reality is the bodily existence of individual human beings, the complex relationship between humans and other organisms, or the vitality of ecosystems and ecological communities. Anthropologist AbdelRahim (2015) argues that "language and literacy have ... provided the means to encode a self-legitimating and self-replicating civilized epistemology" (17) and particularly the "awareness of difference and separatedness, coupled with a narrative that legitimates hierarchy, [which] gave birth to humanism" (9). Such separation is, however, challenged by the posthumanist outlook, which, through recognition of the porousness of boundaries, borders, and identities, suggests the impossibility of such separation. For this reason, posthumanism is immensely valuable as a means of addressing ecocritical issues, and "is often conjoined with radical forms of ecocriticism, animal studies, and object-oriented theories" (Broglio 2017, 34). Each of these critical lenses emphasizes the humanist insistence on sentience and individualism as a key focal point for injustices toward the nonhuman. Through narratives of space frontier exploration and colonization of alien environments, the Chaos Walking novels explore the human relationship to nonhuman others—both animal and alien—and directly challenge the humanist investment in both individualism and sentience as distinguishing features of subjectivity, and the ensuing control these imply over nonhuman Others. While this series goes a long way in reimagining human relationships to nonhuman others and to the environment, however, it fails to go far enough, redrawing humanist lines of control rather than dispensing with them altogether.

Chapter 4 focuses on Neal Shusterman's Unwind dystopia, to explore how YA dystopia disturbs the humanist notion of individual progress and development. This chapter will explore the coupling of progress and technology with capitalism within the series, as well as the way in which the series undermines the traditional humanist bildungsroman format. In many traditional YA dystopias, characters are either depicted as agents, "with the capacity to act independently of social restraint," or as victims within "a prestructured social order within which s/he is ultimately represented as disempowered and passive" (McCallum 1999, 7). Stewart (2007) points out the essentially humanist nature of such plots, writing that "[a]dolescent fiction, because protagonists are usually represented as navigating their way out of solipsism to recognition of their intersubjectivity, often displays humanistic tendencies to the extreme, particularly with their struggle with authority" (25–26). However, as McCallum (1999) argues, for many readers such a portrayal is "simply idealistic and unattainable" (7). This is particularly the case where such portrayals depend not only on the development of unique individual gifts (e.g., Katniss' skill in shooting and hunting in The Hunger Games series, or Tris' "divergent" qualities in the Divergent series), but also on technology that represents a similar uniqueness on the part of the human race: futuristic technologies that depict the evolutionary progression of the human race as a superior species (The Hunger Games arena or the simulations in Divergent: both simulated virtual realities dependent on sophisticated AI technology). In such depictions, the dystopia pits the humanist subject against overwhelmingly hostile environmental conditions only to show that same subject as mastering the conditions and returning them to human control. Humanism, therefore, becomes about the control of human fate or destiny, through technology and within a hostile environment. These dystopias portray the potential fall but ultimate reinstatement of the superior, disembodied humanist subject who remains in control of his or her fate by remaining in control of technology. However, Victoria Flanagan (2014) argues that "writers of young adult fiction have become increasingly eager to discard the established model of dystopian representations of technofuturistic worlds" (5). Depicting a world in which rampant capitalism has rendered bodies posthuman in their similarity to machine-assembled commodity products, the Unwind series criticizes the humanist faith in technological and scientific progress. In doing so, it also criticizes the corresponding liberal humanist faith in capitalist society, which posits the consumer as able to purchase the destiny of his or her choice. The characters in these books pit themselves against the ultimate hostility of nature: a world in which the inevitable outcome of life is ageing, bodily decay, and death. In the attempt to defy death, the natural world has been all but erased in the dystopian society of these novels, as the characters seek to control every aspect of embodiment. Nevertheless, the series ultimately endorses not an ideological shift, but a technological solution, thereby falling back on the very attitudes it purports to critique.

Finally, the third part of this volume explores texts that offer posthumanist alternatives to the humanist outlook that has been more traditional in YA dystopian literature. In chapter 5, a close examination of Philip Reeve's steampunk quartet and prequel trilogy, the Mortal Engines and Fever Crumb series, explores the ways in which YA dystopia disturbs humanist notions of linear/progressive time and the progressive evolution of humanity as a species. One idea that posthumanism seeks to grapple with is the growing assertion in popular culture and media that human progress is superseding evolution itself. An article in *The Economist* in 2011, for example, places the human race firmly in the Anthropocene, seeing us as no longer merely a species but a "geological force to be reckoned with," and one that "dam by dam, mine by mine, farm by farm and city by city . . . is remaking the Earth before your eyes." Popular science, as well as science fiction, bombard us with images of modified human bodies: bodies that can defy space, time, and biology. The problem with this posthuman representation, however, as Katherine Hayles (1999) has famously pointed out, is that it results in an illusory disembodiment of the human subject—the myth that knowledge, data, and information can replace the body and the environment as the habitat of human beings. The posthuman body, therefore, is often seen as the product of human evolution away from a state of nature, but this perspective is very much founded upon a humanist assumption about the separation of human beings from a hostile environment, away from which they must progress. What was once a defensive measure (the formation of human societies for protection against a hostile environment) comes to be celebrated as "natural" and as an evolutionary birthright. Taking this separation from and disregard for the natural world as its starting point, Reeves' series challenge this idea of a controlled progression through linear time toward an evolutionary destiny. Close examination of both the posthuman bodies and circular narratives of the Mortal Engines and Fever Crumb series, with particular attention to the deployment of steampunk philosophies, will reveal that these narratives instead foreground the inevitability of embodiment and the resulting imperative to create sustainable environmental relationships.

Chapter 6 closes the volume with an analysis of the recently published YA graphic novel, *Decelerate Blue*. Rosi Braidotti (2013) sees in the posthuman stance enormous potential to address the many theoretical and practical shortcoming of the humanist ethos, including racial, gender, and class inequalities, and argues that "a posthuman ethics for a non-unitary subject proposes an enlarged sense of interconnection between self and others, including the non-human or 'earth' others, by removing the obstacle of self-centered individualism" (49–50). According to Braidotti, "The posthuman condition urges us to think critically and creatively about who and what we are actually in the process of becoming" (12). In other words, if the humanist construction of the normative human subject can be understood as the foundation upon which issues of racism, sexism, environmental exploitation, and so on have been built, then posthumanism not only nullifies that normative subjectivity but offers a new and stronger pluralistic and mutable subjectivity upon which solutions to these issues can be constructed. Like the Unwind series, *Decelerate Blue* grapples with the concept of the human control of technology and, through technology, human fate. The novel depicts bodies, which, once again, are rendered posthuman by an investment in technology, biomedicine, and capitalism; however, this graphic novel is a prime example of the solarpunk genre, which reimagines technologies outside of humanist contexts. Turning the traditional basis of the dystopia on its head, in *Decelerate Blue* the environment is shown to be hostile only to those who seek to violently control and fight against it, and technology becomes a means of reconnecting with a natural world that is both dangerous *and* nurturing. It is the humanist need to control the environment through technology that renders both environment and technology threatening in this novel, and once the humanist need to control is relinquished, exciting new possibilities for an entangled existence emerge. Furthermore, in reimaging the human relationship to technology, the novel also seeks to reimagine human subjectivity and as a result offers alternatives to the exploitative frameworks, which have become the norm in much of humanist society. *Decelerate Blue* celebrates technology not as a form of individual control, but as collective and shared action that distributes power equally. In both form and content, it offers an alternative to the humanist dystopias depicted in other YA dystopian texts.

NOTES

1. Within this collection I used the term "environment" to refer not only to physical space, but also to social and cultural contexts.

2. For a comprehensive discussion of the different critical developments and positions or posthumanism and the posthuman, see Seaman (2007) and Wolfe (2010). Wolfe makes clear the distinction between the posthuman state and different critical approaches to that state including transhumanism and posthumanism. In particular, Wolfe discusses the posthuman theory of Katherine N. Hayles (1999) in its celebration of the posthuman as a state of "triumphant disembodiment" (xv), placing it more in line with transhumanism than posthumanism in its retention of classic humanist faith in reason and disembodiment.

Chapter One

Carrie Ryan's Forest of Hands and Teeth

Sex, Infection, and Hopelessness

Carrie Ryan's postapocalyptic zombie thriller presents a dystopian image of humanity plagued by violence, repression, and biological deterioration. As such, it feeds into a growing craze for "zombie apocalypse" narratives, which has manifested itself through box office hits such as the Living Dead films and *The Walking Dead* TV series; bestselling books such as *Pride and Prejudice and Zombies* (2009); and zombie-themed video games, parades, and festivals, as well as a host of other products and events. The zombie has been equally popular with cultural theorists who see the zombie as a zeitgeist figure; Thomas Morrissey (2013), for example, argues that "the swiftness and mysterious nature of zombie apocalypses speak to the pervasive sense of insecurity that lurks in the minds of many post 9/11 Americans" (193). Such a growing fascination with the zombie feeds into a host of tropes, but all share a single theme in common: these narratives speculate about the end of humanity as a result of rampaging infection. Infection is terrifying because it is both omnipresent and amorphous: it is both unseen and yet everywhere, versatile, changeable, and seemingly uncontrollable. As a catalyst for apocalypse it holds seemingly illimitable dystopian potential, pitting human beings not only against the environment but also their own bodies. In an interview with Catherine W. Griffin (2012) in the *Pennsylvania Literary Journal*, Carrie Ryan explains her motivation for choosing this particular dystopian trope for her writing:

> I'm fascinated by how people not only survive really overwhelming circumstances, but also how they find ways to do more than just survive. People may face the end of the world and yet they still fall in love and make friends and actually continue to live their lives . . . [the] human spirit is remarkable. (38–39).

Clare B. Curtis (2010) argues convincingly that postapocalyptic events in fiction rarely depict the end of humanity; instead they depict a return to "a state of nature" and "focus on the very idea and possibility of starting over, with all the potential hope and utopian imaginings that starting over implies" (2); this, it seems, is the very idea that Ryan draws upon in her series. However, what is striking about The Forest of Hands and Teeth trilogy— especially in light of Ryan's assertion—is the lack of hope that pervades the narrative. The series tells the story of two generations of women, struggling for survival in a world transformed by the rise of an infection that causes the dead to return to life as mindless, infectious monsters. Following the conventions of YA dystopia, all three narratives explore the impact of such drastic changes on the fundamentals of human existence; in the case of this trilogy, the focus on the intertwined bildungsroman narratives of self-development and romantic fulfillment allows the series to interrogate the viability of traditional family structures predicated on specific, controlled sexual relationships and acts. While the traditional humanist conception of the binary human/nature divide supports traditional family structures as a defense against hostile environments, Ryan's novels (and other zombie narratives) depict how zombie infection—particularly through sexual acts—embodies a posthumanist dissolution of the human into the environment, destroying traditional family structures and therefore foreshadowing an end to human civilization as we know it.

DEATH, INFECTION, AND SEX: THE POSTHUMAN BODY

By persistently juxtaposing the zombie narrative of infection with the bildungsroman narrative of romantic fulfillment, zombie YA narratives such as The Forest of Hands and Teeth series (Ryan 2009, 2010, 2011) depict the human body as fundamentally posthuman by placing emphasis on the permeability of the boundary between self and environment. Jones (2011) describes the zombie narrative as concerned with "infection across binary divisions" (52); Gerry Canavan (2010) agrees, pointing to the "biopolitical origins of the zombie imaginary" (433). Often remarkably vague about the origins of the epidemics that cause zombification, zombie narratives nevertheless often focus on the physical breach of the human body through acts such as biting or scratching; focusing on the ways in which environmental contaminants can pass through the skin boundary into the blood and throughout the body, such narratives echo discourses about sexually transmitted disease all too familiar to most YA audiences. For Jones (2013), in the zombie narrative "fear stems not from the zombies themselves, but from human susceptibility to infection," mirroring the fact that "sex too is commonly allied with pathogenic infection and interpersonal pollution" (200). The zombies "enact a debased inversion of human reproduction, playing into the global fears over viral epidemics and sexually transmissible diseases" (Curry 2013, 82).

However, the significance of this coupling of ideas about infection and sex lies not only in the perceived vulnerability of individual bodies, but also in the ways infected bodies threaten social structures as a whole. Applying queer theory to a posthuman exploration of AIDS infection, Halberstam and Livingston (1995) pick up on this idea in *Posthuman Bodies*, discussing how infection affects not only individual bodies but entire populations: "disintegration operates like a virus and infects people with fear . . . the randomness of the disease means that everyone is affected by the infection of so many" (15). Boluk and Lenz (2011) apply the same argument to zombie narratives, writing that "A zombie outbreak, much like a plague epidemic, is an event in which the anxieties associated with social connectivity come to the fore—the more boundaries between self and other are broken down in plague time, the more the contagion spreads" (7). The logical extrapolation from such a conclusion is that, in the wake of infection, socially cohesive human societies predicated upon sexually generated nuclear family structures disintegrate as reproduction becomes asexual and uncontrollable. Lauro and Embry (2008), whose "Zombie Manifesto" half-jestingly sets itself up as a posthuman successor to Donna Haraway's essay "Cyborg Manifesto" (2016), argue that "the physical boundary between zombie and not-zombie is effaced, through its bite" (99); however, from the zombie's bite what is transmitted is not something extra, but instead a "lack" or incompleteness—reproduction of something that is not human, and which severs the human control of the body. The zombie's bite is not about nourishment, but about reproduction; its penetration of the human-body boundary allows it to reproduce, exactly like a viral infection. It is this fear of infection and bodily encroachment which permeated The Forest of Hands and Teeth series.

The Forest of Hands and Teeth (Ryan 2009), the first book in the trilogy, opens with the brutal image of Mary's mother, contaminated by the unconsecrated as she grieved for a husband who had already "returned" as one of them. From the moment Mary's mother is touched by the undead, she is considered infectious, and transformed instantly from a member of the community to something less-than-human, the subject of the village's anxious gaze. Mary explains: "If she was merely scratched they will monitor her even though she couldn't be infected that way" (8). From Mary's graphic description of her mother's hands, "sticky" and "covered with her blood" (8), to her speculation about whether her mother has been bitten or merely scratched, Mary's mother becomes the object of an intense anxiety about the breaching of the body's boundaries by an inhuman other. Interestingly, this scene also plays with a standard trope of YA literature: the protagonist's loss of a parent or parents as the starting point for the bildungsroman narrative. In fact, the scene also evokes YA bildungsroman romance by making Mary's mother's escape the result of Mary's neglect as she pursues her own romantic interests. Thus, the breach of Mary's mother's body is foreshadowed by Mary's own bodily encounter with Harry as they hold hands and think of marriage; the loss of Mary's mother simultaneously frees Mary to pursue her own relationships and self-development.

The Dead-Tossed Waves (Ryan 2010) opens with similar imagery as an undead "Breaker" rips through the group of teenagers who have illegally breached the protective walls of their seaside town in search of freedom and excitement. Gabry (Mary's adopted daughter) explains that "the only safe places are those protected by walls and fences" because "the dead will never stop once they scent human flesh" (9–10). Here the town becomes a metaphor for the human body itself, with the breach of one foreshadowing the breach of the other. After Mellie, one of the girls bitten in the attack, returns, Gabry describes how even though "[h]er eyes are still clear . . . [h]er skin bronzed and smooth" (23), nevertheless the infection has rendered her less-than-human, "crawling to her feet, teeth bated and hands grasping" (22). The infection, passed from bite to blood, acts immediately to replace humanity with something inherently other. Once again, Ryan implies the risk of infection as inherent to the YA bildungsroman romance: just as Mary's first encounter with the unconsecrated was triggered by the loss of a parent and the pursuit of a romantic relationship, Gabry similarly leaves the safety of her mother's protection behind when she enters the fairground to pursue a relationship with Catcher. The joining of their bodies as they kiss is mirrored by the Breaker's breach of Mellie's body.

The Dark and Hollow Places (Ryan 2011) opens with what is perhaps one of the most explicit discussions of infection, as Annah encounters an infected woman on her way home. Annah describes "the raw circle around her wrist, festering with infection. The flesh edging the wound puffs and oozes, and I recognize it as a bite" (3). The image refocuses Annah's attention from the woman's humanity, "eyes smudged by tears of sweat" (3), to her status as a threatening Other, "She'll be one of them soon" (4). As the woman uses Annah's presence as a means of mourning her lost humanity, Annah (and, subsequently, the reader) is forced to contemplate the role infection plays not only in eroding one's own sense of humanity, but also in revoking one's membership within human communities as the infected individual becomes a threat to the humanity of others.

What these narratives depict ultimately, however, is the triumph of pathogenic or nonhuman reproduction over socially controlled human sexual reproduction. This is made all the more clear when the juxtaposition within the narrative of fear of infection with sexually loaded romantic tropes figures the zombie infection as a result of sexually motivated social relationships. Curry (2013), for example, sees a primary purpose of the narrative zombie as being to "interrogate the ways in which the desire to consume becomes written onto the body of the young female protagonist" (82). This idea of the conflation of female desire and infection is most obviously visible in the scene in the first book which serves as the culmination of Mary's brief respite with Travis, in the abandoned village. For the time in which the two are trapped within the house, an uncomfortable accord is reached between them as they battle to both acknowledge and ignore Mary's sexual desire; made more difficult by the close proximity of Harry, to whom Mary is supposedly engaged, and Cass, to whom Travis is engaged, it is Mary's lack of control over her desire for Travis that hangs heavy in the air as the two attempt to shut out the outside world and the inevitability of their sanctuary's temporary nature. However, when the hordes of unconsecrated finally breach the walls of the house, it is not only the sense of sanctuary they lose, but also the illusion of control over Mary's body. As hordes of unconsecrated pour into the house, Travis's injured leg prevents him from defending her and she is overwhelmed by the incoming tide of undead: "the shock of a thousand bee strings travels up my legs. I refuse to look at the source of the pain, don't want to see the Unconsecrated teeth that might be piercing my flesh, sending the infection deep into my body" (232). Pulled finally to safety, Travis's previously erotically charged touch turns to hysteria and fear as he frantically searches Mary's skin for signs of an infectious bite. His fingers "prod" and he "screams" questions at her (233), in a scene that suggests loss of ownership as well as fear of physical breach, similar to the aftermath of a sexual assault. Mary's response, also similar to common responses to sexual assault, is one of shame: "I am afraid to meet his eyes" (233). As Curry (2013) suggests, Mary's "aggressive female sexuality has the effect of enforcing a link between femininity and death" (83). By having this close encounter juxtaposed so closely to Mary's indulgence in forbidden sexual relations with her friend's fiancé, Ryan implicitly links infection to sexual excess.

A similar connection is portrayed in *The Dead-Tossed Waves* (Ryan 2010) as Gabry struggles to come to terms with her feelings for both Catcher and Elias. Catcher's continuing rejection of her sexual advances leaves Gabry both frustrated and humiliated, until finally Catcher explains that his immunity to the infection might not stop him from being infectious. Gabry's response is one of bodily discomfort: "I suck in a quick breath . . . sitting here now in his lap I feel instantly vulnerable. I swallow, my throat straining as I push down the sudden fear that leaps around me" (273). Their physical proximity combines with the sexual imagery to equate Gabry's vulnerability to infection with her lack of sexual control as she pursues two men at once. In the face of Catcher's insistence to Annah in the third book, that he cannot get close to her because he might be infectious, Annah nevertheless feels his rejection as personal and physical, stating that, "His pronouncement makes me feel cold and ugly. Unwanted" (Ryan 2011, 84). As with his earlier sexually charged encounters with Gabry, Catcher's uncertainty about his infectiousness destroys not only his availability as a sexual partner for these women, but also translates into an embodiment of female sexual shame. Women's sexuality, therefore, is a site for control and anxiety in these novels, as the historical hysteria about women's sexuality purity is translated into a literal threat to the continuation of the species. By focusing on female protagonists, these bildungsroman novels frequently frustrate their heroine's attempts to define themselves through sexual relationships, as the ever-present threat of infection denies them "safe" partners. Mary, Gabry, and Annah are all positioned as Eve characters: they break rules (don't cross the fences) and pursue forbidden desires (such as Mary's desire for Travis and for the sea), and in doing so they "invite" infection in their drive for self-development. At the same time, the risk of infection denies them not only a romantic partner, but a stable traditional family unit. Unlike the traditional YA romance heroine, none of these young women will achieve a happily-ever-after marriage to balance the loss of parents with which each narrative begins. Although they pursue it passionately, marriage and family remains beyond their grasp.

What is ultimately at stake in these depictions is the viability of a future human society. Where reproduction is at risk, so, too, is the possibility of children. Discussing a variety of zombie narratives, and particularly Whitehead's *Zone One*, Sorensen (2014) describes how the figure of the child is frequently utilized to "embody the promise of reproductive futurism—that growth is inevitable" (581); such narratives "make the [human] act of reproduction heroic in itself," a bulwark of defense against the viral zombies who are "the masters, and monsters, of reproduction" (590). Catcher's infectiousness prevents him from undertaking sexual/romantic relationships, but there is a strong possibility that he might reproduce asexually, aggressively. His restraint and self-control are shown in contrast to the impulsive, self-indulgent irresponsibility of the women; at the same time, Catcher is the antithesis of the bildungsroman hero, as he lacks a future and therefore a reason to learn, grow, and develop. Despite the infection's failure to turn or kill him, Catcher has effectively ceased to function as a humanist subject, as he can neither gratify himself nor contribute to his community, and instead remains suspended in time—a conduit for the virus rather than a bastion of humanity.

Where normalized sexual relations are made impossible by the risk of infection, the family—a fundamental building block for human society—is shown to be at risk. For Halberstam and Livingston (1995), "the story of the victory of the middle class and the hegemony of its family, discipline, and rationality," and by correspondence "the birth of human culture," can be located in "a system specifying who may be allowed to fuck what and how, producing mandates, prohibitions and selective freedoms in the circulation of fluids—breast milk, semen, money, gifts, information" (11). In other words, it is controlled sexual reproduction that forms the basis of the family, and the family that forms the basis for liberal humanist society. With this in mind, it is easy to see why the novels center such hysteria on the control of the young, sexually active female bodies of the protagonists. Controlling these women becomes a means of bolstering a vision of human society and civilization, which is shown to be increasingly unviable. Traditional YA bildungsroman romances work hard to ensure that the journey of female protagonists through independence and self-discovery ends with a reinstatement of family values: Katniss will marry Peeta, Bella will marry Edward, and Hermione will marry Ron, to give but a few examples. In *The Forest of Hands and Teeth*, however, this neat reinstatement of humanist family values falters, as infection makes controlled bodies and therefore the stable family a near impossibility to achieve.

In *Posthuman Bodies* (1995), Roddey Reid coincidentally describes families in a posthuman society as "dead but never quite: the undead. Zombielike" (178). He writes that within humanist philosophy the "refrain returns over and over again that 'family' unites us all and sets aside divisions of race and class (and presumably, gender)" as well as distinguishing the "human" from the nonhuman as a marker of civilization (184). At the same time, however, he describes the family as "a tactic for reinscribing and protecting the so-called normative 'humanity' of (straight) upper-middle-class whites" using family, or lack thereof, as a benchmark for humanness (186). Following Foucault's postmodernist social theory, he argues for the family as a tool for imposing social discipline on the liberal humanist body (194). However, the zombie as the ultimate symbol of uncontrollable sexuality and infection undermines the viability of the family by elevating individual survival above social cohesion and liberating sexual desire while simultaneously restricting human reproductive capacity. For Jennifer Rutherford (2013), in the zombie narrative "it's not just romantic love but the whole language and social organization of love and family that is brought into question" (5). Cassie Ozog (2013), in an exploration of family in the zombie film *Zombieland*, explains that "the fight for survival means the rejection of solidarity or group cohesion, and the fight for survival does not include helping others along the way" (131). In place of the triumphant narrative of the endurance of human relationships—and therefore human society—that Ryan hoped to portray in her series, what is actually depicted in *The Forest of Hands and Teeth* (as well as many other YA dystopian romances) is the dissolution of sexually predicated family-oriented humanist societies.

This begins in *The Forest of Hands and Teeth*, as we see Mary's traditional nuclear family torn apart by both infection and the indulgence of selfish desire over communal safety: infection claims Mary's mother because her desire to rejoin her husband is stronger than her love for her remaining family and her duty to her community; it is telling that it is her mother to whom Mary's memories reach when she nurtures her illicit desire for Travis, and her selfish desire to find the sea and a sense of independence from what remains of her community. Her desire for Travis is a further indication of how infection has weakened the bonds of family, as the destruction of the village by the unconsecrated is what provides the opportunity for rigid rules pertaining to marriage and childbearing to be abandoned, and her own desires to be pursued. As has already been discussed, although these desires pertain to finding a husband and family of her own, the novels will constantly depict the failure of Mary and the other women to achieve these desires.

The dissolution of family is depicted most vividly throughout the second two books in the series, with the introduction of a cult known as "Soulers," who worship the undead and willingly allow themselves to be infected so as to live forever. Most shocking about these depictions is the juxtaposition of genuine and strong bonds of family affection and loyalty with scenes of violence and death. In *The Dead-Tossed Waves* (Ryan 2010), for example, Gabry watches a group of Soulers as they allow a young boy to be turned:

> The woman who'd been standing in front of me runs down the hill and jumps onto the stage, falling onto her knees next to him. She pulls the boy into her lap, his blood seeping around them both. She takes a collar and slips it around the boy's neck. Then she folds him in her arms, squeezing him in a desperate embrace . . . her face wet with tears. (144)

This scene depicts a mother doing what she believes to be the best she can for her beloved child, in the face of overwhelming odds against human survival. Nevertheless, it is the mother's desperation to hold on to what she loves that exposes her son to pain, infection, and death. Because so much of what is considered "human" in this society centers around the protection of family members from infection, the Soulers are despised by the rest of their society as "inhuman" in their willingness to deliberately infect loved ones. Nevertheless, the novels strive to reveal the genuine love and care that underlies the Soulers' beliefs, thus reinscribing the idea that what makes us *all* human is our desire to protect our loved ones from the ultimate threat of nature: disease, infection, and death. The Soulers furthermore demonstrate the futility of that desire. In *The Dark and Hollow Places* (Ryan 2011), for example, Annah encounters a woman grieving over her undead husband, with whom she has been locked in a cage for the amusement of Recruiters. The woman, whose husband was once a Souler, explains "He's the one who really believed in all of this. There's nothing left inside him anymore. I'd know if there were" (291). Not only does the Recruiters' cruel practice of caging people to fight the undead strip them of humanity and tear apart the few families and bastions of community that remain; the Soulers themselves stand for the futility of humanity's attempt to cling to the family as a mode of protection against a hostile environment in which death and infection run rampant. Against the pervasive power of the infection to replicate itself, the bonds of family prove to be a hindrance, based as they are upon the fulfilment of individual drives and instincts as a foundation of social cohesion.

Catherine Buckley (2013) describes the new craze for undead romantic heroes and heroines in YA culture, arguing that for "the young adult (YA) reader and movie audience, then, these monsters have been transformed into misunderstood romantic heroes" (215). As she explains, however, "the message that true love conquers all, even a virus or death, and can be forgiving of murder may be an overly optimistic message" and even potentially dangerous (223). This is a quagmire that Ryan has stumbled into, largely by refusing to recognize the failure of love, society, and the human to triumph. Ultimately, The Forest of Hands and Teeth series calls the viability of these fundamental humanist assumptions into question, but nevertheless refuses to abandon or replace them.

Perhaps the most heart-rending example of this in the series is when, in *The Forest of Hands and Teeth*, Mary finds an unconsecrated baby still lying helpless in its crib, abandoned and infected, no doubt when its family was infected. Mary describes the baby as "ashen ... her mouth open in a perpetual yet silent scream" (193). There is pathos in the helplessness of the infant, who "lies there kicking her fat legs against the footboard of the crib, eternally calling for her mother. For food" (193). The emphasis on both food and reproduction is what is intended to appall and shock the reader in this description, as the "natural" human functions of sexual reproduction and mammalian feeding have been undermined by the superior reproductive ability of the zombie infection. In this scene, Travis' dream of a family and a home in spite of everything that has happened is shown to be hopeless, as Mary drops the infected infant out of the window. Here, it is simply not possible that "love will conquer all," for the virus, it is implied, will make family and future impossible for all lifeforms except itself. The disease has not only harmed the infant, it has harmed Mary as well—the fear of infection overrides her maternal instinct to love and protect, rendering her almost as inhuman as the baby itself as she unfeelingly disposes of it. Despite the stark impossibility of stable family implied by this scene, however, the novels cling doggedly to the romance narrative formula.

The Dead-Tossed Waves and *The Dark and Hollow Places* are likewise haunted by the image of an abandoned child, as we learn that Annah abandoned her sister Gabry (Abigail) alone in the forest as a young child, barely more than a baby. The image of the young Gabry alone on the path, bleeding and frightened, calling for her sister and surrounded by the undead, will recur with frequency through both books. This abandonment is echoed by another, toward the end of *The Dark and Hollow Places*, when Catcher abandons a mother and child desperate for food, because he is searching for a way to free his friends from the island where they are imprisoned. When he returns, the mother is dead and the child is sobbing and terrified; Catcher attempts to carry the child to safety, but is forced to admit his failure: "he was screaming and crying and I was trying to keep him safe. That's all I was doing was trying to keep him safe and they got him" (265). Catcher's initial abandonment of the child is compounded by the mother's inability to stay alive and protect her son, further compounded by Catcher's subsequent failure to save the boy. Each new abandonment drives home the idea that humans are powerless to protect their offspring against the more efficient and successful reproduction of the infection.

Richard Teleky (2015), discussing his students' fascination with zombies, writes that they expressed "a vague sense of unease," eventually admitting that "they feared there was no future for them, that the future had been used up" (517). Predicated upon the dissolution of both the body and the family, this suggests that perhaps the fear associated with zombies stems from the depiction of human society in zombie dystopias as doomed to dissolve back into the ever-encroaching wilderness of a hostile natural environment.

APOCALYPSE AND THE HOSTILE ENVIRONMENT

In depicting the dissolution of humanist bodies under the pressures of infection, zombie narratives ultimately depict a breach of the boundary between the human and the environment; the conventions of the horror and dystopian genres render such a breach as fundamentally something to be feared. In a 2009 article in ISLE, Simon Estok famously offers the term ecophobia to describe what he sees as a pervasive "contempt for the natural world" (204). Commenting on this article, Tom J. Hillard (2009) discusses how "this darker side of nature writing, with its emphasis on fear, inevitably intersects with an examination of gothic fiction and literature," (688) which he describes as exploring "physical, psychological, and social limits and boundaries" (690). With these stipulations in mind, it is not a huge leap to seeing how the intersection of posthumanism and environmentalism leads inexorably to both horror and dystopia, both genres concerned intimately with fear. This fear of the environment is evident throughout The Forest of Hands and Teeth series.

For Curry (2013) the first novel can be seen as "inscribing the wilderness as a space both of threat and salvation" (15). Mary's first encounter with the world outside of her village, for example, intermingles the physical sensation of bodily experience of the natural world with the heightened perceptions of fear: "Suddenly I'm on my hands and knees in the fresh air, pine needles digging into my palms. I hear birds, I feel dry grass under my bare toes and I am disoriented—confused—until the first moan begins" (*Forest* 33). Engaging all five senses to present this environment to the reader, Mary's description emphasizes both safety and the sterility of the spaces she has previously inhabited, as the physicality of the forest undermines her understanding of her body as separate from her environment. Her fear is a direct result of the deliberate way in which the village, led by the Sisterhood, have equated the Unconsecrated to the forest, and gone to great lengths to isolate themselves from that natural space through the erection of fences and barriers. Like Mary's body, however, the village proves less defensible than its inhabitants would like; fences are fragile, constantly under threat from both the forest, which threatens to pull it down, and the Unconsecrated who press against it, hungering for the living within. Infection has rendered the human animalistic, and has thus rendered natural spaces fearful. Both the forest and the Unconsecrated stand as a symbol of the fragility of human distinctness.

The same holds true in *The Dead-Tossed Waves* (Ryan 2010) of Gabry's first foray beyond the safety of the town and even the ruins, into areas unmediated by human interference. The beach at first seems idyllic: "[t]he sand is still warm, retaining the heat of the day, and thick with tangles of seaweed and driftwood" (78). Nevertheless, Gabry responds with fear, feeling "open and exposed" (78); free of the walls and fences of the town which protect her, this space seems to Gabry to be hostile and threatening, a natural environment made for supporting Mudo and infection, not for humans. This idea is reinforced as the undead then begin to appear, rising from the sand that, at first so welcoming, has in fact been concealing them from their prey. In *The Dark and Hollow Places*, the Dark City serves similarly as a bastion of human civilization against the threatening and hostile environment. As Annah speculates, what is at stake is the reabsorption of the human into the natural: "The Earth will spin, the stars will rearrange themselves around one another and the world will crawl with the dead who one day will drop into nothingness: no humans left for them to scent, no flesh for them to crave. Everything—all of us—will simply cease to be" (249). AbdelRahim (2015), writing from an anthropological perspective, argues for a direct link between fear of the natural environment, and the formation of human societies: "[P]aradoxically, the whole civilized premise rests on the promise of safety from predators and diseases that, ironically, are civilization's own making" (219). In other words, the humanist narrative takes as its starting point the vulnerability of the human animal within a hostile environment figured as inherently "other," and uses the structures of civilization as a defense which both enables and justifies its own predation on that environment. In such a binary construction, which takes conflict for granted, fear is the inevitable response to the natural environment, and that fear is amplified by posthuman and posthumanist depictions of the dissolution or penetration of bodies and societies. Ryan depicts a future in which humanity is overrun and rapidly disintegrating into a hostile natural environment.

Throughout the series, the undead are described in animalistic terms, aligning them closely to the natural environment. As Mary stares at her wonderingly, for example, after the fall of the village to the Unconsecrated, Gabrielle is described in terms that call to mind not a corpse, but a dangerous predator: "she raises her head as if she is sniffing the air, something catching her attention from the comer of her eye" (*Forest* 135). In *The Dead-Tossed Waves*, Gabry insists "They're monsters. They only want to kill us and eat us and infect us" (220). Nevertheless, she explains that her insistence springs from horror at contemplating the alternative, "[t]hat there's something left of who they are trapped in a body that wants only to consume us" (220). For Curry (2013), "These zombie figures . . . are naturalised as non-sentient and ontologically inhuman . . . closer to the natural than the human, these Forest-dwelling creatures are predicated on an ecophobic rendering of a debased and degraded natural world" (68). The response of the humans in the series to the undead is that of the prey to the hunted: they fear the humility and ultimate inhumanity of being eaten by something stronger and inescapable. In his discussion of ecophobia, Simon Estok (2014) explains that "imagining a menacing alterity of the natural environment . . . means imagining materials and their intractable grip on our lives and deaths" (130). Ryan's ecophobic depiction of the reabsorption of the human into that natural is accomplished by emphasizing the vulnerability of human bodies and human society to penetrating natural forces.

In a final twist of the knife, zombie narratives such as the The Forest of Hands and Teeth series voice the suggestion that the very hostility of the natural environment may be the fault of humanity itself. Rutherford (2013), for example, sees one motivation for the popularity of zombie narratives in the increasingly global sense of threat to the environment: "[h]azards which used to assault local environments now threaten the planet affecting all humanity and all human life—unforeseen, imperceptible and beyond rational control" (8). Balaji (2013) confers, suggesting that the fascination with zombies and the "undead apocalypse" is appropriate to "a turbulent period in which wars, financial collapse, extreme climate change and technological revolutions" (xi) have destabilized society. As Sarah Juliet Lauro (2011) explains, "the modem zombie . . . is more related to evolutionary forces than to forces of evil," aligning itself with ecological threats such as climate change in "a natural progression that comes to look like retaliation for humanity's abuse of its environment" (55). She sees in many zombie narratives the horror of "the natural world's indifference to the plight of humanity as it battles extinction" and the suspicion that "the destruction of humanity is in the long-term interest of the planet" (57). She argues that the zombie narrative depicts both "the transition from a fear of nature to a fear of humanity" as well as, simultaneously, "a return to a mythic enchantment of nature" (63) and "the pre-Enlightenment conception of nature as something that was not within man's power" (62).

In The Forest of Hands and Teeth series, dystopian descriptions of the world that came before the "Return" implicitly criticize a culture of mindless consumption. The Dark City in *The Dark and Hollow Places* is a fallen New York City, described by Annah as she remembers visiting a museum exhibit: "shiny bulletlike machines that sped through the tunnels called subways, sloping parks with families picnicking while kids clutched balloons. Buildings that stood tall, the glare of light bouncing off them so bright that even from the dingy picture I wondered how people back then didn't go blind" (93). Annah's description focuses on the excess of the city, expressed in mass consumption of energy (the bright lights), materials (the tall buildings), and goods (the balloons and picnics), all of which failed to insulate the inhabitants from the infection when it hit. *The Dead-Tossed Waves* begins with a scene in a ruined fair-ground, perhaps (given its proximity to what was once New York City) Coney Island. However, this fairground is a gothic ruin, a ghost of what was once a site of the mass consumption of food, entertainment, and energy. Gabry describes the rollercoaster, "its humps rising from the decaying ruins like the back of some serpentine monster" (11), "the old buildings that have been stripped bare or tumbled in on themselves" (12), and "the carousel with the faded animals, the chipped red and green and purple and blue paint along its peaked roof" (15); each description speaks of the excess and consumption of a past age, now decaying and serving as the hiding place and breeding ground for a new species to exist in. The infection has consumed and repurposed both the bodies and the civilization of the human species for its own uses. Such descriptions provide a graphic illustration of the binary divide between human civilization and the natural world, showing humanist civilization as marked by consumption of resources without regard for the consequences.

Rushton and Moreman (2011) explain that in zombie apocalypse narratives "the persistent message being that to live is to struggle, and that we as humans need it to be that way," as it allows for "a celebration of human engagement and effort" (5–6). However, this drive toward a fundamentally humanist hopefulness is missing from a dystopia such as Ryan's, in which no amount of "human engagement and effort" is able to stop the relentless dissolution of humanist social structures and human bodies. Instead, it is closer in formulation to what Pollock (2011) describes as the environmental apocalypse, distinct from other apocalyptic situations in that the survivors "do not have . . . a clear marker of 'before' and 'after' . . . like zombies, they 'survive' in the sense of living on or beyond, but do not enter the temporal cycle where they would get to start over from scratch" (175). Ryan's series, which uses the trope of infection to undermine the foundations of humanist society, collapses the difference between zombie and human and, therefore, between human and environment, exposing the unsustainability of exploitative human civilization.

HUMANIST HOPELESSNESS

Overall, The Forest of Hands and Teeth series dismantles the humanist notion of civilization, without providing a viable alternative. Morrissey (2013) claims that within the series, "The voracious and stupid hunger of the Mudo is challenged by irrepressible youthful hope and exuberance driven by the desire for posthuman liberation" (194). However, in light of the endings of each of the three novels, it is difficult to see where this optimism comes from.

The Forest of Hands and Teeth ends with the frustration of Mary's hopes for a life untainted by the Unconsecrated; having fought her way through to the ocean, she finds that it, too, is overrun with the undead: "Already the ocean is washing around the Unconsecrated on the beach, pulling them back into the water, reclaiming them" (*Forest* 308). The image of the ocean, the ultimate symbol of hope for Mary and the cultural embodiment of vastness and illimitableness, awash with more infectious undead carries the implication of finitude, of a complete capitulation of the human world to infection and dissolution. The ocean, from which all human life originally sprang, has now become a breeding bed for a new and far more dangerous species. An image of similar ambiguity forms the end of *The Dead-Tossed Waves*, as Gabry and Catcher move away from a vast horde of the undead, "endless, stretching beyond the horizon and spreading around me like forever. They heave and moan, frothing over each other, cresting and falling. . . . They ripple and swell, the bodies of the Mudo, like the ocean. Like the dead-tossed waves" (395). Cut off from the life they have known by the collapse of the bridge that spanned the canyon in which the Horde has been sleeping, Catcher and Gabry move toward a future where annihilation is foreshadowed by the Horde's awakening. Despite Gabry's insistence that "There has to be more" (403), the ending of the novel suggests nothing but further death, pain, and eventual erasure for these couples fighting desperately against an ever-multiplying and interpenetrating enemy. *The Dark and Hollow Places*, which concludes the series, ends with a return to earlier dreams: Annah dreams of the ocean as described to her by her father Jacob, the boy who escapes the village with Mary in *The Forest of Hands and Teeth*. However, much as the reader knows the Horde is greater and more powerful than the mass of escapees from the Dark City, and that Catcher remains infectious, the reader also knows—as does Catcher—that the ocean is a false dream of hope.

In her discussion of posthumanism in children's fiction, Zoe Jaques (2015) argues for the importance of finding "alternative modes for conceptualizing the relationship between the human and the wider world" (16). This is precisely what Ryan fails to do. For Pat Wheeler (2013), the cli-fi dystopian apocalyptic text speculates on "the continuing evolution of human beings in post-apocalyptic futures that offer very different social and public environments" (59); however, when the cli-fi dystopia is superimposed upon the zombie narrative, the future is portrayed not just as different, but as humanistically hopeless. As Rutherford (2013) suggests, "zombie fictional works drive the future into a cul-de-sac of no return" (9). Ryan, by providing neither the bleak relief of complete annihilation nor the hope of humanist postapocalyptic revival, leaves readers with the difficult task of interrogating both the sustainability and the desirability of societies based on humanist values.

Bigger and Webb (2014) argue that one of the greatest values of fiction is that it "juxtaposes different opinions, requiring the reader to deliberate and decide, to take a stance" (132). Carrie Ryan's The Forest of Hands and Teeth series is ultimately subversive of humanist philosophy, in that each voice it presents to the reader is fundamentally incapable of sustaining humanist values. Although superficially modelled on the YA trend toward romantic fulfillment and self-development, in reality these novels show both ambitions to be unattainable, thereby undermining the very foundations of humanist society. However, The Forest of Hands and Teeth series ultimately fails to provide a viable alternative to the humanist model for civilization, choosing instead to depict the dissolution of the human body and of human society, and to imply the defeat of humanist hope by an overwhelming hostile environment. Ryan ultimately depicts the inability of humanism to endure indefinitely.

Chapter Two

Lois Lowry's The Giver

Biotechnology, Wilderness, and Government

If The Forest of Hands and Teeth series explores the hopelessness of the individual trapped within a humanist relationship to the natural world, then The Giver series (Lowry 1993, 2000, 2004, 2012), conversely, is concerned with the relationship of humanist societies to the natural world. The relationship—whether it consists of relationships to other sentient creatures, or to landscapes and spaces—is an enduring theme in human literature and culture, and for good reason. As Francis Fukuyama (2002) states in his fundamentally humanist exploration of a posthuman future, "what we consider to be the highest and most admirable human qualities, both in ourselves and in others, are often related to the way that we react to, confront, overcome, and frequently succumb to pain, suffering, and death" (173). Fukuyama's statement reveals an underlying defensiveness in the humanist relationship to environment: the environment here is something to be "overcome" and the source of "pain, suffering and death," and it is through this confrontation that the humanist human being becomes "human." Of course, such confrontation can happen on two levels: the level of the individual and the level of the collective. At the collective level, the banding together of human beings into collectives, communities, and eventually societies ruled over by government authorities, as many philosophers including, famously Kant and Hegel have argued, has enabled human beings to resist and control their environment, allowing better protection from other animals and human groups, security from environmental changes such as climate and natural disasters, and better management of resources such as crops, livestock, fuel, and so on. Humans choose to give up a measure of free will and autonomy in return for the protection that subservience to a collective affords.

It is at the personal level, however, that relationships to the natural world are formed, and such relationships are often considered fundamental to humanist subjectivity. However, these relationships are often antithetical to the needs of the collective: because environment and civilization are seen as binary opposites, so, too, are personal emotion and social responsibility. Human collectives—societies, communities, governments, civilizations—therefore, are the means of managing humanist subjectivity. In such a formulation it is only through the suppression of individual emotions and desires—so called "natural" behaviors—that civilization can be sustained. Humanist civilization, therefore, is predicated upon a fundamental principle, "the premise promulgated by Enlightenment humanism that a distinct and separate humanity is in essence divorced from his ecological embeddedness" (Curry 2013, 47)—in other words, the binary division between nature and culture. At the personal level, the relationship to the environment is often figured as an emotive one, in which human beings must learn to control negative emotions and foster positive emotions, so as to balance the needs of the collective with the desires of the self.

This is an aspect with which Fukuyama (2002) is particularly concerned; in *Our Posthuman Future,* Fukuyama devotes many pages to the dangers of biotechnology—and specifically neuropharmacology—to liberal humanist subjectivity. Among other examples, Fukuyama speculates on the impact of mind-altering phamaceuticals (such as Prozac and Ritalin), designer babies (a result of IVF, fetal screening, and germline genetic engineering), prolonged life expectancy, and cloning on the tenuous characteristic we call "human nature." Biotechnology, according to Fukuyama, has the potential to radically alter the human mind and body, in ways that are difficult to predict in both the short and long term. In particular, Fukuyama worries about the ways in which altering the human body will impact upon other aspects of humanist society, such as human rights, equal opportunity, and cultural diversity. While such technologies are the ultimate triumph of the human being over hostile nature, offering protection from death, aging, disease, and other lifeforms, they are also a threat in and of themselves. Ostensibly a means to facilitate the functioning of the individual within the limitations of society and civilization, such technologies also have far-reaching consequences for our relationship with the environment, as they reinforce the environment/civilization binary and limit the capacity of human beings for meaningful emotive relationships to the "natural" world.

Issues such as these are reflected in much literature, and especially literature for the young where, as Hintz explains, the bildungsroman mode common in YA utopias and dystopias often means that these types of text "contain at least two major elements: the developmental narrative and a consideration of political organization" (Hintz 2002, 254). Hintz describes *The Giver* in particular as embodying "explorations of personal autonomy and growth" as "not merely tropes of the young adult genre but a way of using the transition from adolescence to adulthood to focus on the need for political action and the exercise of political will within a democratic society" (Hintz 2002, 254). In Lois Lowry's The Giver quartet, both personal and collective relationships to the environment are explored, but both are used to explore the ways in which human societies manage the division between nature and culture. Lowry depicts societies in which this division is managed with greater or lesser success, without ever questioning the inherent harm in such a division.

ALIENATION FROM NATURE AND THE DESTRUCTION OF THE HUMANIST SUBJECT

At the personal level, The Giver series explores the dangers of a society that protects inhabitants too vigorously against a perceived hostile environment, and in the process threatens the humanity of its inhabitants. The use of biotechnology as a trope within the series critiques the alienation of individuals from nature, without necessarily questioning the need for a divide. One of the most controversial aspects of biotechnology—and one which makes a frequent appearance in YA dystopian fiction—is its use for modification of human behaviors and bodies. From neuropharmaceuticals to control "abnormal behavior," to genetically modified "designer babies" and gene modification to control physical appearance, sexual orientation, aging, and so forth, these technologies take the human conflict with the environment—whether that means an environment of Others or a physical space—to the extreme.

As Fukuyama (2002) argues, to modify the human body or brain in any way is to fundamentally change the relationship of that individual to the environment, while Greely (2017) identifies "safety, fairness, coercion, and naturalness" as critical ethical, social, and legal questions pertaining to bioscientific advances (217). Using Ritalin as just one example, Fukuyama (2002) discusses the overuse of the drug within the United States as a means of modifying "undesirable" behaviors in children in order to facilitate their socialization into liberal humanist society: Ritalin, far from treating any disease or deficiency (problematic terms in themselves) in the child, in fact modifies "natural" behavior for the convenience of patents, educators, and other disciplinarians (47). That such practices are an important and growing feature of human society is, for Fukuyama, a serious concern; that his concern is not unfounded is implied in the fact that the publication of the Ritalin prescribing information on the FDA website both points to its widespread usage and to implicit sanctioning of the listed side effects and risks (FDA 2017). For the patient who takes this drug, the advantage incurred in terms of increased attention span within situations of collective governance (such as the classroom) may well involve a trade-off in terms of an altered emotional state: nervousness, insomnia, libido changes. Such trade-offs are not only sanctioned by governments, but are also actively encouraged by official authorities ranging from federal agencies and state regulations, to doctors, pharmacists, teachers, and therapists, all of whom contribute a vested interest in processes that distance the child from his or her "natural" state in order to facilitate a smooth-running society. In other words, Fukuyama traces the process by which the "natural" behavior of the child or young person is rendered "unnatural" by collective social agreement: affect and emotions (such as joy, excitement, exuberance, anger, and sadness) are demonized, regulated, and abolished for the sake of social cohesion. This is a sinister picture, illustrative of a trend in modern humanist society described by Foucault (2008) as "biopolitics," or the control of the government over whole populations in every aspect of life; under the guise of concern for the well-being of individuals, government policies and practices support control of the individual for the sake of collective governance. This is similar to the type of posthuman political speculation described by Hughes (2017), in which the humanist claim that "[a]ll the weaknesses of human governance stem from our mammalian programming for emotion over reason, tribalism, and dominance" is used to justify human bodily alteration (172).

At the same time, according to Steve Fuller (2017), conventional politics is "ultimately about charting the career of *Homo sapiens*" (161, original italics); in other words, government is in part about the mobilization of collective power to fuel the evolution of human beings in a hostile environment for greater control and faster development, a desire that has been formally recognized in the field of transhumanism, which James Hughes (2017) defines as expressing "the ancient human aspiration to be wiser, longer lived, and to transcend the limitations of the human body" (133). Technology is the means not only of controlling the negative aspects of embodiment for the collective good, therefore, but also about promoting and creating improved embodiment. The body in humanist society is seen as a site for both regulation and enhancement by biotechnologies, with the trade-offs experienced by individual human beings both sanctioned as necessary and celebrated as liberatory. These enhancements help protect human society from the threats of hostile nature: Alzheimer's disease, infant mortality, Down syndrome, infertility, infection, limited fresh water, crop shortages, natural disasters like hurricanes and floods, old age, and death. Of course, such benefits are often more readily felt at the abstract level of the collective rather than by individuals: the eradication of Down syndrome, for example, may come at the expense of many individual aborted fetuses and untold parental heartbreak; unlimited genetically modified foods crops may spell the end (by poverty and starvation) of the individual subsistence farmer. In humanism, therefore, technology can be a double-edged sword that promotes the human race at the expense of the individual. For Fukuyama and humanists like him, the government-sanctioned use of biotechnology to control and suppress the individual is untenable, destroying true "human nature" by destroying human relationships to "nature"—both sentient others and the "natural" environment. Regulation of natural emotive responses to the environment are controlled for the "good" not of the individual, but of the society and the human race as a whole. There is in humanism, therefore, a constant trade-off between society as the protector of the human against the environment and society as the barrier between the human and its relationship with the environment.

When spread across wide sections of society, what do such trade-offs mean in terms of human beings' relationships to one another and to their environments? Lowry provides one answer in her depiction in *The Giver* of a supposedly utopian community. Throughout this first novel in the quartet, the regulation of human impulses toward the environment and each other by means of biotechnology are part and parcel of a repressive governmental regime designed to facilitate a society seen as advanced, utopian—the epitome of "civilization." In this society, all aspects of life are controlled, including the environment and "human nature." Natural weather extremes, for example, such as sunshine and snow have been erased, as have human sensory perceptions such as warmth and cold. Drugs have not only eradicated pain and sickness, but also emotion. People feel neither love nor hatred; jealousy and envy have been abolished and with them the motivations for conflict. Strict rules and laws govern exposure to the landscape of river and fields, while a program of eugenics breeding has almost eradicated natural personal variation. This society, in other words, depicts humans beings being protected in the most extreme way from the "nature" half of the binary, but ultimately at the expense of fundamental humanist traits.

The first and most striking example of this in The Giver series comes when Jonas first learns about the "pills." His "mother" explains that the pills are taken by every member of the community, starting from when they begin to have "stirrings." As Jonas muses:

> Stirrings. He had heard the word before. He remembered that there was a reference to the Stirrings in in the Book of Rules, though he didn't remember what it said. And now and then the Speaker mentioned it. ATTENTION. A REMINDER THAT STIRRINGS MUST BE REPORTED IN ORDER FOR TREATMENT TO TAKE PLACE. (*Giver* 47).

What is telling in this passage is the conflation of control with "treatment," essentially figuring non-compliance with the "Book of Rules" as akin to sickness, in an eerie echo and exaggeration of the widespread prescription of drugs such as Ritalin to children. What makes this so extreme, however, is the fact that taking the pills in this society is no longer a matter for doctors, but is instead universally required—a matter for government rather than medical regulation.

Levy (1999) writes that "Lowry has intentionally constructed its society to solve many contemporary problems, particularly those likely to be of significance to twelve year olds and their parents" (52); these pills do not solve only the problems pertaining to adolescents, however, because all adults take these pills with a few notable exceptions—the pregnant and the old. What becomes clear very quickly is that the pills are designed to suppress the undesirable aspects of human embodiment—the "natural," "animalistic" and sexual emotions and sensations that connect human beings to each other and to their environment. As Davis (2014) explains, "the community has clearly privileged the more benign forms of emotions and erased the others" (55–56). However, it would be more accurate to state that the community has regulated not against less benign emotion, but against extreme emotions. Emotions such as love, hate, envy, and remorse are valued in humanist society as uniquely "human" natural characteristics; at the same time they are the very characteristics that create conflict, and which therefore need to be regulated and managed for humanist civilization to be sustained. By depicting their complete annihilation, Lowry paints a chilling picture of what happens when technology attempts to improve upon nature.

Jonas is unaware of what he is missing until he discovers love—simultaneously through the memories from the Giver and through his attachment to Gabriel. After Jonas first experiences the memory of love, and shares it with baby Gabriel, we see Jonas' dawning revelation of what he is missing: "The next morning, for the first time, Jonas did not take his pill. Something within him, something that had grown there through the memories, told him to throw the pill away" (*Giver* 162). By making Jonas' revelation instinctual rather than something he is taught directly, Lowry implies that the instinct to feel and to love is "natural": something intrinsic to human beings.

In a similar manner, Claire in *Son* is exposed to maternal instinct and love as a result of an oversight: after her disastrous cesarean birth, those in charge forget to reestablish her on the pills, resulting in not only her ability to feel emotion but also her growing awareness of what is wrong with her community. The birth mothers discuss the pills together: "I began to be aware of my own feelings. Not just in my head, but—well, *physical* feelings too" (*Son* 114), and "It's really boring . . . when you're between births, and taking the pills. *Nothing* is much fun. You don't really notice it, though" (*Son* 115). Claire realizes that the cessation of the pills allows the girls to sustain their pregnancies, but she is also aware that it is the reason for their sense of community and comradery—and for the low esteem in which they are held by the rest of the Community. Biotechnologies such as the pills allow the community to erase the "natural" behaviors of human beings which cause conflict, protecting them from themselves. However, as Lowry's depiction in

Son makes clear, this protection also renders them inhuman automatons, unable to respond to or even see the unnaturalness of their condition. Furthermore, the necessity of withholding the pills from pregnant mothers suggests the limitations of technology over nature: the natural process of pregnancy and birth, it is implied, something that could not take place under the influence of the pills, and therefore the emotions and feelings the pills suppress remain fundamentally important to life itself. Lowry implies strongly that in relying on these nature-suppressing technologies, the members of the community are deluding themselves and doing untold damage in the process.

What are lost in these exchanges of technology for nature, furthermore, are the qualities of individualism as well as moral capacity, both of which are highly prized in liberal humanism as functions of reason and therefore exclusively human traits. Fukuyama (2002) highlights the entanglement of humanity and society, rejecting Rousseau's theory of the "wild" state of natural man and arguing instead that "human beings are by nature cultural animals, which means that they can learn from experience and pass on that learning to their descendants through nongenetic means" (13). He therefore makes a strong case for the biological and evolutionary, as well as social, necessity of human civilization, essentially suggesting that civilization is a "natural" phenomena based on evolutionary necessity. Although humanism celebrates the human capacity for emotions such as love and suffering, therefore, these are prized only when they contribute to the greater good of humanist society; where emotion runs wild and is indulged by the individual, it is often deemed unnatural and inhuman. This seems to be a perspective challenged in The Giver quartet, in which the pills—supposedly the foundation of this cohesive and successful civilization—are in fact a hindrance to biological reproduction as well as true social cohesion, ultimately resulting in the dissolution of the society over the course of the novels. Lowry suggests that by inhibiting feeling and emotion so aggressively, society becomes repressive and ultimately self-destructive. As we see throughout *The Giver*, a direct correlation is posited between "humanness" and a relationship with "nature," undermining the humanist binary division.

What the reader comes to understand in *The Giver* and later in *Son* is that as well as stifling human "nature," the pills also destroy the connections of the people in the community to the natural environment—in fact, to any environment. As Hintz, Basu, and Broad (2013) point out, *The Giver* "presents a world of stifling 'sameness' devoid of color, emotion, and memory" (3): significantly the taking of the pills to stifle feelings is linked intimately within the novels to an alienation from physical enjoyment of the environment. The commitment to "sameness," in other words, disregards "all environmental and individual incongruities such as colors, cold, figurative meaning in language, seasons, and so on" (Cengiz 2017, 18), and communal harmony is sustained because "there is no contact with the natural world"

(Hintz 2002, 261). Jonas learns the pleasures of snow and sunlight, for example, through the Giver's memories: "the speed, the clear cold air, the total silence, the feeling of balance and contentment and peace" (*Giver* 103). Here the emotions of contentment and peace are directly linked to the experience of physical sensations in an interactive environment: the cold, the feathery softness of the flakes, and the feel of the wind rushing past him. These sensations, like the warmth of sunshine, will become symbolic throughout the series, carrying the significance of positive human emotions such as love and courage, which have been lost to most members of the Community. Furthermore, the Giver explains the reasons behind the loss of these qualities: "Climate Control. Snow made growing food difficult, limited the agricultural periods. And unpredictable weather made transportation almost impossible at times. It wasn't a practical thing, so it became obsolete when we went to Sameness" (*Giver* 106). Control of the self, in other words, is figured as equating to control of the environment, and is achieved through a loss of the emotive connections which make control difficult.

In a manner similar to the loss of sensations such as cold and warmth, the members of the Community also lack the ability to see color, "symbolizing the sacrifice of that which gives beauty and meaning to life" (Hubler 2014, 231). When Jonas begins to receive the memories and stops taking the pills, color returns to him: "he could see all the colors; and he could *keep* them, too, so that the trees and grass and bushes stayed green in his vision. Gabriel's rosy cheeks stayed pink, even when he slept . . . he had seen oceans and mountain lakes and streams that gurgled through woods" (*Giver* 164). The examples Jonas cites equate connection to other humans beings—Gabe's rosy cheeks—and connection to the natural world—the trees and grass, and the wilder terrains he knows only from memory. Both wild terrain and wildlife have been denied to the citizens of the Community, to the extent that animals have become creatures of myth: we learn that within the community in *The Giver* "Many of the comfort objects, Like Lily's, were soft, stuffed, imaginary creatures. Jonas's had been called a bear" (*Giver* 23). In *Son*, the evolutionary disadvantages of this strategy become apparent: outside of the Community, Claire is "fearful of the smallest of creatures" (*Son* 156) and, unable to correctly identify medicinal plants, she apologetically explains "I'm only learning colors. They're as strange to me as birds" (*Son* 165). As AbedelRahim (2015) argues, an understanding of and close relationship to the natural environment has been fundamental to the evolutionary success of human beings: "To have successfully lived and flourished in the diversity of wilderness, communities of life and nonlife have had to rely on the intelligence of their members to know how to be in the world, how to collaborate with other living and non-living beings, and help life be" (4). However, she also discusses the fact that such a relationship is both arduous and threatening: it requires effort, practice, and skill, and exposes individuals and communities to the constant threat of a wrong judgment or failed relationship. Society—civilization—according to AbdelRahim, mitigates this threat. It places human culture defensively in opposition to nature, sharing the risk and making survival easier. In extreme, this is the trade-off made by the citizens of the Community. Lowry suggests strongly in this first novel, then, that a strong, positive bodily relationship to nature is fundamental to the evolutionary survival of the human race, and that humanist civilization is antithetical to such a relationship. In this sense, *The Giver* seems on the surface to challenge humanist philosophies.

It is significant that Lowry makes a direct correlation between "natural" human individuality which makes, for example, a mother's love of a child possible, and a relationship to the "natural" world of weather, flora, and fauna. Fukuyama argues that civilization—so long as it is based upon humanist values of justice, equality, and so on—is a natural feature of the human species, a result of the very spirit of collaboration identified by AbdelRahim. Collective authority, however, when it becomes too strong, can take this protection too far, relinquishing the relationship to nature, which hones human skills in favor of complete control and domination over nature: this, according to AbdelRahim, places the environment at risk and, according to Fukuyama, places humanist subjectivity at risk. In humanist philosophy, therefore, there is a constant tension between the natural environment viewed as the very source of "human nature" and the natural environment viewed as a constant threat to human survival. Science and technology, furthermore, are radically implicated in both attitudes toward the environment, becoming tools for the enforcement of the separation of nature and culture, as well as for the supposedly "natural" evolution of the human entity. If the community portrayed in *The Giver* and *Son* shows how socially-sanctioned rupture from the environment can destroy human nature, the communities portrayed in *Gathering Blue* and *Messenger* are equally adamant about the hostility of the natural world to vulnerable societies. Lowry may challenge the humanist drive to control nature and embodiment, as we have seen, but she ultimately falls back upon the humanist insistence that such control is necessary.

HUMANIST SOCIETY AS A DEFENSE AGAINST A HOSTILE ENVIRONMENT

While the novels themselves explicitly criticize alienation from the natural environment as harmful to the development of humanist values such as individualism, moral and ethical reasoning, family cohesion, and so forth, they also emphasize the importance of these values as the means of keeping a hostile environment at bay and under control. Humanism, therefore, both fosters and is damaged by alienation from nature. As is clear from *Gathering*

Blue, *Messenger*, and *Son*, this alienation is in part a defense mechanism against an environment perceived as at least potentially hostile. Civilization offers protection to the humanist subject—both the physical protection from environmental threats such as wild animals, starvation, and climate, but also protection from the ontological reality of humanity as merely one fragment of a greater environmental whole. To do so, however, it exploits both the environment and the individual, using the hierarchy that prioritizes the human over the nonhuman to also prioritize some humans over others. With exploitation and control of the environment justified in terms of human survival (the anthropocentricism which, according to AbdelRahim, will pave the way for humanism), exploitation and control are normalized, paving the way for the degradation of the humanist values upon which civilization is founded. Civilization, in other words, is a self-destructive cycle.

In *Messenger* in particular, this degradation is figured crudely as giving rise to selfish capitalism; capitalism is the catalyst that causes civilization to begin to fail. As Curry (2013) argues, "Capitalism, as a product of the neoliberal free market, rewards the self-actualising individual and marginalises discourses of dependence, community or collective empowerment" (43); this is exactly what is shown to be occurring when the Community falls under the sway of the Trademaster. We first learn of the Trademaster's power to destroy community when Matty hears those who have traded argue for the closing of Village's borders to further refugees:

> One by one the people spoke, and one by one Matty identified those who had traded. Some of those who had been among the most industrious, the kindest, and the most stalwart citizens of Village now went to the platform and shouted out their wish that the border be closed so that 'we' (Matty shuddered at the use of *we*) would not have to share the resources anymore. (*Messenger* 85).

Here we see the very reasons for human community—better access to resources and better protection from a hostile environment—undermined by a selfish focus on the individual. The Trademaster destroys community by stealing positive human qualities—much like the pills in the Community did; as Mentor explains later to Gabriel in *Son*, "I had traded away the most important part of myself. I turned selfish. Cruel. The pretty widow didn't want a man like that! So I had made a meaningless trade, and I had turned into a person I hated—but a handsome one! And young!" (*Son* 361). Such individual selfishness is positioned as "unnatural," and renders the community vulnerable to the hostile environment surrounding it—the Forest. The resulting focus on individual desires in the novel, therefore, shows the aspects of civilization pertaining to exploitation taking precedence, and as a result undermining the very protective aspects civilization is supposed to offer. Just as *The Giver* does, *Messenger* offers stark criticism of humanist ideals such as rationality and individualism when they are taken to extremes; again, although Lowry does not acknowledge it, there is an implicit suggestion that the underlying assumptions of humanism itself might be flawed.

Throughout all four novels in the quartet, the reason for communities such as Village and the Community is shown to be the hostility of a harsh and unforgiving environment: the binary opposition between civilization and nature is therefore the humanist assumption being explored in these novels. At the start of *Gathering Blue*, for example, Kira explains that "Fear was always a part of life for the people. Because of fear, they made shelter and found food and grew things. For the same reason, weapons were stored, waiting. There was fear of cold, of sickness and hunger. There was fear of beasts" (*Gathering Blue* 3). This community holds together despite a lack of human feeling and emotion because it has no choice in the face of a hostile and threatening environment, in which hunger, cold, and danger are omnipresent. In *Son* the ocean and the cliff equally mark the boundaries of human civilization, circumscribing the limits of human ability: "the ocean was turbulent and unpredictable, with dangerous currents and constant wind" (*Son* 136). The most striking example of this hostility, however, is found in *Messenger*, in which we learn that in response to the human disengagement from feeling, nature has become actively malignant. As the inhabitants of Village become more and more set on closing their borders to incomers, the forest prepares to support their decision, actively attacking anyone who strays into it from within an established community. As Matty struggles to bring Kira home to her father, he describes how "Forest was shifting, moving, thickening, and preparing to destroy them" (*Messenger* 134). Here the forest is not only malignant, but personified—an active force against which humans must strive.

The reader eventually comes to understand in *Son* that the hostility of the natural environment is a direct result of the Trademaster's actions. Significantly, the Trademaster himself seems to be aligned with the natural environment outside of civilization: as Gabe swims to meet this malignant force, he experiences the "relentless churn and pull" of the river, a "brisk wind" that chills him as "the shadows darkened and enveloped the swaying shrubbery and trees" (*Son* 373). At first, the implication in *Messenger* is that it is not nature itself, but human perceptions of nature, which render it hostile: when Matty defeats Forest's attack he sees that "It was an illusion. It was a tangled knot of fears and deceits and dark struggles for power that had disguised itself and almost destroyed everything" (*Messenger* 168). The implication is that the "it" is the Trademaster, and that Matty has healed not the forest, but the harm done by the Trademaster to the Villagers. There is enormous potential in this conceit for critical examination of the humanist assumption of man's separation from nature. However, in *Son* when Gabe finally defeats Trademaster, we learn that "It had never been human" (*Son* 391). By placing the threat externally, in an inhuman creature which emerges from the forest and mobilizes the environment against the humans from which it steals the humanist values on which civilization is founded, Lowry inadvertently reinscribes the binary of nature/civilization.

Just as in *The Giver* the too-aggressive enforcement of the nature-culture divide resulted in the crumbling of humanist values, in *Gathering Blue*, *Messenger*, and *Son*, the dissolution of humanist values leaves the community vulnerable to a hostile natural world. As Bradford et al. (2008) argue, then, "The trilogy does not trace the formation of an ideal community: in *The Giver* and *Gathering Blue*, such communities are desired but not attained by protagonists" (108), and this holds true as well for *Messenger* and *Son*, even though the latter ends on an optimistic note. Each protagonist eventually falls back on humanism as the solution to a problem, whether it be that the gifts of the individual permit the defeat of a hostile natural environment, or of a manifestation of a corrupt society, or of a powerful and dehumanizing government.

THE HUMANIST HERO SOLVES HUMANIST PROBLEMS

In *Gathering Blue* and *Messenger*, Lowry depict societies which, in direct contrast to that in *The Giver*, are weak in their lack of advanced technology and human skill to protect them from a threatening natural environment. Similarly, in *Son* she depicts a fishing village equally vulnerable in its lack of protection from a threatening natural environment. In all three of these societies, furthermore, the lack of skill and technology is implicitly blamed upon a lack of humanist values among the inhabitants. Thus, the threat of the environment increases in proportion to the failure of a properly managed humanist nature/culture divide. Culture can be restored and nature controlled, in these depictions, by humanist heroes who display extraordinary humanist skills.

A threatening and hostile environment is a key feature of much dystopian fiction; in such novels, the decay of human civilization is often mapped symbolically onto a degraded physical space, which in itself forms a testing ground for the development of individual humanist subjectivity. Curry (2013) argues that this is especially the case for the YA bildungsroman form, stating that in these novels "tension can be perceived between the common construction of subjectivity as a stable, autonomous category and an acknowledgement that the visibly decaying landscape must nevertheless impact upon the identity formation of its inhabitants" (46–47). For many ecocritics, this attitude of conflict toward natural spaces in a dystopian future is a direct result of what is perceived as a negligent and alienated attitude toward natural spaces within human societies as they currently stand. Regarding the "segregation of space" such as wildlife reserves and national parks, for example, Curry (2013) argues that: "western environmentalism has arguably failed to envisage the human subject as already ecologically embedded" (133). Curry's argument is that solutions that depend on specific types of control over the environment can only ever exacerbate ecological problems because they perpetuate the same mindset of control and separation upon which exploitation is founded. In other words, humanism causes the problem of a degraded landscape by insisting on a separation of nature and culture, which justifies exploitation and results in a hostile environment.

However, that same hostile environment will in turn foster humanist heroes whose exemplary humanist subjectivity will restore human civilization and reestablish control over the environment. The result is that the environment, and particularly natural spaces, are both feared and celebrated for having fundamental impacts on humanist subjectivity; where such subjectivity forms in the "right" way, the relationship to nature will be positive and nurturing, but where it goes wrong, the degraded landscape, which is the result, is the ideal testing ground upon which it can be fixed. As discussed in the previous section, throughout the series we see human beings struggling against an environment which, in the face of their own degraded societies, is actively malevolent and hostile. What is clear from each of these depictions is that the hostility of nature derives in whole from the absence of sound humanist values in these communities. Because they lack the technological protections and skills which, in *The Giver*, are taken to extremes, their environment has become threatening, rendering them as vulnerable animals in a fierce evolutionary battle. Only when the appropriate humanist values have returned to these societies via extraordinary humanist heroes is a proper, safe equilibrium with nature restored: one in which human beings are free to construct their subjectivity against a benign and nurturing natural environment.

Writing in 1987, the philosopher Cheney argues that "an answer to what might be our moral relationship to the nonhuman environment depends upon (1) a complex understanding of what it is to be a human being, what it is to respond to another human being as a human being . . . and (2) an understanding of how those complex webs of relationships that constitute the human moral community might expand to include the nonhuman" (105). What Cheney does not acknowledge in this formation is that, by keeping the human firmly at the center of the moral compass, any ethics of relationship to the environment is one rooted in the assumption of separateness and thus, inevitably, conflict. Like Cheney, Lowry allows her narrative solutions to depend on a particularly gifted humanist subject to establish control over the environment. At the end of *The Giver*, we are introduced to the idea that individuals have special—supernatural—powers and gifts: "Using his final strength, and a special knowledge that was deep inside him, Jonas found the sled that was waiting for them at the top of the hill" (*Giver* 224). It is significant that in this novel, Jonas does not attempt to heal his community; instead he uses his gift to foster his own subjectivity and will, fleeing the Community and beginning afresh elsewhere. Although Lowry does not openly acknowledge it, Jonas' decision to flee rather than fix is symbolic of the inability of humanist solutions to fix humanist problems.

Later, Kira will use her gift of prophecy to save her community from selfishness and inhumaneness just as Jonas and the Giver do, Matty's gift of healing will likewise save Village, and Gabe's gift of veering will do the same. In each instance of individual skill and innate giftedness, these protagonists use control to restore their communities' control over the hostile environment around them. Matty's healing powers, for example, allow him to save Kira from the attack of the Forest—an attack, it is strongly implied, which has been brought on by the hostility of human civilization to the Other. Later, Gabe's gift will enable him to defeat the Trademaster by exerting stronger control over the hostile Forest and the powers of nature than the Trademaster himself can. Critically, the special powers of these protagonists hinge upon humanist ideals and values: rationalism, technological prowess, a strong sense of individualism, and positive emotive capacity (love, friendship, loyalty). These ideals are placed in opposition to that which lacks them—the Trademaster, the Forest, the Community, and the Sea—in a formulation that equates the Outside and the Other with chaos, wildness, danger, impersonal hostility, and negative emotive capacity (hunger, hatred, and loneliness). In each case, human communities exist in opposition to hostile, outside, natural forces which are defeated by a remarkable humanist hero or heroine.

The series, therefore, having established the nature/civilization binary, suggests that humans survive in a hostile world only as a result of special powers, over which they can exert control over their environments. Jonas' gift enables him to survive the cold by recalling memories of warmth, Matty's gift forces Forest to recede, and Gabe's gift calms the turbulent river as he crosses to confront the Trademaster. Their gifts frequently circumvent natural forces such as illness, death, time, and space. Critically, what is restored in these depictions is not a relationship of reciprocity with nature, but one of clear-cut separation and control. The humanist conflict between nature and culture, therefore, remains intact through each happy ending. While the novels posit a positive outcome for those who adopt humanist ideals, the natural environment remains a source of conflict and threat.

It is this conflict that is both managed by and maintained by human civilization, in the form of governments and authorities. This is why Jonas' and Gabe's escape from the community at the end of *The Giver* cannot be and is not the end of the story, because wherever they find community, they must also struggle to maintain their humanist subjectivity in relationship to the perceived environment. The power structures that maintain civilization actively manage the human relationship to the environment, attempting to avoid both the dehumanization that results from alienation, and the threat that results from too much closeness.

What these novels demonstrate, therefore, is the self-perpetuating cycle of humanist logic, in which the insistence on the nature/culture divide inevitably erodes the very humanism on which it is founded, only to be reinstated by a humanist hero to begin the cycle again. Lowry's novels suggest that what is needed is not a reimagination of the human place within the cosmos, but instead a sharpening of the humanist skills that supposedly place us above and beyond nature: skills such as cognitive capacity, technological advancement, and rationality. The novels are based upon a circular humanist logic that refuses to confront the underlying problem that all human "control" is temporary, and therefore illusory.

For Latham (2004) this circularity—at least in the first novel—is tempered by hope: "The novel . . . serves to reintegrate readers into the power structures of our own society while at the same time empowering them as potential agents of positive social change" (135). Other critics such as Stewart (2007) are much less forgiving, arguing that "*The Giver* fails to address alterity, reinforces cultural continuity, and actually diminishes opportunities to think in terms of difference because of its overriding humanist impetus" (26). She argues that "[w]hile it appears that Jonas's actions are quite radical, they are actually very conservative . . . the individual takes precedence over the community" (25). Bradford et al. (2008) make the point even more clearly, arguing that "Lowry's depiction of exceptional individuals destined to act as catalysts for reform is mapped onto humanist ideas concerning an essential human nature which exists outside social and cultural formations" (110–11).

In their insistence upon the ability of gifted humanist subjects with enhanced humanist traits to maintain control over nature and restore crumbling societies, Lowry's novels encourage readers to remain trapped within the cycle of destructive alienation from and fear of the natural environment. Lowry, when asked if young adults can handle pure dystopia, replies: "Young people handle dystopia every day: in their lives, their dysfunctional families, their violence-ridden schools. They watch dystopian television and movies about the real world where firearms bring about explosive conclusions to conflict" (Hintz and Ostry 2003, 199). What she does not add, however, is that in many of these depictions, young people are not called upon to consider the radical measures that might be necessary to end the dystopias they experience at every turn.

This radical measure is the acknowledgment of the nature/culture divide as illusory and damaging. While such a move is almost impossibly difficult, entailing a radical alternation in deeply embedded ideas about government and society, as Åsberg (2017) argues, "In the context of the ecological crisis, we simply can no longer afford the modern divide of non- or subhuman and human, nature and culture" (193). This is an acknowledgment that The Giver quartet, in its commitment to humanist values, simply refuses to make.

Chapter Three

Patrick Ness's Chaos Walking Trilogy

Language and the Nonhuman Other

If there is one area that brings the posthuman into greater focus than any other, then the human colonization of space may be it. Narratives of space exploration and development, whether they appear in the dramas of science fiction or the rhetoric of science and politics, juxtapose ideas about human development and progress with questions about human interactions with both nonhuman lifeforms and environments, while simultaneously questioning human exclusivity in the face of the vastness of space. In the West, these narratives have been shaped by humanist values: as a quick glance at NASA's 2018 strategic plan (NASA 2018) reveals, liberal humanist rhetoric about "exploration," "human expansion," and "knowledge" is easily elided with neoliberal market-driven politics which emphasizes "commercial" interests and "industry." With this in mind, it is easy to see how space exploration has been pursued with potentially devastating impact on the environment, both in terms of material damage, and in terms of the ethical and philosophical relationship of human beings to their environments. Noeil Sturgeon (2009) utilizes a postcolonial ecocritical lens to describe extraterrestrialism as an extension of the "frontier myth" in US discourse: this myth, he explains, has consisted in the West of "[s]eeing Third World peoples as primitive populations or cheap labor rather than complex cultures, conceptualizing natural resources in the Global South as available for 'development' and presenting ideologies of the 'free market' as a narrative of inevitable and desired evolutionary progress" (82). Sturgeon furthermore explains that this frontier myth is effectively without bounds: the same logic that has celebrated violent expansion into the Third World and Global South is frequently extended to discourses concerning space exploration and colonization, assuming the use of extraterrestrial resources to be a "natural" right of human beings.

There are, in addition, environmental implications associated with the frontier myth. The narrative of human expansion into space allows the problematic relationship to earthly environments to be displaced, on the assumption that in a "new" environment, the problems of the past can be overcome. Such an assumption is an extension of the "technological" solution to environmental problems found in much mainstream environmentalism, underpinned by faith in human evolution—frequently equated to technological development—to overcome what comes to be seen as merely one more hurdle in the survival of the species. Technologies such as exoskeletal spacesuits or body enhancements enabling astronauts to regulate body functions in space, faster-than-light space vehicles, and permanent space-station environments are all technological dreams about what human beings would need to colonize a new and hostile environment.

In this development of technology that enables human beings to "evolve" beyond their "natural" environments, there would seem to be an obvious route into consideration of the posthuman. Elaine Ostry (2004) views the technological advances of the twenty-first century as spurring on the development of posthuman science fiction; she writes that in the face of the "technobody," adapted by both bioengineering and machines, "[w]hat it means to be human has never been more flexible, manipulated or in question" (222). While much mainstream environmentalism has focused on technology, attempting to find technological solutions to environmental issues—including, coincidentally, extraterrestrial exploration—the Chaos Walking series (Ness 2008, 2009, 2010) shows the futility of such a solution, demonstrating that both social and environmental problems stem not from physical environmental pressures, but from so-called human nature. Chaos Walking, in other words, is science fiction which does not begin with the premise of the technologically altered human being, and which instead explores the failure of technology to solve the problems of human "nature."

Ostry (2004) identifies in many posthuman YA science fiction texts "the line of thought that science has lost control and needs to be reined in" (242), a view echoed by Kay Sambell (2004); in contrast, the Chaos Walking trilogy makes clear that it is the people and not the technology that is at fault. Furthermore, it does so through a focus specifically on issues of language. This is significant in posthumanist terms, as it draws attention to the roots of liberal humanism in Enlightenment philosophy, and particularly Cartesean philosophy, which pinpointed language as a measure of reason, and both as the foundation upon which the posit a binary opposition of mind and body. This division of mind and body has, in turn, supported a growing human disdain for the material, including both human and nonhuman bodies, and the environment (Graham 2002; Fromm 1996). At the same time, language—as the indicator of reason—has become the marker by which the human is distinguished from the nonhuman, allowing binary divisions (such as human/ animal, human/slave, human/nature) to become hierarchical and human beings to self-proclaim themselves as superior (Braidotti 2013; Derrida 1997). Language, then, in posthumanist criticism is seen as a means of distinguishing the "human" from the "nonhuman" for the purpose of hierarchical categorization and control. However, posthuman representations challenge language as a measure of reason and as valid grounds for categorization and control, revealing the linguistic barrier to be fluid, mutable, and leaky. The dystopian mode in the Chaos Walking trilogy stems directly from the revelation of the linguistically based dichotomy between human and nonhuman as illusory.

For language to be the focus of dystopia is not unusual: David Sisk (1997), for example, identifies in twentieth-century dystopias "a central emphasis on language as the primary weapon with which to resist oppression, and the corresponding desire of repressive government structures to stifle dissent by controlling language" (2). He cites Benjamin Lee Whorf's 1940 theory that "language gives shape and structure to human perceptions" (12). According to Sisk (1997), one reason for the rapid growth of the dystopian genre in the twentieth and twenty-first centuries has been the fact that "people are becoming more aware of the implications of language controls" and that "the growth of mass media and new information technologies has provided more avenues through which such controls can be identified" (164). This view is shared by Magdalena Mączyńska (2011), who argues that the Chaos Walking trilogy specifically "sprang from a crucial characteristic of the contemporary world, namely the overflow of information" (73). In the Chaos Walking trilogy, the myth of a human superiority based on reason is exposed when human beings are denied exclusive control of and access to language, and therefore of nonhuman Others. Through the exploration of language and reason across species boundaries, Patrick Ness calls into question the humanist binary formulations that separate the human from the nonhuman sentient lifeform, suggesting that illusory binary as a root cause of conflict between human beings and the wider environment.

LANGUAGE, SENTIENCE, AND INTERCONNECTION: INTERACTING WITH THE SPACKLE/LAND

What Graham Huggan and Helen Tiffin (2010) identify as postcolonialism, animal studies and environmental studies' shared "concerns with conquest, colonization, racism and sexism, along with . . . investments in theories of indigeneity and diaspora and the relations between native and invader societies and cultures" (6) are also of key interest to posthumanist studies, as the underlying causes of conflict between human, Other, and environment are explored alongside humanist discourses of colonization and development. Each of these disciplines engages with a central dilemma: the humanist assumption that (some) humans have the right to control land, resources, and lives because they hold essential "human" qualities lacked by others. For example, many postcolonial historians have discussed the justifications common to European colonization and the slave trade that indigenous populations were less civilized, less evolved, less intelligent, and even less human than their European counterparts, making it acceptable to colonize them for their own good. Similar arguments have been used to justify the incarceration of the mentally and physically disabled, the use of animal subjects in drug and product testing laboratories, and even the abortion of human embryos: the argument is that those who are "more" human—more intelligent, more civilized, more emotive, and so on—have a right to control those who are "less" human. Similar logic extends to the environment, which is seen as a resource which can be owned, controlled, and exploited by human beings. A hierarchy is thus formed with some human beings (historically white, European heterosexual males) at the top, other human beings (women, children, the disabled, indigenous people, homosexuals, and so on) lower down, animals lower down still, and the non-sentient environment at the bottom. Postcolonial studied indicate the ways in which humanist colonization has led to both environmental and social exploitation of Others: as Val Plumwood (2003) argues, in the colonial imagination non-European lands are understood as "spaces" which are "unused, underused or empty," and the people indigenous to them are "primitive," "less rational, and closer to children, animals and nature" (53), while Sarah Reese (2014) argues that "indigenous cultures are often associated with the natural environment, and . . . are subsumed as a part of a perceived non-human otherness" (247).

Critically, language has traditionally been one of the primary markers by which these hierarchical categorizations have been established. Elaine L. Graham (2002), for example, describes how revelations about the language capacity of chimpanzees sparked popular and scientific debates about the genetics, evolution, and cultural superiority of *Homo Sapiens* (23–24). The clue, of course, is in the name: "sapiens" or *sapere*—to be wise—identifies reason as a key marker of humanness, eliding measurable science with subjective judgment. Those who have self-declared themselves as "wise," under humanist logic have a seemingly "natural" and "scientific" right to control those who are less "wise." In posthuman terms, the humanist subject has often assumed the right to power over nonhuman Others. Derrida's concept of *l'animot*, expressed in *The Animal that Therefore I Am* (1997) indicates why this might be so: Derrida argues that possession of recognized language abilities conveys upon the human subject an illusory sense of difference, separation, and uniqueness, which, in turn, allows the denial of the agency, subjectivity and power of those whose language is not recognized. Language (a supposed sign of reason) is the marker by which the humanist subject defines himself in contrast to the Other, as well as the means by which the Other is labelled and described. The namer and describer gains individual subjectivity even as the Other is denied the same. In postcolonial terms, Roberta Seelinger Trites (1997) explains that "those who are denied language are denied their full potential as humans" (62). Both postcolonial studies and environmental studies identify as a problem the fact that "'others' may speak but their speech is often pre-positioned so as not to be heard by those in power" (Huggan and Tiffin 2010, 191). Language, therefore, is a key component of the process of Othering inherent in colonization, justifying the abuses of the humanist subject.

In the Chaos Walking trilogy, these concerns are brought into focus through the portrayal of the indigenous inhabitants of New World, dubbed the "Spackle" by the colonizers, and the "Land" by themselves. Lacking externally vocalized language as well as written language, the Land communicate with one another by means of a telepathically shared language known as the "Voice"; this telepathy is shared by the male human settlers as well (although not the female), who struggle to adapt to the sudden openness of their thoughts that occurs soon after they land on the alien planet. From the start, therefore, the narrative in Chaos Walking directly links issues of colonization to issues of language. According to Parrinder (2001), the concept of colonization of the Other is inherent in humanist philosophy: "The scientific revolution—and thus the history of modern Western civilization—begins with the acts of learning from other worlds symbolized by the names of Columbus and Galileo" (4). The first example we see in the series of such Othering occurs when Todd, encountering the puzzle that is Viola's lack of Noise for the first time, reflects on the Spackle while gazing on one of their abandoned huts:

> There's writing on the outside of this one, the only written words anyone has ever seen in the spack language. The only words they ever saw fit to write down, I guess. The letters are spack letters, but Ben says they make the sound *es'Paqili* or suchlike, *es'Paqili*, the Spackle, "spacks" if you wanna spit it, which since what happened happened is what everyone does. Means "The People." (*Knife* 15).

Here, the juxtaposition of Todd's dismissive and hostile attitude toward the Spackle with the physical evidence of their annihilation indicates the way in which language has been used by the settlers as a benchmark for sentience, and therefore respect. Human language has named the indigenous people while simultaneously denying them emotive and cognitive capacity based on their supposed inability to communicate; the similarity of the proffered name "es'Paqili" to Spanish (with *es* clearly indicating *the*) calls to mind parallel processes of language colonization practiced by Europeans in the Americas. In contrast, the human settlers are able to maintain their humanist subjectivity by insisting on themselves as the only lifeforms on the planet with "proven" sentience—a written and spoken language. The colonizers explain their initial hostility to the Spackle, whose presence on the planet presumed empty was unpleasant surprise: the "deep space probes didn't show any signs of intelligent life" (*Monsters* 353). The combination of technology and language has been used to label and categorize the indigenous people of the planet by humans who are willing to form relationships based solely on their own, humanist criteria. Later, when Todd kills the unarmed Spackle, it is their difference in language that enables Todd to convince himself of his opponent's inhumanity: "No words come out clear, just pictures, skewed up strange and with all the wrong colors" (*Knife* 272). The Spackle's failure to conform to Todd's expectations about both sentience and conflict allow Todd to alienate him and distance himself, making the murder inevitable. Similarly, when humans enslave the Spackle in Haven/New Prentisstown, dominance over these other sentient creatures is ensured once again through control of language: "the noise was the only way they communicated. . . . It turned out we didn't really need them to talk to us to tell them what to do. . . . So who cares if they needed to talk to each other? [The cure] makes them docile. . . . Better slaves" (*Ask* 100). In this passage it is suggested that the colonizers enforced their perception of the Spackle as nonhuman by enforcing the lack of language and sentience that they had themselves assumed the Spackle to suffer from; as with their naming of these people as "Spackle" rather than "Land," the settlers use language to create the environment of nonhuman others they both expect and require to maintain their humanist subjectivity.

However, this process of Othering through language is fragile precisely because it assumes an uncomplicated relationship between sign and signified. Huggan and Tiffin (2010) draw attention the problematic nature of linguistic representation, reminding us that "the power of the sign lies in its embodiment" (193); when linguistic representation fails to match embodied reality, the invincibility of the humanist subject begins to waver, creating what Huggan and Tiffin (2010) describe as "the vexed question of interspecies communication" (192). This happens primarily through the human exposure to Noise, which removes both language control and exclusive access to language from human subjects. Explaining the title of the series, Todd explains in *The Knife of Never Letting Go* that "The Noise is a man unfiltered, and without a filter, a man is just chaos walking" (42). What this description reveals is that it is *language* which is revealed as artificial—a "filter," and the *chaos* (as the settlers see it), which is "natural."

While the settlers have always relied on their control of and access to language as the tool that gives them superiority, the Noise reveals that it is a tool they have actually not yet learned to wield properly. What they have seen as control over their environment is revealed to be little more than deafness to the totality of what they cannot control: as Todd explains it, "Everything on this planet talks to each other. . . . Everything. That's what New World is. Informayshun, all the time, never stopping, whether you want it or not" (*Knife* 390–91). Surprisingly, it is Aaron who first voices this realization: "Language, young Todd" explains Aaron, "binds us like prisoners on a chain" (*Knife* 27). The humanist insistence on language as a means of understanding, controlling, and categorizing the environment—a process that ensures a stable individual subjectivity (I am that which can communicate with or name an "other")—is revealed to be limited, and that subjectivity itself is shown to be illusory. According to Adrienne Kertzer (2012), "the male settlers appear to be suffering a collective trauma produced by a lack of boundaries between the self and the group as a whole" (11). With every man's thoughts open to both other humans and to other sentient life forms, individual subjectivity becomes increasingly hard to maintain. As the collapse of human settlements across the planet further indicates, without a stable sense of human individual subjectivity, domination and subjugation are likewise made difficult.

As a solution to this inherent problem of the humanist language of Othering, therefore, Ness portrays not separation, governance, or domination, but instead a merging of languages that moves beyond humanist ideas of subjectivity. In the Chaos Walking series, the conflict portrayed between the Land and the human settlers ends only when the human beings learn to understand the limitations that a humanist understanding of language has placed upon them. Noeil Sturgeon (2009) explains how in many science fiction and environmental narratives, "the possibility of global annihilation is portrayed as the only means of bringing the world together" (91). However, it is not the threat of mutual annihilation that eventually ends the conflict; instead, it is the human capitulation to a new form of (nonhumanist) language that offers the possibility of peace. When Ben first awakes from his enforced coma with the Land, he speaks to 1017, and "though he shows it to us in the language of the Clearing," Ben nevertheless also "shows it in the perfect, unmistakable voice of the Land" (*Monsters* 386). Ben's ability and willingness to overlook the differences in communication, and thus subjectivity, between the Land and the humans is what maps a path forward and beyond conflict. As the Sky explains to 1017, "If this one can immerse himself so far into the Land with such obvious understanding and feel himself part of the Land . . . does it make him an ally? . . . Does it provide us more hope for the future than we ever thought possible? If he can do it, can others? Is there more understanding possible?" (*Monsters* 423). Here, the elision of the Land with their Voice is made explicit; Ben's immersion in their communication is described as an absorption into the people themselves. It is an experience Todd will later describe as being able to "hear the voice of the planet," when he "lives within it, lets himself be part of it, lets himself ride the current of it without losing himself" (*Monsters* 564–65). It is this complete immersion into the subjectivity of others—at the expense even of his individual feelings and desires—that makes Ben the hope for the future of New World. He explains to Viola why they must not take vengeance on 1017 for accidentally shooting Todd, even as Todd lies dying in his arms: "Because I hear them. . . . All of them. All the Land, all the men, I hear every one of them" (*Monsters* 578). Later, Ben will become the link between the Land and the now-evolving human settlers, helping them adjust to their new language abilities and their accompanying new sense of subjectivity: "Echoing through him is a language not of the Land but not quite of the Clearing either, some deeper combination of the Clearing's spoken language and the Land's voice but sent along the Pathways, along *new* Pathways" (*Monsters* 529). Ben's experiences of this new form of language reveals to him in turn a new type of subjectivity, in which the needs of the collective become more important than the needs of the individual.

Marta Komsta (2017) defines Noise as "a male-only condition of open consciousness which becomes accessible to the outside environment" (41), as opposed to the Voice, "the telepathic conduit for the unified primal consciousness of all sentient beings, which functions as the utopian antithesis to the individualized consciousness of humans" (42). What Ness is insisting, therefore, in his juxtaposition of these forms of language, is that the hierarchical Othering, which is inherent in human communication, gives rise to humanist exploitations and, ultimately, to conflict. In contrast, language that rejects the isolated and individualized humanist consciousness—which performs, in other words, non-hierarchical Othering—also avoids humanist conflict with nonhuman Others and the environment. As 1017 describes it, "The Land is all one, is it not? The Land has no *others*, it has no *they* or *those*. There is only one Land" (*Monsters* 114). As he struggles to regain his own language, the language of the Land, 1017 encounters a "group of young ones singing the songs that will teach them how to sort out the history of the Land from all the voices, how to turn and twist and weave the mass of sound into one single voice that will tell them who they are, always and forever" (*Monsters* 156–57). In his narrative of self-recovery, he describes the language of the Land as "almost unspoken, shared among them so quickly I could almost never follow it, as if they were just different parts of a single mind. Which of course they were. They were a mind called the Land" (*Monsters* 197). What Ness is portraying here is language that is in complete contrast to that of the human settlers, who use language—and eventually weaponized Noise—to control one another, and thereby create inevitable and ever-recurring conflict and violence. Patricia Kennon (2017) argues that "The traditional hero's quest conventionally concludes with the hero's confrontation with the wild things that challenge the authoritative regime of patriarchal power and his ultimate mastery over those dangerous exotic and alien Others" but that in the Chaos Walking series Ness "challenges this dualistic, patriarchal and hierarchical system of manhood and the nonmanly" (26). The series does not only reimagine manhood, however; it also reimagines humanity as a whole. It does this by using language as the basis for a new understanding of human subjectivity, based on non-hierarchical understanding of nonhuman Others.

LANGUAGE, SENTIENCE, AND SENTIMENT: INTERACTING WITH ANIMALS

Disappointingly, however, the Chaos Walking series falls short of realizing the full posthumanist implication of such a radical approach to language. While the series focuses heavily on depicting progressive interactions between the human settlers and the humanoid indigenous Land, portrayals of relationships between humans and nonhuman animals are more problematic. This is significant in light of the work that has been done linking animals studies, posthumanism, and language. In traditional humanism, the distinguishing feature upon which the binary division between human and animals has been maintained is that of language, seen to be the key indicator of "reason" in Cartesian terms. It is the supposed inability of animals to demonstrate reason through communication, which has justified their relegation to a lower hierarchical status than humans. As explored at length by Jacques Derrida in *The Animal That therefore I Am* (1997), animals have traditionally been denied the linguistic privilege of response, as well as the agency to return the gaze of the human being. Huggan and Tiffin (2010) describe the way in which narratives have traditionally dealt with animal subjects by "relegating them to the background of human activity or reading them as more-or-less transparent allegories of ourselves" (173). They point out that in Western culture, "[s]ince at least the Middle Ages, animals have not been accorded moral agency, nor . . . [until recently] any rights whatsoever" (191). They also argue that "hesitant as we are to accord complex emotions to animals, we are equally reluctant to admit out own involvement with them" (194). Cary Wolfe (2014) describes "the concept of 'rights,' in which ethical standing and civic inclusion are predicated upon rationality, autonomy and agency," as "central" to "a model of subjectivity and experience drawn from the liberal justice tradition" (91)—in other words, from the liberal humanist philosophical tradition. He attributes the ethical marginalization of both animals and the disabled to "the too-rapid assimilation of the questions of subjectivity, consciousness, and cognition to the question of language ability" (92). Wolfe makes a key argument, furthermore, about humanist attempts to end exploitation and control over Others by expanding the category of "human" to include more and more of those traditionally excluded; he writes that "a fundamental problem with the liberal humanist model [is] that in its very attempt to recognize the unique difference and specific ethical value of the Other, it reinstates the very normative model of subjectivity that it insists is the problem in the first place" (98). In Chaos Walking, this pertains not only to the treatment of animals, but to the way in which human characters label access to or lack of Noise/Voice as a disability.

What animal studies—particularly in relation to posthumanism—have revealed is the way in which an increasingly complex understanding of both animals and anthropocentrism have begun to break down the human/animal binary, problematizing the role of language in demarcating a clear boundary line. Francis Fukuyama (2002) argues that animal studies theories tend to "erode the bright line that was once held to separate human beings from the rest of the animal world" (144); they do so by revealing the abuses described by Derrida as occurring through language against animals, as well as emphasizing the complex emotional and cognitive processes of animals which, while different to those of human beings, are nevertheless far from inferior. In the Chaos Walking series, animals experience the same effects of Noise and Voice as human beings, whether they are indigenous species or those introduced from Earth by the settlers. Just as the thoughts of human men are opened up to one another and to the Land, so, too, are the thoughts of animals. The result is that animals are revealed to have complex modes of communication, and to be in possession of both reason and emotive capacity. Throughout the series, Todd in particular frequently encounters animals whose reason is sounder than his own, and who display an equivalent—if not superior—emotive capacity. For example, as Todd struggles with the decision as to whether to return and help Ben and Cilian or move forward as Ben insisted, Manchee reminds him, "Promised, Todd" (*Knife* 57). Manchee's comment, couched in the deceptively simple language permitted to nonhumanoid animals in the series, nevertheless reveals a complex understanding of abstract human concepts such as faith, loyalty, and honor. It also displays Manchee's involvement in the processes of logic and reason that guide Todd's flight from Prentisstown. Angharad, Todd's beloved horse, will later also show her affection and loyalty through language, when she insists on helping to "Save Boy Colt" (*Monsters* 531). Her utterance displays not only her love for Todd, but also her ability to follow the plans and strategies being formed by the humans around her, and acquiesce to her role in them.

The same cognitive and emotive capacity is portrayed in the indigenous animals in the series. 1017, for example, describes an encounter with the Sky's mount, a Battlemore: "*Return,* it shows as I approach the paddock fence. The only word of the Burden it knows, taught it by the Sky, no doubt. *Return,* it shows, and it is gentle, welcoming" (*Monsters* 157). Here, the Battlemore is granted not only the emotive capacity for affection, but also the ability to learn language and to switch between linguistic registers appropriately. That it could learn a new word from the Sky furthermore suggests that the linguistic openness of the Land to each other extends to other lifeforms as well, making the animals an integral part of the New World community alongside humanoid entities. In a formulation that echoes strongly the later portrayal of the Land and the Voice, Todd experiences relief from the Chaos of noise on his flight from Mayor Prentiss and Aaron when he encounters a herd of indigenous animals grazing a vast plain:

> If I had to imagine being on the sea, this is what I'd imagine. The herd surrounds us and takes up everything, leaving just the sky and us. It cuts around us like a current, sometimes noticing us but more usually noticing only itself and the song of HERE, which in the midst of it is so loud it's like it's taken over the running of yer body for a while, providing the energy to make yer heart beat and yer lungs breathe. (*Knife* 243)

Unlike his encounters with individual animals, who are almost anthropomorphized in their reciprocal relationships with humans/humanoids, here the animals are shown to have a subjectivity, which is both alien to that of humans and superior in that it lacks the conflict and chaos which torment humans on New World.

The result of such portrayals is that the human characters are forced to acknowledge the illusory nature of a human/animal binary opposition based on language. There is great potential in this realization for humans to modify their behaviors and attitudes toward the animal-other, in tandem with the series' focus on human/nonhuman relationships through interactions with the Land. While the human characters come to accept the subjectivity, agency, and equivalence of the Land, however, the series pays little attention to the obvious parallel to be drawn between the sentience of the Land and the sentience of other, nonhumanoid animals. For Sarah Reese (2014), in relationships with the nonhuman other "the intensified sense of otherness, based on a lack of common language and experience, in turn entails an intensified level of violence as a part of the appropriative encounter" (239); while Ness is at pains to overcome this tendency with regard to the Land, the series nevertheless portrays relationships with animals that are abusive, exploitative, binary, and hierarchical. Disappointingly, the series makes no attempt to problematize these portrayals. The very first words offered by Todd to the reader in *The Knife of Never Letting Go* reveal his inherent disdain for animals as based on his perception of language: "The first thing you find out when yer dog learns to talk is that dogs don't got nothing much to say. About nothing" (3). Over the course of the next half of the novel, Todd will come to understand that this perception is incorrect, in the same way that he is forced to realize that his perceptions of the Spackle are incorrect. The regret and psychic trauma he feels over the murder of the Spackle foreshadows his later betrayal of Manchee, whom he sees "confused and scared and watching me leave him behind" before hearing "a CRACK and a scream and a cut-off yelp that tears my heart in two forever and ever" (*Knife* 350). Nevertheless, Todd does not hesitate long about sacrificing Manchee, who ultimately counts for less than humans such as Viola in the fight for survival.

While it might be argued that Todd will later come to see the error of this position through repeated encounters with the Spackle, his growing awareness of the equivalence of other life forms will not prevent him from sacrificing other animals. Anghared will be ridden into battle, made vulnerable because of her subservience to Todd despite his awareness of her clear ability to communicate, reason, and love. Later, Acorn, too, will be sacrificed: despite Viola's awareness of his condition, he will be run until he collapses beneath her in her determination to reach Todd: she will see "pain wracking through his Noise, not just from his front legs, which I can see are broken, but the tearing in his chest which caused him to collapse in the first place, it's too much, he's run too hard" (*Monsters* 542). It is telling that Ness ascribes Noise rather than Voice to these creatures, even as he portrays them in clear communication with human beings and humanoids: animals in the series, although extended respect and affection, remain the property of human beings, subservient to them and to their needs and desires. While the humans may mourn their sacrifices, they do not hesitate to demand them.

Even more frustrating is the way in which the series explicitly acknowledges the parallel that can be drawn between the abuse of animals and the abuse of other sentient individuals labelled as nonhuman, without extending the realization that a change of attitude and relationship is required. A good example comes in *The Ask and the Answer*, when Todd and Davy are asked to put identifying metal armbands on the Spackle prisoners. These armbands, the reader is told, are the same ones used to brand sheep; by creating a permanent wound under the band, these markers prevent the band from ever being removed. The application of the band to the Spackle is, therefore, a deliberate erasure of their subjectivity—their equivalence to humans. When Todd tries to prevent this abuse to one of them, the Spackle in questions lashes out at him, injuring him badly. Todd, in frustration, likens the Spackle to herd animals, calling them "[s]tupid, worthless, effing animals" (*Ask* 211–12). While Todd will come almost immediately to condemn this attitude and regret it in himself, at no point does his awareness of the wrong done to the Spackle translate into an awareness of the same wrong done to the sheep: while it is wrong for the Spackle to be tortured and branded because of their obvious sentience, the equal sentience of the sheep is never acknowledged. Patricia Kennon (2017) argues that Noise "threatens to collapse regulatory boundaries between colonizer and native, human and alien, self and other" (28). While this may be true between the humans and the Land, it does not, in this series, extend to all sentient life forms.

While the Chaos Walking series makes important first steps toward eroding humanist hierarchies based on language, therefore, it nevertheless falls short of abandoning an anthropocentric world view. This is significant when one returns to the idea of anthropocentric colonialism, and its implications for human relationships to the environment, as we shall see in the next section.

KNOWING THE LAND: ENVIRONMENTAL IMPLICATIONS

What the Chaos Walking series reveals in its exploration of language over technology in the colonization of Space is that it is anthropocentrism, more than anything else, that lies at the root of human problems, both with each other and with the environment. Zoe Sophia (1984) explains that within dominant cultures, extraterrestrialism functions as a "safety valve" that permits expansion into outer space as a means of avoiding terrestrial environmental and social problems; this "safety valve" is based on "the assumption that space exploration contains avenues for environmentalist solutions" (Sturgeon 2009, 88). The Chaos Walking series gives lie to the idea that a fresh start can be obtained by colonizing other planets, as it reveals that such a technological response merely delays, extends, and exports problems such as animal abuse, environmental degradation, and social justice issues such as resource appropriation.

One inroad into the importance of language in environmental studies can be found in the field of ecosemiotics. Ecosemiotics can be defined as as a field rooted in the "sense of an identity as realized environmentally in communication" (Siewers 2014, 6). Siewers (2014) argues that environment is both environmental and semiotic, creating what he terms "ecosemiospheres" or "regional landscapes of cultures interacting with nature" (6). He further argues that "humans live 'in' their thoughts, in the sense of thoughts that are signs and are environmental, rather than 'having' thoughts in the sense of modern capitalist anthropology" (8). Faull (2014) gives one example, explaining that "the way we represent the world around us in a painting or a map actually constitutes the reality of that world to us" (206); the same, it can be argued, is true of how we describe the world to ourselves and others through language. In other words, human beings' environmental "reality" is constructed as much through language as it is through matter. In Chaos Walking, the language of the settlers constructs an environment that is threatening and hostile. The settlers originally left Earth, as Todd has been taught, because "Old World's mucky, violent, and crowded" (*Knife* 163). What is clearly an allusion to human pollution, environmental abuse, and violence is, in this statement, translated into a hostile environment, with the land itself marked as the aggressor in place of those who defiled it. They move to a planet which is a paradise in comparison: the novel at various points described abundant meadows, forests, and fertile farmland, as well as the swamps in which the Land bury their dead. Nevertheless, this land is figured by the settlers as hostile and threatening as a result of the lifeforms against which the human settlers must compete for survival. When Todd first flees Prentisstown through the swamp, he encounters an indigenous crocodile, for example, whose communications consist entirely of the hunt: "FLESH and FEAST and TOOTH" (*Knife* 58). Similarly, at the end of *Monster of Men*, Todd describes the marine creatures as "all mouth and black teeth and horrible slime and scales" (*Monsters* 67–68), calling to mind the marine serpents that feature so critically in Coleridge's *Rime of the Ancient Mariner*. The Mariner will eventually learn to reappraise his environment in light of his own prejudices; for the human settlers on New World, however, these creatures are seen as embodiments of a planet hostile toward them, and with whom they must contend for supremacy. Their ability to hear the thoughts of others within the environment does not aid them in overcoming this view; they interpret what they hear in the context of an expectation of conflict, grounded in the evolutionary view of nature as "red in tooth and claw."

In a similar way—and for similar reasons—the human settlers vie against each other for supremacy, with language at the core of the conflict. The human men victimize the women because "They couldn't stand the silence. . . . They couldn't stand women knowing everything about them and them knowing nothing about women" (*Knife* 392). Mayor Prentiss likewise uses his control over Noise not to find his place within this new environment, but instead to master those within it who oppose him: "It's every word, crammed into yer head all at once, and the whole world is shouting at you that YER NOTHING YER NOTHING YER NOTHING and it rips away every word of your own. . . . A flash of words and I'm nothing" (*Ask* 201). In his analysis of ecological discourses, Jason Groves (2009) argues that "war has become the trope that gives ecology meaning" (31). This is the imperative that drives the humans on New World, and particularly the Mayor, to see control as the only means to survival. The novel equates the control of the environment—Noise—with human's control of one another, culminating in the Mayor's triumph over Noise which is described by Todd as "like nothing, like a dead thing, no more shape nor Noise nor life in the world than a stone or a wall, a fortress you ain't never gonna conquer" (*Ask* 10). Noise is an inevitable product of life, and to conquer it is to destroy life itself.

The series explicitly equates environmental problems with this anthropocentric aggression through exploration of relationships between the human settlers and the Land. For Marta Komsta (2017), "'the land' highlights the implicit connection between the inhabitants and their environment as an indication of a community that transcends the limitations of individual consciousness" (50–51). The series, therefore, seems to advocate a move from environmentalist positions that look to technology and frontier logic toward a deeper, more holistic ecological position. As Lenz (1994) explains, "whereas traditional environmentalists and conservationists have tended to see the human role as that of lord of the natural world, deep ecologists see human beings as one species in a community of beings, in a horizontal rather than a vertical relationship to all others" (159); this concept of a "community of beings" is exactly what Ness seems to be advocating for by the end of the series. Sturgeon (2009) describes the underlying philosophy which makes frontier logic so damaging, writing that:

> The underlying logic of extraterrestrialism is separating from the mother, claiming independence from her, putatively admiring her from a distance but in reality violently rejecting any possibility of identification with femininity and its connection to the body, the earth, and the messy, unpredictable qualities of the basics of reproductive work. Extraterrestrialism is thus deeply connected to the desire for control of nature (and women), particularly the promotion of violence . . . as an adventurous, heroic, and necessary aspect of human evolution and achievement. (85)

It is this anthropocentric and humanist "hero" mentality that characterizes the original settlers, and particularly men like Mayor Prentiss, who see not only the planet, but also women, nonhuman others, and other men as adversaries to be conquered; this viewpoint is both expressed through and supported by language. The state in which the reader first encounters the human settlers on New World matches that identified by John Stephens (2010) as a tendency in children's environmental literature "whereby threatened or damaged nature is matched by threatened or damaged lives" (207). It is only by radically altering their attitude toward language—and thereby the associated anthropocentric and humanist assumptions about nonhuman others—that the settlers can move beyond damaging practices and attitudes. Magdalena Mączyńska (2011) argues that "Todd's ability to distinguish good from evil and then to choose rightly brings to mind natural law" (83), a view that ascribes an inherent morality to human nature and which elides reason with moral hierarchies. However, it is in fact Todd's openness to *learning* the voices of others—from his ability to "read" Viola to his ability to empathize with 1017 and to understand even Mayor Prentiss—rather than any *inherent* morality which makes Todd so revolutionary. In this way, the novel proposes an alternative to the frontier myth of evolution as continual conquest. Ben tells Todd, "I think I might be the next evolutionary step for my people" (*Monsters* 424). Emphasis shifts from the hero as individual conqueror (Mayor Prentiss) to communities of interrelated and interdependent subjectivities represented by Ben's relationship to the Land. Through characters like Todd, Bradley, and Ben, Ness suggests the next evolutionary step is not one of conquest, but one of learning new ways to communicate and new forms of subjectivity—learning from and living with, rather than conquering, the nonhuman other.

In contrast to The Forest of Hands and Teeth, therefore, the Chaos Walking series works hard to dethrone the individual from the position of primary concern. As a result, the series ends on a note of hope rather than hopelessness, and while the degraded Earth in the Forest series is shown as ultimately hostile and unknowable, the world of Chaos Walking is shown to be accessible to those who are willing to abandon individuation for collective community. These novels seem to redefine the concept of utopia itself: by deemphasizing the importance of the individual, the novels suggest that once the individual is no longer of primary concern, utopia and dystopia look very similar to one another. Despite the series' failure to commit wholly to communion with *all* nonhuman others, the insistence on the reimagining of relationships through language as non-hierarchical and non-individualistic at least points the way toward a posthumanist future. Chaos Walking does not necessarily abandon the humanist drive for control over nonhuman others, but it does, to a certain extent, begin to question the assumption of separateness as well as the hostility of nature.

Chapter Four

Neal Shusterman's Unwind

Posthuman Recycling and the Death of the Hero

As bioengineering becomes an increasingly sophisticated technology, the ethical implications for the humanist subject are becoming correspondingly complex. The seemingly straightforward utopian ideals of technologies designed to improve and preserve human life are inevitably undercut by anxieties about misuse and misappropriation: in a society that places human wellbeing first and foremost, any technology that supports this priority is not only good ethics, but also good business. In *The Machine in the Garden*, Leo Marx (1967) describes at length the way in which, early in the formation of US society and politics, the humanist ideal of individual liberty and equality was appropriated to support the development of a neoliberalist society based on free trade, industrialization, and exploitation of natural resources. With developments such as cloning, organ transplants, and stem cell research becoming more and more sophisticated, however, the very definition of "natural resource" has become problematic. Furthermore, the way in which discourses of science often elide their complicity in capitalist free market systems disguises that fact that "humans often alter their conduct and self-understanding once they become aware of scientific measurements, categories, and interventions" so that "[t]he moving target that is human nature is constantly being fed back into those sciences that seek to capture it" (Pettit 2013, 1055). Science within free market capitalism, therefore, has powerful potential to both define and commodify human subjectivity by making consumer desire the subject of and the product of scientific endeavor. Exploring controversies surrounding the issues of abortion and bioethics in particular, Neal Shusterman's Unwind dystology (2007, 2012, 2013, 2014) depicts a future world in which unwanted children can be "recycled" at the age of adolescence, to make use of their body parts as a "natural resource" of the nation, available for exploitation by a market of greedy individual consumers. Scrutinizing the implications of this concept, this chapter will examine the impact of technology on the humanist narrative of individual development, to show how the disruption of this narrative may have positive implications for an environment increasingly at risk from the neoliberalist exploitation of resources for individual gratification. Specifically, it will examine how, by mapping the effects of consumer culture directly onto the human body, the humanist hero of neoliberal capitalism is revealed as nothing more than a marketing ploy which, if undermined, might give way to more sustainable communities based on collective empowerment.

FREE MARKET CAPITALISM WITHIN A HOSTILE ENVIRONMENT

Because humanism places the individual in a place of fundamental importance, liberal-humanism is able to take the *gratification* of the individual as a primary goal. As Victoria Flanagan (2014) has described, humanism as a philosophy "places the rational, autonomous and cohesive human self at its centre" (12), and as such, it is a philosophy that is situated ideally to support and promote the ideals of liberal, free market capitalism, which emphasizes the power of individual (autonomous) consumers making individual (rational) market choices which support their (cohesive) identities and subjectivities as consumers. Within such a framework, the traditional binary separation of civilization/nature becomes even more important: civilization is measured by its gratification of the humanist subject, while nature becomes the source of the materials and resources needed to achieve that gratification. To the extent that natural environments resist or deny individual gratification, on the other hand, they are seen as hostile—to civilization and to individuals. Nature in the Unwind series is the source of denied gratification; it is the source of disease, aging, and death, against which civilization—in the form of science and technology—must fight. It is not surprising that the unwinds in the series are frequently aligned with natural spaces; therefore, when Connor first becomes an unwind, we see him escaping from the rigidly controlled space of the highway into the woods, a space where civilization struggles to penetrate, and where unwinds have a chance to escape the civilization that seeks to commodify them. As we shall see later in this chapter, unwinds are frequently associated with natural spaces in this way; they occupy caves, woods, and deserts, and are symbolically aligned with animals. Unwinding is shown to be the antithesis to this "naturalness," and the series therefore sets up liberal-humanist capitalist and technology-driven society as the antidote to an environment that is perceived as hostile, threatening, and un-nurturing. Nature in Unwind fails to support the humanist subject.

In humanism, the development of the autonomous self of the humanist subject is of paramount importance; in liberal-humanist capitalism, that autonomous self develops as a result of specific consumer choices. This is especially the case in YA culture, which routinely encourages young people to understand "who they are" in terms of the clothes they wear (buy), the music they listen to (buy), the brands they identify with (buy), and so on. In his 1982 essay, "The Body in Consumer Culture," Mike Featherstone makes the convincing argument that "[c]onsumer culture latches onto the prevalent self-preservationist conception of the body, which encourages the individual to adopt instrumental strategies to combat deterioration and decay . . . and combines it with the notion that the body is a vehicle of pleasure and self-expression" (18). Featherstone's argument suggests that within liberal-humanist capitalism, human subjectivity—predicated on the development of the rational *mind*—involves the subjugation and control of the *body* in a binary formation that is ultimately antagonistic. Furthermore, this binary hierarchy emphasizes the importance of consumer choice as the exercise of the free and rational *mind* in overcoming the limitations and failings of the human *body*. Within this economic context, the humanist subject's development is directly equated to the consumption of "products" and "resources"; as Shusterman's Unwind will demonstrate, everything, including the human subject, becomes a resource to be exploited by other human subjects in the quest for personal development.

In terms of YA literature, this understanding of liberal humanist subjectivity is especially important when one considers the primacy of the bildungsroman mode, which makes this quest for personal development the cornerstone of the YA genre. Michael M. Levy (1999), for example, argues that "the traditional *bildungsroman* hero gains control of his world by becoming more knowledgeable in both practical terms . . . and moral terms" (115), and that science fiction, therefore, with "its emphasis on change, the discovery of new knowledge, and the conquest of new worlds" is an ideal fit for this mode of narrative (117). With this in mind, it is clear that by aligning knowledge and technical mastery with agency and autonomy, typical YA speculative fiction constructs the bildungsroman hero as a humanist hero, whose subjectivity is based on mastery of the world around him. In her exploration of posthumanism in YA representations of technology in fiction, Flanagan (2014) likewise observes that much of children's and YA literature is concerned with the "construction of agency based on the principles of individualism, action and autonomy," and that this is especially true of YA fiction, which frequently "revolve[s] around the adolescent character's acquisition of independence" (14). Roberta Seelinger Trites argues in *Literary Conceptualizations of Growth* (2014) that "maturation, as it is conceptualized within adolescent literature, links cognition inviolably to embodiment" (8); taken together these arguments imply that mastery of the body (physical "growing up") is inextricably linked in YA fiction to cognitive ability (autonomy of the mind). Flanagan (2014) makes the point that, in their concern with humanist ethics pertaining to control over the body and its modification, dystopian texts concerning the application of biotechnology to the YA body are more properly transhumanist in focus than posthumanist, depicting young characters as "disempowered or subordinated subjects" of adult manipulation, and driven narratively by the need to reassert individual autonomy and agency along humanist lines (16–17).

This is the position in which most of Shusterman's main characters start off: Conner and Risa, for example, are introduced to the reader first and foremost as victims of adult selfishness who must grow up fast and learn mastery of the physical world around them in order to survive the persistent attacks on their lives. For Connor, his first moment of real "growing up" comes when he is on the run from the Juvie Cops, concealed in the cab of a sympathetic trucker who has agreed to let him hitch a lift. Terrified at first that the trucker will turn him in for a reward, Conner is nevertheless quick to trust him, and to trust his safety to him. It is not, however, the trucker who gives Connor away, but the cell phone he still carries, switched on, in his backpack. Furious at his own stupidity, Connor realizes that the phone has enabled his father to track him and lead the Juvie Cops directly to him; "he wonders how many other kids are caught by their own blind trust of technology" (*Unwind* 18). Characteristic of childhood, that blind trust is something Connor will need to leave behind quickly in order to survive. Tellingly, the scene elides trust in adult authority with trust in technology, and the phone is depicted as a crutch that ties Connor to childhood, dependency, and vulnerability: this is not a technology over which Connor has mastery, but instead one that he is dependent on, and that is used to master him. As the series progresses, Connor's journey into adulthood will be marked by a series of more masterful encounters with technology, from his ability to mend machinery at the Graveyard, to his understanding of how the 3D organ printer might be mended. He will also become correspondingly more adept at learning who to trust, from his developing relationship with Lev, to his failure with Starkey, and finally his understanding of Sonia's significance. Connor, therefore—superficially at least—follows the typical path of the bildungsroman hero.

Risa similarly begins the series with a failed demonstration of technical mastery, which will leave her vulnerable to the hostile intentions of selfish adults. When the reader is first introduced to her, she is on stage performing a complex piano recital. Nervous, she slips up and makes one mistake after another until finally the piece ends with a lukewarm reaction from her audience. It is then that Risa reveals the reason for her nervousness: as a state ward, if she fails to live up to the expectations of the state home, she will be unwound as a cost-saving exercise. Like Connor, Risa allows herself to trust in a teacher's platitudes when he assures her she will be fine, but she tellingly observes: "he can afford to believe it. He's not fifteen, and he's never been a ward of the state" (*Unwind* 20). Her use of the word "afford" indicates the way in which she has already been conditioned to consider life as a commodity, which one can either "afford" to hold on to, or be forced to sell or give up by those with more power and resources. Her initial skepticism is proven correct when her teacher turns out to be wrong: she is chosen for unwinding a week later and finds herself "loaded onto a bus" (*Unwind* 25) like the merchandise she has become. Like Connor, Risa's growth throughout the series will be marked by her increasingly technical mastery as she learns to be competent at not only music, but also medical work—including coming to terms with first the loss and then the return of mobility. Also like Connor, Risa's increasing technical mastery of her own abilities will correspond to a growing understanding of the complexity of the people she encounters, including Cam and Connor himself. On the surface, her journey is one of self-discovery, which allows her to master the world through mastery of her own body as a means of forging meaningful relationships.

In a fascinating exploration of how dystopias such as Unwind reflect on real-life practices of organ donation and transplantation, Wohlmann and Steinberg (2016) discuss the fact that within the medical industry, the "preferred narrative is one of success, medical triumph and technical dexterity, which is challenged when patients' experiences disprove the body-as-machine metaphor"; they argue that this disruption is one that Shusterman actively explores by "framing the story of a transplanted individual along the lines of a coming-of-age narrative" (e26). A similar correlation between body and commodity is noted by Sara Wasson (2015), who notes that the "process for marking tissues off as transferable, as acceptable for transplant in legal and cultural terms, echoes many of the detachment processes that typically accompany commodification in late capitalism" (6), and cites metaphors of "organs as machine parts; organs as waste; organs as vegetation; and organs as gifts" (9) as active in this process of cultural detachment. Within Unwind, the humanist subjectivity of characters such as Connor, Risa, and Starkey is powerfully undermined by their commodification. When faced with the panel who will pronounce on her unwinding, for example, Risa is unsurprised when they discuss her in terms of "educational standards," "money," and "5 percent of our teenage population" (*Unwind* 23) and observes that it is "business as usual for them" (*Unwind* 21). Already conditioned to consider herself as their property, she thinks of herself in this scene in fragmentary terms, equating her achievements, talents, and skills to specific monetary values within a master budget beyond her control. This initial, discursive conflict will become more explicit and physical as the series progresses, with both Connor and Risa eventually incorporating body parts from other unwinds involuntarily into their own bodies; modified against their will, both characters lose their sense of self as a result of society's insistence on their "repair." Subjectivity itself, in this society, is shown to be a valuable commodity that individuals battle over: for these adults to maintain a market in modified subjectivity—you can have the new liver you want, the different colored eyes, or the younger heart to make you "feel like a new you from the inside out!" (*Unwholly* 52)—they must, by necessity, destroy the subjectivity of the children they commodify and dismantle. In typical humanist bildungsroman mode, therefore, Shusterman's characters are fighting for subjectivity, autonomy, and freedom.

The way in which the acquisition of independence and autonomy is depicted, however, is critical in determining whether a text will be conformist of subversive in its approach to liberal-humanist capitalism. Comparing the classic adult dystopia about transplantation, *Never Let Me Go*, with Shusterman's Unwind, for example, Richard Gooding (2014) argues that the YA bildungsroman trend "may recoil at assaults to a liberal humanist model of the self as autonomous, self-directing, and rational" (111–12). In texts where the focus is on the triumph of the humanist hero, the dystopia is likely to focus on the ways in which commodification of the body undermines humanist understandings of subjectivity and autonomy: Connor's and Risa's autonomy and personal growth, for example, are threatened by the impending division of their commodified bodies as addendums to other people's consumer subjectivities. However, a closer examination of dystopian depictions of biotechnology in YA fiction reveal that the dystopia is as often likely to result from liberal humanist capitalist practices as from the destruction of the humanist subject. Katherine Hayles (1999) describes liberal humanism as grounding itself "on the notion of possessive individualism, the idea that subjects are individuals first and foremost because they own themselves" (145), free from enmeshment within and constraint by market relations (3). Exploring the depiction of biotechnologies such as organ transplantation in children's fiction, however, Naarah Sawers (2009) argues that many contemporary discourses concerning organ transplantation "raise alarms about supply while simultaneously normalizing the practice of transplantation within western conceptual universes" and depicting access to organs as "a moral right for the wealthy" (171). Her paper explores the disjunction that exists within liberal humanist capitalist society between an idealism that "credits the individual human body with dignity and the right to freedom" (171) and an economic system that would allow that freedom to capitalize on the "increasing economic value" of "human and non-human flesh" (172). Where humanist philosophy suggests that the mind has ownership of the body, in other words, that mind exercises a freedom that enables it to commodify and relinquish the freedom of the body. The humanist mind is free to make choices, therefore, but within the context of capitalism those choices become limited to *market* choices, and constrained by economic contexts. This constraint is symbolized particularly in the descriptions in the series of the "tithed" children: raised by their parents specifically to become "sacrifices," these children come most often from wealthy families, and are the ultimate metaphor for the true cost of consumer society. They represent the way in which a wholehearted devotion to the liberal-humanist free market system can make horrific assaults on life and liberty seem like sensible market choices.

With both tithes and unwinds, the humanist rational mind's ownership of the body is shown to be contested in consumer society. Sawers (2009) explains, "consent [to donate or modify one's body] is a problematic concept with the growing divisions of privilege and fantasies (of desire) that accompany the liberal free-market and new biotechnologies" (175). Within the series, the humanist philosophy that separates mind from body and allows the mind to rule the body opens the door for both the modification of and commodification of the body by *any* mind. Thus, parents are able to sell their children's bodies by virtue of their superior rationality as adults, while the consumption of children's body parts by adults is justified by a market that positions such practices as an acceptable form of self-development for those same "rational" adults. It is this point of view that allows a nurse to shout at Risa in *Unwholly* that "People out there are dying for lack of parts, but you and your selfish friends in the resistance would rather let good people die" (157). In this light, the dystopian situation in the Unwind series is as much about the way in which the characters are enmeshed within an inescapable liberal-humanist free market subjectivity as it is about the threat to their humanist subjectivity: the immediate threat to their freedom and autonomy takes second place to the fact that that freedom and autonomy were always an illusion of the market system.

This illusion is made explicit when a third key character of the series, Mason Starkey, is first introduced as the Juvie Cops arrive to arrest him. Unlike Connor and Risa, Starkey is quick to abandon his initial impulse to trust; he, does, however admit that "Every Unwind believes in their heart of hearts that it won't happen to them—that their parents, no matter how strained things get, will be smart enough not to fall for the net ads, TV commercials, and billboards" (*Unwholly* 4). Starkey's observation, which comes at the beginning of the second book when Connor and Risa are well established in their bildungsroman trajectories, reveals the lie that undermines the movement from childish dependence to adult mastery: in this world, adults and children are equally vulnerable to the market that has conditioned them to think of subjectivity in terms of products, consumption, problems, and market solutions. Neither children nor parents, in his depiction, are "smart" enough to become fully autonomous and free in a market system that commodifies even resistance practices (such as the Graveyard).

The most comprehensive exploration of the liberal-humanist free market capitalist tensions within the Unwind series is Heather Snell's "Ready Made for the Market" (2016), in which ethics of selflessness and charity are contextualized as inextricably bound up in neoliberal cultural. Snell identifies an inherent contradiction in neoliberal culture, in that individualism is both a marketable commodity and a threat to the system. Describing how the series depicts a society in which "goodness is synonymous with obedience and overachievement, and badness with the performance of an individuality that stands out and therefore threatens to disrupt the high-functioning uniformity of the status-quo" (102), Snell argues that, in the series, seemingly "good" acts such as charitable giving and recycling—both keystone practices of soft environmentalism within neoliberal culture—in fact reveal the "inescapability of neoliberalism" (107) as they work to both commodify the individual and to disguise horrific practices. With this in mind, Unwind's dystopian transplantation of commodification and recycling practices onto the human body reveal and emphasize the way in which seemingly ethical choices within a consumerist framework both bolster and disguise liberal-humanist capitalist philosophies and practices that are non-sustainable and destructive: practices that are the real root of the dystopia.

This concern, furthermore, can be extended beyond the human body: as we shall see in the next section, the criticism of liberal-humanist capitalism implied by depictions of recycled bodies opens onto wider debates about the exploitation of environments and the humanist assumption of a detachment from nature. Just as the very basis for the commodification of bodies is the assumption that nature itself is hostile, so, too, does the recycling of bodies within this series reveal the inadequacy of this assumption.

THE ENVIRONMENTAL IMPLICATIONS OF RECYCLING THE HUMAN

In environmental theory, a key concern is the growing disjuncture between market demand and available resources, whether those be human, natural, or even geographical. However, a rift exists between environmentalist approaches that emphasize individual acts such as recycling or wildlife preservation, and deep ecologist positions that emphasize radical, collectivist change and that seek to promote recognition of the "intrinsic value in nature" as opposed to nature's value only as a commodity for human use (Garrard 2012, 24). This latter position recognizes the "inescapability of neoliberalism" (Snell 2016, 107) and its pervasive influence in much soft environmentalist practice that reinforces the habits of individual consumption—habits that are themselves at the heart of the problem.

This tension is frequently played out in children's and YA literature, especially where a didactic approach to environmentalism is adopted. For example, Clare Echterling (2016) argues that "most contemporary children's environmental picture books and easy readers published in the United States focus overwhelmingly on individual environmentalist acts and lifestyle changes, overlook the connections between environmental degradation and systemic social problems such as class disparities, and ultimately oversimplify environmental crisis" (283). She points, for example, to the US EPA's "A Student's Guide to Global Climate Change" as promoting solutions "within the private sphere" and which are about "making good choices" (284). The commonplace approach to environmentalism in children's texts, she argues, "places climate change squarely on individual citizens" (284), "reinforces neoliberal individualism" (286), and omits "any information about the effects of industry" or its collusion with government (284). In other words, these texts position environmental awareness as just one more consumer choice among many. In a world where resources for the manufacture of consumer products is increasingly limited, practices such as recycling, giving to or buying from charity shops, and even conservation of endangered wildlife can be read as attempts to shore up unsustainable relationships with the environment.

This position is made graphic in Unwind by the text's imposition of such practices on the human body itself, with individual consumption and market demand for human body parts supported and driven by the literal recycling of teenaged bodies. Making explicit use of the discourses of consumption and recycling, Unwind reveals the problem to be not the limited nature of resources, but the attitudes that make the consumption of resources a necessity. Scattered throughout the series are faux advertisements and "public service announcements" that make explicit the positioning of unwinding as both recycling and charity. One, for example, discusses the use of unwound parts for wounded soldiers, as well as sick or dying "husbands," "children," and "wives," and to support the families of those working in the transplantation industry: "We all know someone who has been positively touched by unwinding" (*Unwholly* 145). The word "touched" suggests the consent, generosity, and complicity of the unwind in its explicit invocation of the language of donation; an active verb, it implies autonomy as well as affect. Furthermore, the sanctity of the family and the sacrifice of serving soldiers are both utilized as justifications for unwinding, eliding the violence to both the individual and the family that underlies the practice. The first person "we" presumes the complicity of the reader, further normalizing the process of unwinding within the market system, and justifying it as redemptive. A "Letter to the Editor" discussing the rewound character Cam works in a similar way:

the writer asks "why not avail ourselves of the finest attributes of these Unwinds to build a better being?" (*Unsouled* 97). In both of these examples, the implications are clear: unworthy unwinds are justifiably coopted as commodities because their parts are recycled as charity offerings: the waste of this society is being turned back into something useful and worthwhile within the system. As Wasson (2015) explains, "the metaphor of waste . . . is a mediating category enabling the alienation and commodification of tissue" that "sees waste as *rendered valuable* through the operations of capital and biotechnology" (10; original italics). By emphasizing unwinding as charitable and as an act of recycling waste, these pronouncements throughout the series disguise the violence done toward the humanist subject by other humanist subjects within a liberal-humanist free market system. However, the contrast between these ads and the narrative they punctuate bring this metaphor into focus, encouraging the reader to question not just their deceptive rhetoric, but (hopefully) *all* similar rhetorics of charity and recycling. Real-life newspaper and media extracts, with which many chapters are prefaced, further encourage this perspective: discussing real-life practices such as the exploitation of third-world "donors" for first-world organ-transplants (*Unwholly* 167), these extracts encourage readers to question whether similarly exploitative practices underlie other normalized consumer practices in which they partake.

The series draws a further parallel between recycling and unwinding by equating the commodified unwinds to the natural environment. Heather Snell (2016), for example, discusses how euphemisms throughout the series such as "the eco-friendly 'Cold Spring' . . . signal how neoliberal ideology conceals the horror of the order it supports" (101). Wasson (2015) has pointed out the way in which the discourses of farming and natural-resource exploitation are used throughout the series to align unwinds with other exploited resources: one advertisement, for example, offers "millions of healthy young neurons *harvested* from prime Unwinds" (*Unsouled* 35, my italics). In a letter to Lev, Connor describes the graveyard as a "ranch" under threat of takeover by "the big beef companies" (*Unwholly* 177), a metaphor that explicitly compares the unwinds to cattle for the meat market. In another chapter titled "Harvest," the character Roland, who has been Connor's nemesis for most of the first book, is shown being unwound in graphic detail. The language in these scene is reminiscent of a butcher's shop or slaughter house: the surgeons discuss him in fragmentary pieces, ignoring his pain and terror as they address his "abdomen" (290), "strong abdominal muscles" (290), and "Left parietal lobe" (293), carefully lifting each new piece of him away. The scene finally dissolves into metaphors of nature as Roland describes how "Yellow figures lean all around him like flower petals closing in" (291), and "memories bloom" (292). These floral images suggestively align Roland with the natural world, in stark contrast to the cold and clinical procedure he is undergoing, which itself aligns him with a farm animal being slaughtered and butchered for the supermarket.

The language of farming and of natural resources likewise permeates the descriptions of the harvest camps. The inmates are given exercise to "build muscle mass" (*Undivided* 89), and are unwound in the "Chop Shop" (*Undivided* 90), descriptions that once again evoke the slaughter and butchery of livestock. At the same time, great effort is taken to make the camps themselves sound like wholesome, natural environments: a great deal of money is paid to the gardener at "Horse Creek Harvest Camp" to plant "pumpkins growing within the swirling colors of toad lilies, monkhood, and other autumn blooming flowers" right outside the Chop Shop entrance in the "tranquility of a bucolic day" (*Undivided* 90). The overall effect is to align the unwinds with the natural world, disguising their reality as highly processed commodities within a market-controlled environment. This is further emphasized when Lev and Connor become aligned with the Arápache people, Native Americans who live on a deliberately isolationist reservation. Both explicitly and implicitly drawing on a history of political and economic exploitation, the series' positioning of the boys within the deliberately protected wilderness spaces of the reservation again equates them to a destructively exploited natural resource. In contrast to the world outside of the reservation, where the greed for resources and commodities is so great that even children are being consumed, the reservation is both restrained and connected to the natural world:

> The Arápache have steeped themselves in both their culture and modern convenience. Plush leather furniture speaks of wealth, but it is clearly made by hand. The neighborhood—if one can call it that—is carved into the red stone cliffs on either side of a deep gorge, but the rooms are spacious, the floors are tiled with ornate marble, and the plumbing fixtures are polished brass or maybe even gold. (*Unsouled* 147)

The rejection of conspicuous consumption by the Arápache is in line with their rejection of unwinding, and serves to link the one to the other: unwinding is, in their eyes, equivalent to the mass slaughter of animals for leather or the destructive use of petrochemicals in place of natural materials; all are natural resources exploited by liberal humanist capitalism to feed the greed of the liberal humanist consumer. Just as recycling unwanted teenagers to feed the demand for organs is not, for them, ethical or viable, neither is the recycling of natural resources into more products for conspicuous consumption. The reservation is, therefore, symbolically filled with items that are handmade and speak of a finite but valuable existence: the guitars made by Una, the recorded music of tragically unwound Will Tashi'ne, and even Pivane's hunting rifle. Tellingly, however, Connor also notes the way they have, nevertheless, succumbed to the lure of modern convenience, suggesting the pervasiveness of neoliberalism even in the protected space of the reservation. Nevertheless, the reservation represents what comes to be seen as the alternative to destructive capitalist exploitation of the natural world for the gratification of liberal-humanist subjects: the reservation is about community, collective action, and the entanglement of subjectivities and relationships, and it is this fundamentally posthuman ethos that Connor and his friends come to adopt in place of the humanist subjectivity of the traditional bildungsroman. As the characters' individual subjectivities deteriorate under the pressing weight of commodification, the series intimates that by replacing the humanist drive for self-fulfillment with a vision of collective purpose and empowerment, an alternative, more sustainable subjectivity might be possible.

THE HIVE MIND: POSTHUMAN BODIES FOR SALE AND THE ERASURE OF SELF

In *How We Became Posthuman* (1999), Katherine Hayles discusses the influence of cybernetics theory, and specifically Maturana's theory of autopoesis, on reconceptualizing the liberal humanist subject as "not consistent with laissez-faire capitalism . . . with the idea that each person is out for himself and devil take the hindmost" (143). Similarly, in discussing the posthuman in children's and YA literature specifically, Victoria Flanagan (2014) states that posthumanism "views subjectivity as networked and collective" (21). It is this attitude that Shusterman seems to advocate for in the Unwind series. Bugajska (2016) argues that Shusterman "draws attention to the discourse of the media, stigmatizing teenagers as a mob" (15); at the same time that he does this, however, Shusterman also draws attention to the positive force that any collective subjectivity can wield. In Unwind, the horror of unwinding reveals the problematic nature of the humanist hero, and makes individual development seem like a futile and puerile goal, implicated in the destructive and puerile exploitation of natural resources. However, depictions of *re*winding offer an alternative, posthumanist possibility: in place of individualist liberal humanist subjectivity, instances of rewinding throughout the series champion collective, communal subjectivity as a more sustainable option.

Sawers (2009), in her analysis of Anderson's *The Scavenger's Tale*, argues that "[i]n an advanced-capitalist, neo-liberalist society, dominant discourses engender separation and thus work oppressively" but that narratives of biotechnology can resist such discourses by "articulating affective connections that extend beyond the autonomous self" (178). This is exactly what Shusterman achieves in Unwind, by making the narratives of characters such as Connor, Cam, Risa, and Lev less about their development into autonomous individuals, and more about their recognition of their interconnectedness within networks removed from liberal humanist capitalist frameworks. When the humanist bildungsroman narratives of these characters fail under pressure of their fragmented, commodified subjectivity within neoliberal society, they develop not as autonomous individuals, but as key parts of a collective subjectivity.

Perhaps the most obvious example of this in the series is the character Cam. Created by the sinister corporate entity behind unwinding, Proactive Citizenry, Cam is a "rewind" composed of the deliberately handpicked individual components of hundreds of unwound teenagers. While their unwinding was justified by a rhetoric of waste, Cam is marketed by his creators as the ultimate recycled commodity. As his creator, Roberta, explains, "it is the task of science to take what we already have and build on it. Not create life, but perfect it" (*Unwholly* 140) and Cam "recombine[s] both our intellectual and physical evolution into the finest version of ourselves, the best of all of us combined" (*Unwholly* 140). He is described as "the new golden child of humanity" (*Unwholly* 292) who deflatingly becomes the launching point for "a whole new line of trend-setting patchwork clothes" (*Unwholly* 292). Cam is therefore not, in essence, different to the unwinds of which he is composed: his subjectivity in humanist terms is contested ("Your request to sign your own document has been denied by the court" (*Unsouled* 212)) and his ownership of his own body is qualified by his conformity to a subject-position as commodity. Nevertheless, Cam proves highly resistant to occupying this subject-position, and it is the fragmentary nature of his posthuman body and mind that enable him to rebel against it. As Roberta and Proactive Citizenry labor to bring his disparate parts into line in service of the unified and cohesive subjectivity they are attempting to forge, Cam comes to see himself as "a factory full of strike-prone workers, or worse, a clutch of slaves forced into unwanted labor" (*Unwholly* 56), which is, of course, exactly what he is. Nevertheless, in his rebellion against Proactive Citizenry, it is each of those disparate parts working together that enables him to succeed, from the portion of his brain that remembers having a crush on Risa, to Will Tashi'ne's hands which, through music, lead him to Connor on the reservation, and even the eyes of "a boy who could melt a girl's heart with a single glance" (*Undivided* 166), which allow him to charm Roberta as he brings Proactive Citizenry crashing to its knees. Wohlmann and Steinberg (2016) describe Cam as an exemplar of "recent developments in young adult fiction, in which the impact of technology is presented as potentially enabling" and in which posthuman subjectivity is "emphasized"; his story "speaks about gradual growth, the search for identity and an organic, interactional and performative relationship between body, self and social context" (e27). He is represented as both "a single 'he' from the outside and as a fragmented being and an accumulation of various individuals from the inside" (e28). Critically, none of these individuals retain their cohesive humanist subjectivity, but nor is their subjectivity wholly replaced by a unified subjectivity of Cam's own: when the series ends, even his relationship with Una remains entangled with the past and subjectivity of what remains of Will Tashi'ne in him. Instead, Cam represents a community of subjectivities, all working together to reject the system that seeks to commodify them. However, crucially this rejection is not based on a reassertion of their subjectivity: they are not rewound or restored, and they never acquire a right to commodify others as the typical bildungsroman hero might. Cam, in the end, does not attempt to assert his subjectivity by mastery over others or his environment. Instead, he accepts his condition as a collective entity, whose subjectivity and well-being is entangled with that of others.

The same is true of the two other depictions of rewinding in the series: the revival communes formed by Cy-Fi and his fathers, and the reunification staged by the Admiral of his son Harlan. Neither of these examples represents a literal rewinding: in place of the literal stitching back together of the individual who has been unwound, they instead involve the coming together of the individuals who received the transplanted body parts, in order to "reunite the Unwind they share" (*Unsouled* 123). As this language used by Cy-Fi to describe the revival communes indicates, this is not a process of consumption and it does not contribute to individual subjectivity: instead, this is about sharing—of resources and of subjectivity. It begins at the end of Book 1, when the Admiral and his wife bring together all the recipients of Harlan's parts, "putting their son together in the only meaningful way they can" (*Unwind* 331). What is significant in this scene is the focus on the character of Emby, who received one of Harlan's lungs in his youth to combat the pulmonary fibrosis that was killing him. Although the Admiral repents his decision to unwind Harlan, Emby's backstory is offered as the reason why Harlan could never be rewound physically: neither Emby's nor Harlan's right to subjectivity is given precedence over the other's, and to rewind one would be to kill the other. Both boys are marked as victims of the liberal humanist free-market system, which both insisted upon and then commodified their subjectivity, and in place of this flawed system, the Admiral creates a collective community that honors both but destroys neither. Harlan was recycled to save Emby, but only so that Emby could himself become a commodity in the parts market. The Admiral chooses not to recycle Emby as a means to fulfilling his own desires; instead both accept a finite but meaningful existence as an essential part of a bigger, entangled, affective community.

For Trites (2014), Shusterman's depiction of the entanglement of mind and body, revealed especially through these instances of "rewinding," demonstrate "the lie of the Cartesian split, that legacy of the Enlightenment which leaves us believing what Einstein calls the 'delusion of consciousness'" (70). Instead, in place of the Cartesian split, these depictions suggest subjectivity to be an amalgam of bodily, emotional, and mental experiences, and position individual consciousness as subordinate to collective affect. In doing so, they provide an alternative subject position to that of the individual consumer who must recycle in order to preserve access to desired commodities: by revealing the body upon which consumer demand is based to be entangled within affective communities, the text suggests that resources should be respected and conserved not because we desire them, but because we *are* them. The novels, therefore, offer sustainable cooperation as an alternative to selfish recycling for further consumption; instead of endless meaningless reuse, the series privileges meaningful and terminated experiences. The individual will end, Shusterman implies, but the society will live on.

Sadly, the promise embodied in Shusterman's exploration of posthumanist subjectivity is not sustained through the ending of the dystology. As Snell (2016) explains, "the real tragedy of this otherwise uplifting ending is that only the discovery of a new technology—3D organ printing—sparks radical social change and not, as one would hope, a paradigm shift that would require genuine self-sacrifice in a world where parts are not readily available as commodities in a global market" (109). The acceptance of this new commodity technology at the close of the series is the real dystopian element in Shusterman's world, providing as it does yet another way of supporting and disguising the fact that the real problem is the commodification of the body enabled by the humanist hierarchy of mind over body within a liberalist free-market system. Further capitulations mark the end of the series: Connor is literally rewound into a cohesive whole of himself, and cements his relationship with Risa; he is also reunited with his parents in an emotional scene that implies that reestablishment of the nuclear family. Una gets married to what remains of Will Tashi'ne in a similar move toward unification, as well as starting a relationship with Cam, and Grace strikes a lucrative commercial deal on the organ printer. Each of these moves, like the neat solution of the printer itself, serves to reestablish a sense of humanist subjectivity and to disguise the fact that its devastating effects will continue. Shusterman's ending is chilling in its capitulation to the "inescapability of neoliberalism" (Snell 2016, 107) and humanist capitalism.

On the other hand, the raw and graphic speculations within the novel about what these liberal humanist values look like when taken to their free-market extremes do serve as warning. As Snell suggests, "Perhaps what is needed most right now are . . . books that take greater risks by modelling present and future worlds, which, while not perfect, inspire us to take a radically different direction" (123). The glimpses Shusterman provides for readers of collective, entangled affective communities are one such model which, even if not ultimately adopted at the end of the series, nevertheless can inspire an alternative approach to environmental practices. As Stacy Alaimo (2014) points out:

> Activists, as well as everyday practitioners of environmental, environmental health, environmental justice, and climate change movements, work to reveal and reshape the flows of material agencies across regions, environments, animal bodies, and human bodies—even as global capitalism and the medical-industrial complex reassert a more convenient ideology of solidly bounded, individual consumers and benign, discrete, products. (187)

Shusterman's depiction of the way in which consciousness, and therefore agency, flows between entangled subjects works to undermine such ideologies and dethrone the consumer and the product from their places of primary importance. With examples as complex and multifaceted (literally) as Cam and Harlan to consider, readers are given a glimpse of the way in which we are all entangled with the other subjectivities who have been commodified to enable us to feel like cohesive humanist subjects.

Echterling (2016) makes the important observation that "a great deal of ecocritical work on children's literature has focused on YA dystopian fantasy" and while "this work is important and astute . . . other, less trendy types of children's books deserve sustained critical attention too, as they deal quite differently and often more directly with environmental issues" (286). While this is true, it is the sustained and critical reflection on current situations, missed opportunities, and future possibilities enabled by YA speculative fiction that makes this genre such a rich medium for posthumanist reconceptualization of environmental ethics. As Bradford (2010) suggests, YA dystopian texts "invite a critical and participatory style of reading" and thereby "[encourage] readers to reflect on the consumerism and the neoliberal politics of their own time and to imagine the 'what-if' implications of a world in which these tendencies dominate political and economic life" (136). The posthuman reconsideration of the liberal humanist subject in a free market economy allows for a radical reimagining of the very foundations of exploitative, non-sustainable consumer culture.

Chapter Five

Philip Reeve's Mortal Engines Series

Posthumanism, Evolution, Apocalypse, and Time

What is progress? This concept, so pervasive in every facet of Western global capitalist society, is nevertheless difficult to pin down. The *Oxford English Dictionary Online* (2017) lists, in the second part of its entry, the following definition: "Advancement to a further or higher stage, or to further or higher stages successively; growth; development, usually to a better state or condition; improvement." This seemingly transparent term has become politically and culturally loaded in Western culture, however; according to an opinion piece in *The Atlantic* entitled, "Is 'Progress' Good for Humanity?" for example, progress has been mis-sold to the West by proponents and celebrants of the Industrial Revolution as "a new world based on wage labor, easy mobility, and the consumption of sparkling products" (Caradonna 2014). What this comment unpacks is the way in which, in the popular imagination at least, progress has come to be inextricably identified as driven by the twin forces of technology and consumerism. "Progress," in the Western imagination, seems to hover somewhere between utopia and dystopia, seemingly representative of both evolutionary success and the defeat of evolutionary constraints. It is, furthermore, a fundamentally humanist concept, placing the human species at the front of an evolutionary race through time and space. As the article in *The Atlantic* suggests, however, the ingrained notion of "progress"—and particularly technological progress—as a human evolutionary prerogative is just as likely to engender questions and anxieties: How much of this so-called progress is merely illusory, and what does this vision of continual progress cause us to lose sight of? In other words, what are we leaving behind us in our constant need to be moving, and are we really getting anywhere?

These are the questions that lie at the heart of Philip Reeve's epic seven-novel steampunk dystopias, Mortal Engines (2001, 2003, 2005, 2006) and Fever Crumb (2009, 2010, 2011a). The original quartet of four books, recently supplemented by the Fever Crumb prequel trilogy, has been described as employing "an eclectic, postmodern and very often comedic mode," to describe "a military and ideological struggle between the dystopian capitalism of the traction cities and the dystopian deep ecology of the Green Storm" (Bradford et al. 2008, 16). Taking as a starting point this critically perceived struggle within the novels between civilization and natire, this chapter will argue that posthuman representations in the Mortal Engines series can be understood as disruptive of humanist concepts of linear time and evolutionary progress through the deployment of steampunk tropes. In place of the humanist celebration of human evolutionary progress, these representations of the posthuman support a posthumanist understanding of time, history, and being as cyclical and regenerative, encouraging readers to view symbiotic (rather than parasitical) relationships with place and environment as necessary to human survival.

HUMANIST AND POSTHUMANIST TIME, PROGRESS, AND EVOLUTION

One of the core principles underlying much humanist philosophy is the understanding of time as linear and progressive, particularly for human beings; taking theories of evolution as a starting point, humanist philosophy measures time according to specifically human epochs and posits history as the story of the ascension of man and the drive for human progress and development. In this humanist perception of time, the evolutionary progress of human beings is a story of human movement, through increasingly sophisticated technology, away from the "natural" constraints of other species and into a position of domination in terms of rationality, culture, language, and, above all, control over nature. Kate Soper (1995) describes this story as providing a backdrop for the inherently humanist binary opposition of nature/culture, explaining that "nature" as a cultural concept is frequently understood as "a spatial and as a temporal marker" (187). Soper describes the desire to "get back to nature" as an attempt not only to enter a spatial location or environment, but also to escape from the effects of time, progress, and—perhaps—evolution itself. That is to say, it is a product of the humanist perception of nature as hostile, something from which human beings must struggle to escape through ever-more developed civilizations. This understanding of the nature/culture dichotomy is in keeping with Leo Marx's influential exploration of the American pastoral tradition in *The Machine in the Garden* (1967); Marx traces the celebration of the bucolic to Virgilian pastoral, in which "[w]e are made to feel that the rural myth is threatened by an incursion of history" (21). In both Soper and Marx's formulations, the natural world is conceived of as timeless and contrasted to a civilized, technologized world in which the march of progress and history pushes nature further and further away.

In one of the most influential assessments of posthumanism to date, Fukuyama (2002) identifies precisely this certainty of human evolution and progress as being fundamental to any stable sense of what it means to be human, but also as being at risk. Focusing on the disruptive potential of the posthuman body, Fukuyama is overwhelmingly pessimistic about a posthuman future in which he envisages the subversion of the evolutionary human being by technology as indicative of the loss of humanist values and ethics, resulting in social and political anarchy and an overall loss of ethical foundations with which to underpin notions of "progress" (6). In a direct evocation of evolutionary theory, Fukuyama insists that "human nature exists, is a meaningful concept, and has provided a stable continuity to our experience as a species" (7); his assertion throughout *Our Posthuman Future* is that human nature is a nebulous but very real ethical quality, threatened by posthuman developments. In direct contrast to Fukuyama, however, Layla AbdelRahim (2015) suggests that the idea of human progress through linear time is a myth: "what we consider to be unquestionable truths in sacred texts or incontestable facts in science are part of a larger story that shares its epistemological foundation with fiction and legends and, concurrently, with science and civilization" (1). For AbdelRahim (2015), both evolutionary theory and religious apocalyptic rhetoric (as discussed below) form part of what she describes as the "civilized narrative" (6), an anthropocentric myth that posits "civilized humanity as the epitome of life on earth" (6, 12, 51). Unlike Fukuyama's assertion that the evolutionary human being is critically important to personal and social ethics, for AbdelRahim the "mythical" nature of this humanist certainty in human progress is precisely what creates the opportunity for exploitation of both human and nonhuman others and the environment. By figuring all human characteristics and achievements as products of a successful evolutionary process, the rhetoric of evolutionary progress suggests hierarchical divisions and boundaries as "natural" and, therefore, disguises their exploitative nature. The rhetoric of environmental threat and hostility already explored in previous chapters, therefore, can be seen as being implicated in this push for progress away from a state of nature.

Critically implicated in such debates is the role of technology, whether that technology is as primitive as the agricultural revolution that AbdelRahim (2015) identifies as the catalyst for the "anthropocentric myth" (6), or as futuristic as the bioengineered "designer babies" Fukuyama (2002) identifies as a future challenge to "dearly held notions of human equality and the capacity for moral choice" (82). As far back as 1996, Lynn White Jr. was arguing that it was the Victorian industrial revolution that irreversibly linked the concepts of scientific knowledge and technological "power over nature," asserting that "[i]ts acceptance as a normal pattern of action may mark the greatest event in human history since the invention of agriculture, and perhaps in nonhuman terrestrial history as well" (4–5). Joel Dinerstein (2006), in his cuttingly lucid account of technology and the posthuman, traces a trajectory from the discourses of the age of exploration—from Christian explorers such as Columbus to philosophers such as Francis Bacon—through nineteenth-century discourses of frontier exploration and finally space-age rhetoric of technological colonization, to show how ideas of scientific progress and technological innovation (including the posthuman or cyborg body) have become synonymous with Christian notions of "second creation" as a justification for the reconceptualization of "nature—natural resources— as a set of raw materials, as 'standing reserve' for human consumption" (578). Leo Marx (1967) makes a clear case for this "faith in progress" (27) as a predominating theme in American literature, with texts such as Hawthorne's "The Celestial Railroad" satirizing and criticizing what was obviously a prevailing popular belief in the myth of technological progress. In the narrative of Western progress, therefore, the human species is engaged on a journey through time and space, away from hostile and threatening natural spaces and behaviors, and toward a future in which we control and dominate both by means of technology.

This narrative of progress is the driving force behind Reeve's depiction of the traction cities in the Mortal Engines and Fever Crumb series. In Buell's (2001) ecocritical "five dimensions of place-connectedness," the third dimension is an acknowledgment that "places themselves are not stable, freestanding entities but continually shaped and reshaped by forces from both inside and outside" (67). In Mortal Engines these processes have been literally embodied in the cities that constantly remake and recycle themselves. When *Mortal Engines* kicks off the first quartet, the city of London is a vast and successful example of what Reeve sardonically terms "Municipal Darwinism" (*Mortal Engines* 10). Composed of seven tiers of buildings, streets, deck plates, and elevators, the city of London is a monstrous composite of old and new: the infamous blue whale from the Natural History Museum, for example, or the age-worn and crumbling edifice of St. Paul's Cathedral perched cheek-by-jowl with engine rooms, unfamiliar temples, and the sinister Guild of Engineers. The whole structure travels unceasingly on huge caterpillar treads powered by fuel-hungry, house-sized engines across the vast wasteland that once was mainland Europe, now referred to as the "Great Hunting Ground" (*Mortal Engines* 3), a term that reflects critically on the evocation of evolution implicit in the term "Municipal Darwinism." In conflating species evolution with urban development, "Municipal Darwinism" foregrounds the cost of endless progress.

In an interview with Michael Bennett in *The Nature of Cities*, Andrew Ross (1999) explains the complex interrelation of environmental concerns and social justice issues that come to play when considering the application of ecocriticism to urban environments; in these areas it becomes very difficult to disentangle discussions of the environment from the tense discourses of social inequality and class-based interests (15–16). Posthumanism, with its emphasis on the degradation and exploitation of all "others" who deviate from the humanist norm, offers a way of seeing this surface conflict of interests as instead a continuum of exploitative situations, all of which need to be addressed for an urban environment to thrive. It is precisely this transformation of the context of urban environmentalism that Reeve portrays. Reeve's depiction of the traction cities extrapolates the capitalist emphasis on endless growth and consumption to its logical extreme: unable to see past the mythical nature of the coupling of human evolutionary progress and technology, the inhabitants of these cities consider it "natural" that cities should hunt each other across the wasteland that was once the earth, consuming each other in a constant snatch-and-grab war for increasingly limited natural resources. The novel makes clear that it is this flawed mindset that has rendered the environment literally hostile: both in terms of destroying all nonhuman life, and in terms of filling the environment with dangerous predators.

There is, furthermore, humor in Reeve's subtle depiction within the novels of characters who persistently refuse to consider what will happen when the last city has been eaten, and the resources finally run out: positioning the earth as an enemy to conquered and plundered just like any other, the rhetoric of the tractionists is so extreme as to be comical. As Chrome, the mad-engineer mayor of London, rhapsodizes shortly before the destruction of the city:

> The Guild of Engineers plans further ahead than you suspect. London will never stop moving. Movement is life. When we have devoured the last wandering city and demolished the last static settlement we will begin digging. We will build great engines, powered by the heat of the earth's core, and steer our planet from its orbit. We will devour Mars, Venus, and the asteroids. We shall devour the sun itself, and then sail on across the gulf of space. A million years from now our city will still be travelling, no longer hunting towns to eat, but whole new worlds! (*Mortal Engines* 274)

Frightening in its complete disregard for the symbiosis of (human) species and the environment, Chrome's ambition imagines a human species freed from the limitations of a localized and particular environment, and divorced from any remnant of the "natural" (i.e., non-constructed). It is a vision of total. The hyperbole of this speech suggests that endless progress is neither logical nor sustainable when it is equated in this way with technology and consumption. However, in the modern rhetoric of "progress," such questions are left hanging by an equally strong urge toward apocalypse—an urge that might explain the well-documented rise in dystopian popular culture.

POSTHUMANISM AND THE RECYCLING OF TIME

Not only does the humanist perspective focus on time as the narrative of progressive human evolution, but it also envisages an end to time. In the Christian ideology that has come to permeate Western culture and society, human progress (both individual and social) is not only a "natural" evolutionary process, but also an inevitable spiritual movement toward apocalypse, the end of time, and the ultimate disposal of the material world. It is the inevitable end result of an ideology that sees the natural world as separate, hostile, and exploitable to which an end will eventually come—as Chrome's speech examined above so humorously reminds us. This ideological stance supports the dichotomy of human/nature, as it envisages the movement of humanity away from a state of nature until, at the last, nature can be dispensed with and left behind altogether. This is in keeping with Dinerstein's (2006) discussion of the codependency in Western culture of concepts of progress and the Christian ethos of the Adamic;[1] just as human technological achievement is naturalized as human evolutionary progress, so are questions of sustainability rendered irrelevant by the rhetoric of apocalypse, which posits the destruction of the physical body and Earth as the preordained and righteous end of history and time. As humanist ideology has moved further and further from its religious origins, however, apocalypse has taken on increasingly negative connotations in modern culture; humanist society continues to place faith in the progress of the species away from hostile nature, but dreads the inevitable end result. This ambivalence toward apocalypse is a key characteristic of dystopia, helping visions of the future to waiver between utopic and dystopic imaginings. What the narrative of apocalyptic dystopia attempts is an escape from the inevitable outcome of an end to the human narrative. These narratives tend to attempt a rewriting or restarting of human history, with the mistakes of the past erased and the human race given a chance to alter the line of the narrative.

In the Mortal Engines and Fever Crumb series, apocalypse—ironically—is not a final end, but is instead a frequent occurrence. This irony, however, is not immediately apparent. Both series imagine the earth as a postapocalyptic landscape following a disastrous ancient (i.e., twenty-first century) technological war, termed the "Sixty Minute War," in which "the Ancients destroyed themselves in that terrible flurry of orbit-to-earth atomics and tailored virus-bombs" (*Mortal Engines* 7). This description draws heavily on the rhetoric of apocalypse described by Berger (1999) as emanating from the

Cold War, in which the inevitable end result of human technology is envisaged as the destruction of both planet and species. Later apocalyptic moments in both series echo this rhetoric: in *Mortal Engines* an ancient weapon named "MEDUSA" gives London the potential to wipe other traction cities and static settlements from the map altogether, but ends with the complete annihilation of London itself, while *A Darkling Plain* goes further and imagines the removal of the entire human species by an ancient orbital weapon known as "ODIN," controlled by the cyborg Stalker Fang. Inherent in this vision of apocalypse is the specter of powerful technology; from weapons such as MEDUSA and ODIN, to the dreaded Stalkers and destructive Traction Cities, technology in this series is shown to be both inextricably human and beyond real human control, almost like a force of nature itself.

Braidotti (2013) describes how "[t]he relationship between the human and the technological other has shifted in the contemporary context, to reach unprecedented degrees of intimacy and intrusion" (89). In a reaction against this, according to Perry Nodelman (1985), YA science fiction—and particularly dystopias—frequently anathemize technology, advocating instead a return to more primitive, and more innocent, humanized, or natural ways of life. Referring only to the first novel in the series, *Mortal Engines*, Noga Applebaum (2010) argues that "Reeve makes a hierarchical distinction between the humanists who seek to preserve culture and the scientists who destroy it" (57), thereby fixing the trajectory of the narrative firmly within an evolutionary drive toward either evolution or devolution. As she explains, "Reeve implies . . . that humanity's gaze must be directed into the past, the realm of the humanities, rather than into the future which he associates with technology and the sciences" (57). Reeve seems, in this first novel, therefore, to be endorsing a humanist apocalyptic vision of human progression away from hostile and finite nature. Although he represents human progress as destructive, violent, and unnecessary, he also represents it as inevitable. Throughout both series, for example, the traction cities become the focus for criticism of the pursuit of technological advancement without recourse to sense, safety, or consequences. As the Stalker Fang explains in *A Darkling Plain*, in justification of her intention to use ODIN against humanity: "I understand that humanity is a plague; a swarm of clever monkeys that the good earth cannot support. All human civilizations fall, Tom, and all for the same reason. Humans are too greedy. It is time to put an end to them forever" (*Darkling Plain* 504). The Stalker Fang's argument draws on discourses of evolution in labelling humans as animalistic "clever monkeys," no more deserving of special treatment than any of the environmental elements destroyed by humans in their technological power struggles. Her description is given further irony in that she herself is a technology that has evolved out of the control of her human makers, deploying humanity's own technology against itself. As such, the Stalker Fang comes to embody unintended consequences. In a similar manner, Fever's discovery in *Scrivener's Moon* that she, the Scriven people, and the Nightwights are all the results of an ancient genetic experiment that has continued to spiral out of control long after the destruction of the ancients by their own weapons (218; 222) suggests strongly that it is the human tendency to meddle with what is not fully understood that will lead to apocalypse. The Scriven will eventually be responsible for the rise of traction cities and the destruction of what remains of the "natural" environment, while the weapons of the ancients, which first devastated the earth, will remain a threat to later civilizations. Each of these storylines, therefore, suggest that the human drive for ever-greater technological mastery in the name of progress is also a drive toward inevitable apocalypse, sundering humanity irrevocably from the sustaining natural environment (which was never really hostile at all) before removing them from it altogether.

The relationship between apocalypse and technology is made even more explicit through the depiction of the traction cities themselves, which appear almost as characters throughout both series. Implicit in Reeve's coining of the phrase "municipal Darwinism" is the idea of the city—as well as the individual—as subject to evolutionary progress (Webb 2013, 157). Throughout the Mortal Engines quartet, cities are shown to be living organisms symbiotically entangled with the humans who inhabit them in much the same way a human being could be seen as entangled with the gut microbiome: indeed, Kay Sambell (2004) describes Reeve's London as "a grotesque human body" (255). This idea of entanglement in evolutionary progress is one that has been explored at length by Robyn McCallum (2009), who aligns Reeves' evolutionary rhetoric with wider utopian and dystopian discourses. McCallum describes how despite Reeves' "representation of urban space . . . as alive and evolving, and hence as a dynamic evolutionary process" (215), the quartet as a whole indicates that "the inability to adapt physically and ideologically ultimately leads to the downfall of the traction cities," as well as indicating "the need for human beings to be active agents and adaptable to changing circumstance if they are to survive both as a species and as social creatures" (223). For McCallum, therefore, Reeve's vision of the human/city relationship is one which does seek to enmesh humans within the environment in an "interdependent web of life," but which also retains faith in and evokes "the power of narrative and the importance of a sense of history which is at its core humanist" (224). In other words, Reeve's novels, by insisting upon progress away from problems created by progress, fail to recognize humanist ideologies of progress as an underlying problem.

When it comes to environmental apocalypse, also, the role of technology remains one of ambivalence in the humanist narrative. Apocalypse in this new iteration is not the movement of humanity away from an earthly prison and into a final, spiritual home in heaven. Instead, apocalypse is a complicated relationship between environment, species, and technology, in which endless human progress is disrupted by the destruction of one or more of these three elements. Much dystopia imagines apocalypse as the disruption of the human-environment relationship by technology, or the disruption of the human-technology relationship by some natural disaster. Because, as Dinerstein (2006) discusses, faith in God has been replaced in humanist philosophy by a faith in technology, however, technology has come to be seen as both the problem and the solution to immanent apocalypse. While technology seems to be helping to speed humanity further and further from "nature," and thus toward the destruction of the natural world once and for all, humanist faith in technology also ironically calls on technology to solve environmental problems. As Alice Curry (2013) explains, "The naturalization of human advancement in the contemporary western imagination centers on the notion that progress and particularly technological progress can provide an ongoing solution to crisis" (43).

However, there are elements of Reeve's portrayals of technology that both challenge and problematize these same ideologies of progress. This is in part an effect of its status as a specifically YA text. A special issue of the *Lion and the Unicorn* in 2004 focused on the ambivalent rhetoric of apocalypse in children's and YA science fiction. For many of the writers in this issue, science fiction's urge to imagine apocalyptic consequences is frequently brought into tension with the humanist philosophical underpinnings of much children's and YA literature. Among many arguments about the tensions within the YA science fiction subgenre, for example, Farah Mendlesohn (2004) describes it as "unstable" in that its authors "attempt to combine the bildungsroman with a realization of one's very small place in a large universe" (286) and that in many YA science fiction novels, "maturity (the growth into adulthood) substitutes for political and social consequences" (290). She discusses the idea that true science fiction is at odds with the tendency of children's and YA literature to return to a safe status quo or starting place at the conclusion of the narrative (291). For Mendlesohn, many children's and YA science fiction texts use science and technology merely as a backdrop for the humanist project of portraying the development of the individual within a narrative of human evolutionary progress. In Mortal Engines, which Mendlesohn recognizes as one of the few examples of "true" science fiction, however, this is not the case. Instead, Mortal Engines ultimately rejects the humanist linear progression toward apocalypse portrayed in the traction cities to instead offer a posthumanist vision of time as cyclical and regenerative, with very different consequences for the environment.

In its engagement with the multiplicity of interpretations surrounding the critical prefix "post," the discourse of posthumanism is inherently concerned with notions of time. For Zoe Jaques (2015), one of the most powerful potentialities of a posthuman perspective is that "it immediately suggests that there might be something above, beyond, and—most crucially of all—after, the human present" (2). As already discussed, a linear concept of time is a key characteristic of humanism; Donna Haraway (2016), in her foundational text of posthuman theory "The Cyborg Manifesto," describes the "myths of origin of Western culture" as characterized by a "longing for fulfillment in apocalypse" (55). For Haraway, however, the antidote to this self-destructive drive lies in the reformulation of myths in a movement away from totalizing visions of humanity toward visions of plurality, hybridity, and interconnection which celebrate survival and regeneration (55, 67). Haraway's focus on regeneration in particular is critical to posthumanist reconceptualizations of time. If, as suggested by Morrissey (2013), dystopias "reflect negatively on our times by positing besieged postapocalyptic societies in need of radical change lest the human race fall even further" (192), then YA dystopias, by insisting on the survival, continuation, and regeneration of the world, necessarily reflect a posthumanist subversion of the narrative of apocalypse that underpins humanist dystopias, positing, in place of a linear progression away from nature, a continually evolving and renegotiated relationship with place and environment.

By depicting the traction cities as themselves a species, subject to both evolution and apocalypse, for example, Reeve disturbs the humanist positioning of the human as central to history, suggesting the displacement of human beings by their own technology in the evolutionary story. As suggested by descriptions of the barren and ravaged land across which the traction cities roam, this displacement carries serious consequences for the environment. For Leo Marx (1967), the metaphorical significance of the railway in American literature was that it threatened to break down the eons-old binary between city and county, nature, and civilization, by introducing "technological power" into rural spaces, "a power which does not remain confined to the traditional boundaries of the city" (32); in many ways, the traction cities have a similar metaphorical significance, allowing the technology of the city to escape from any sense of confinement on a macro scale, colonizing and effacing the "natural" environment. However, as Curry (2013) points out, there are "surprising possibilities for growth and renewal offered by the post-apocalyptic landscape, suggestive of a comparable restoration of human community after apocalypse" (21). In Mortal Engines, the effacement of the natural environment is neither complete nor permanent: the earth appears to fight back and regenerates after each apocalyptic technological disaster much faster than the human populations do. Rather than the destruction of planet and species, therefore, these technologically spawned apocalyptic events end each time with renewal and rebirth—monumental destruction from which both planet and people can start afresh. Although the natural environment remains hostile to these self-destructive human civilizations, therefore, the blame for this hostility seems to have shifted to human civilization itself, and much of humanity's destructive power is portrayed as harmful, ultimately, only to itself. This is not an abandonment of the nature/culture binary, but it is certainly a repositioning of its traditional power dynamics. In other words, the solution offered by YA dystopian literature to the dilemma of human progress is not to end time, but to restart it.

STEAMPUNK, CYCLICAL TIME, AND POSTHUMANISM

Reeve's deployment of human/technology relationships works constantly to undermine the notions of progress and apocalypse traditional to the dystopian genre. Instead, technology in the world of Mortal Engines and Fever Crumb is intimately bound up with cycles of regeneration and degeneration of human culture and nature. It is in part through the deployment of steampunk tropes that the novels achieve this. "Punk" has been around for a good few decades now, and it is easy to forget that it had its roots not just in music and art, but also in literature. As a movement is has diversified exponentially and it is now possible to follow not just the ubiquitous steampunk, but a whole range of different punk "brands": atompunk, clockpunk, dieselpunk, cyberpunk, and solarpunk are just a few that could be named. Despite the way these movements are creeping into the mainstream, however, they still have at their roots a serious philosophical engagement with mainstream culture, which is particularly relevant to theoretical approaches such as literary studies, environmental studies, and new materialism.

Mortal Engines has been persistently categorized not only as dystopian fiction but also as a pinnacle of the YA steampunk genre. Frank Cottrell Boyce's review (2009) of *Fever Crumb*, for example, describes the novel as "a king of steampunk Planet of Slums" and labels it "a heady mixture of the strange and the familiar." This mixture, reminiscent of Freud's uncanny, is characteristic more generally of the steampunk genre. Steampunk as a literary genre is typified by "alternative histories that frequently explore the rise of new technologies in Victorian England and throughout its global empire" (Jagoda 2010, 46); however, it has also come more broadly to be understood as any attempt to imagine the future in conjunction with past technologies, or vice versa (JRRL 2010), a formulation that Alice Bell (2009) terms the "anachronistic fantastic" (7), defined as "an everyday sense of wanting to critique, yet simultaneously have affection, knowledge and some sense of control over what came before" (7). In this sense, steampunk is an apt categorization for the Mortal Engines and Fever Crumb books, in which various iterations of the future are imagined as technologically degenerate: in both series, the technology of the twentieth century is depicted as both present and lost to future generations, whose loss of the knowledge of how to create or properly operate such technology leads them to continually refashion and reinvent it by means of more primitive technologies (such as steam and gas power). Stefania Forlini (2010) describes the steampunk movement in general as typified by a "utopic dimension" that emerges through followers' belief in "their ability to shape a better future through the recycling of the past" (75). Although Forlini discusses at length the tendency within the movement to assume a problematically clear distinction between human and technology which at times undercuts the posthumanist potential of the genre, she nevertheless identifies potential within the genre for the development of "an increased mindfulness toward things and our relationships to them" which might foster "increased sensitivity toward our endangered material environment" (80).[2] As Forlini's argument illustrates, steampunk's insistence upon the inherent recyclability of time, history, and technology offers an alternative to linear concepts of evolutionary history and progress that nevertheless embrace the entanglement of the human and the nonhuman. By making his series a hybrid of this steampunk outlook with dystopian rejection of the illusion of human control, Reeve presents readers with a vision of the future that is intriguingly divorced from the narrative of inevitable human progress.

Throughout Mortal Engines and Fever Crumb, the relationship between human beings and history is told through the re-appropriation of technology through city-dwelling and archaeology. It is through this re-appropriation of old technologies and machines that the series earn their steampunk label, as they imagine a future in which primitive technologies of steam, diesel, and clockwork mechanics enable the human race to continue limping forward through time after more sophisticated technologies have all but destroyed it. However, key elements within the plots of these books work constantly to undermine the characters' own impressions of forward progress. One of these elements is the persistent and yet ineffectual presence of archaeology and history as subjects of study and fascination within the series. In Mortal Engines, the Guild of Historians and the archaeologists who rank within their midst are both the greatest opponents and the source of old/new technologies. Their ambivalence toward MEDUSA makes this clear; although "The Historian's Guild had never been as quick as the rest of London to welcome new inventions from the Engineers, and they made no exception for MEDUSA" (*Mortal Engines* 201), it is nevertheless the Guild of the Historians, Thaddeus Valentine, who made the redevelopment of this weapon possible in the first place. As Valentine's speech to the apprentice historians in *Mortal Engines* makes clear (16), it is the work of historians and archaeologists in recovering the artefacts and knowledge of the past that makes the technological future possible. The historians find themselves caught in an ideological battle: while the tractionists and engineers wish to move forward toward the future and the freedom of the human race from earthly constraints altogether, the antitractionists look nostalgically to the past and wish to move backward in time to a pre-technological past of environmental purity. What both sides ignore is the fact, demonstrated by the historians and their archaeological finds, that time persistently repeats itself and that progress is never straightforwardly forward in its momentum. As Katherine herself explains of the goddess of history, Clio: "the poor goddess was being blown constantly backward into the future by the storm of progress, but . . . she could reach back sometimes and inspire people to change the whole course of history" (*Mortal Engines* 107–8).

The point that history is cyclical rather than linear is further emphasized by Pennyroyal's false histories and Freya's museum in *Predator's Gold, Infernal Devices*, and *A Darkling Plain*, as well as The Scrivener Institute in *A Web of Air*. Jagoda (2010) suggests that steampunk is informed by "the extensible, recombinant, and subjective nature of historical data [which] makes it susceptible to the construction of numerous pasts and futures" (62). Pennyroyal's false accounts of the history of America, for example, demonstrate the way in which history serves not so much as a way of informing progress with compounded truth and knowledge, as a justification for a multitude of goals with both positive and negative consequences. Their influence on Freya's decision to take Anchorage to the dead continent of America, for example, or their influence on the Stalker Fang leading Gargle and the Lost Boys to retrieve the codes for ODIN, shows how history is written and rewritten to serve the needs and ideologies of those who come later. Anchorage, Ark Angel, London, the Green Storm, and the *Traktionstadtsgesellschaft* will all fail to learn the lessons taught to them by history, instead using the tools and information provided by history to repeat the mistakes of the past: war, genocide, and environmental destruction.

The Scrivener Institute in the Fever Crumb series will likewise demonstrate the failure of knowledge and truth to lead to progress: although the physical technologies—the stalkers, stalker brains, and computers—designed by the institute will remain intact, the ability to understand the knowledge, memories, and lessons they have preserved is shown to have been lost, as that knowledge is corrupted and repurposed. The genetic engineering project of the ancients is re-codified by the Scriven people they created as proof of their evolutionary superiority, and renamed as a God to guide their ideological transformation of the earth once again through the use of repurposed technologies—in this instance, the huge, steam-powered engines that will come to power the traction cities of Mortal Engines. The Scrivener Institute, eroded and decayed by a hostile landscape and the inevitable passage of time (and its effects on the human race) is metonymic of the force of nature to undermine any attempt at endurance. Just as the knowledge of the institute will not endure, however, it is also not lost or replaced by new knowledge or truth: instead, it will be remade and repurposed as the circle of time swings round and humans replay their age-old fascination with technology.

London is another good example of this regenerative attitude toward time. Despite multiple instances of apocalyptic destruction throughout the series— it is destroyed during the Sixty Minute War, taken over by the Movement in

Fever Crumb, transformed into a traction city by Quercus in *A Web of Air,* and destroyed by MEDUSA in *Mortal Engines*—London never actually experiences an end of time and existence. Instead, London is made and remade constantly, not as a new and improved version, but as a reconfiguration of old parts and personalities. Buildings such as St. Paul's Cathedral and the London Museum (of Natural History), place-names such as Bloomsbury and Ludgate Hill, and even individual bloodlines such as the Natsworthys are shown to endure through multiple eras and locations, constantly repurposed and yet never really changing. Alice Bell (2009) describes the characters of the series as "obsessed with rediscovery" and suggests that throughout these narratives "science and technology becomes knowledge to be 'discovered' rather than invented, but discovered by people in the humanities" making it "a very human, even socially constructed, enterprise" (14). She describes this narrative focus on rediscovery as suggesting that knowledge and science are timeless (15). Critically, however, the series is careful to emphasize the fact that such repurposing does not constitute progress or forward motion: while the museums and historians constitute repositories of knowledge from which people might learn and progress, like the Scrivener's Institute their contribution to progress is undermined and illustrates nothing so clearly as the transience of any illusion of progress. Like the old computer disks and "seedys" (*Mortal Engines* 21) that are of no use to "the horrible old Guild of Engineers" (22), the knowledge they carry is lost and humans, far from progressing into a future freed from time and earthly constrains, continue to tread and retread the same earthbound circuits. The ancients who built the Scrivener Institute were certain they could escape, through genetic engineering technology, the environmental disaster they had created; the Movement was certain they could escape the growing scarcity of resources and the threat of war by the development of steam-powered traction cities; and London was certain it could escape the degraded earthly environment through the use of technological weapons to dominate resources and conquer space. However, each of these dreams of a future less dependent on the environment is shown to be mere hubris: by the end of the Mortal Engines series, the human race remains firmly earth-bound and as dependent as ever on sustainable relationships with each other and the natural world. In the world of municipal Darwinism, as in the world of capitalism, "Movement is considered not only imperative for survival, but viewed as a sign of social and technological progress" (Bullen and Parsons 2007, 129); it "institutionalizes the law of the jungle and the survival of the fittest" (130). However, contrary to this humanist evolutionary perspective, what Mortal Engines and Fever Crumb persistently insist is that time is fluid, history subjective, and progress and evolution are the illusionary projections of a species that cannot see beyond its own—fundamentally embodied—perspective.

THE INDIVIDUAL, THE ENVIRONMENT, AND THE POSTHUMAN BODY

In a parallel formulation to its deployment of evolutionary tropes of progress, children's literature has been variously identified as invested in the myth of progress through its celebration of the primacy of individual development typified by the bildungsroman form. As Bradford et al. (2008) explain, "Children's texts remain constrained by the intrinsic commitment to maturation narratives—narrative structures posited on stories of individual development of subjective agency, or of *bildungsroman*" (91). With its focus on the importance of the individual and his or her progress toward self-realization, the bildungsroman form that pervades children's literature diverts attention away from the Other except where that Other serves to reflect on the development of the individual. Hintz, Basu, and Broad (2013) describe the way YA dystopias in particular "recapitulate the conventions of the classic *Bildungsroman*, using political strife, environmental disaster, or other forms of turmoil as the catalyst for achieving adulthood" (7); in so doing, these dystopias refigure the environment more as a means to an end than as something that has value in its own right. As we have seen in previous chapters, therefore, the environment becomes something hostile and threatening, against which the young protagonist can test himself or herself. This anthropocentric foregrounding of the individual at the expense of the other (including the nonhuman other) creates what AbdelRahim (2015) defines as "humanism narratives" that "selectively construct humanity and empower the human at the expense of the nonhuman" (20). For Bradford et al., the bildungsroman form is implicated in the failure of the YA dystopia to adequately address environmental issues. More troubling, however, is the fact that such narratives implicate the individual's development of self and agency in a linear trajectory toward the apocalyptic destruction of nature itself. They suggest that the destruction of everything, including the environment, is of little importance in the face of the endurance of the individual consciousness.

A number of characters develop toward maturity in the Mortal Engines and Fever Crumb series: notably Tom Natsworth, Hester Shaw, their daughter Wren, Oneone Zero, Theo Ngini, Fever Crumb, Charley Shallow, and Cluny Morvish. Other characters such as the lost boy Fishcake, or Fern and Ruan Solent, while not main protagonists, will nevertheless prove to be catalysts for societal change as they develop and mature. As Dawson (2006) argues, "all of the young protagonists in *Mortal Engines* and *Predator's Gold* are engaged in an identity quest" (143), and it is through the changing perspectives of these characters as they find their place in a tumultuous world that the plots of these novels unfold. However, Dawson also points out that "no protagonists voice or perspective is privileged throughout the narrative, nor is any protagonist represented as simply heroic" (144), while Bullen and

Parsons (2007) insist that "This is no simple story of good and evil. Tom is not a hero" (132). Kay Sambell (2004) agrees, stating that "Reeve has overturned the conventional hero myth" (262). Throughout the narrative Hester will fail to become a better person, Wren will fail to heal her relationship with her mother, and Tom will fail to save his daughter; Hester, however, will be loved anyway, and Wren will survive and marry in spite of Tom and Hester's failings. Fishcake enacts his revenge on the Natsworthys, but it is ultimately not his actions that kill them, and Fever's heroic attempts to prevent the development of traction cities is marked from the beginning by inevitable failure. Gwen Natsworthy's rebellion will be thwarted, and she will be hanged and forgotten; nevertheless, her descendants will survive as inhabitants of London. What such characters demonstrate again and again is that history will not permit the endurance of the hero: the humanist quest for self-fulfillment will always fail in the face of the demands of embodied experience and the myth of linear time. The individual Gwen Natsworthy does not matter in the face of the constant reappearance of Natsworthys. In place of the individual hero, Mortal Engines and Fever Crumb offer an altogether more intriguing possibility: posthuman steampunk cyborg bodies resist stable embodiment and individual endurance, in place of regenerative embodiment and existence embedded within the environment.

If the traditional bildungsroman YA novel can be understood as emphasizing the development of the individual at the expense of the nonhuman and the environment, then the YA steampunk dystopia seems to undermine this emphasis by depicting posthuman bodies that resist stable embodiment and finite existence. According to Zoe Jaques (2015) the cyborg is uniquely suited to occupy a world in which "the lines between the human and the animal, between the enlivened and the inanimate, between the organic and the artificial, are porous and fractured" (18). Curry (2013) similarly describes the posthuman body as "a continuously evolving human-machine or human-nonhuman hybrid" (68); in this sense the evolution of an entire species becomes transposed onto specific bodies, rendering the consequences of progress within an environment more immediate and impactful. These bodies resist the drive of the bildungsroman toward self-fulfillment and/or apocalyptic self-destruction (whether individual or societal) by presenting bodies that are intimately entangled with environments in ways that erase the individual. For these posthuman bodies, embodiment within a specific environment means that identity fails to remain stable, binary, or hierarchical because it develops as a result of cycles of change and regeneration. In such a formation, the endurance of individual personalities is rendered irrelevant as they continually change and flux contingent with embodiment within a specific albeit fluctuating environment. Importantly, a key consequence of this enduring embodiment is that the environment is no longer positioned as a hostile enemy against which the individual can strive for self-development, but is instead shown to be a constantly present, regenerative, and nurturing force, supportive of entangled embodiment.

The steampunk cyborgs of Mortal Engines and Fever Crumb, known as Stalkers, are excellent examples of this type of embodiment. They hybridize not just the human and the machine but, through the deployment of ancient and poorly understood technologies, the past and the present. Constructed from the reanimated bodies of the dead, these Stalkers cannot, like mortal human beings, chase individual development at the expense of the environment because their near-immortality binds them to a physical world that is constantly changing. Removed from the trajectory of linear time, it is from these steampunk cyborgs that a more posthuman perspective on embodiment within time emerges. Grike (Shrike in UK versions of the texts) is a Stalker of the Lazarus Brigade; already old when he makes his first appearance in *Mortal Engines*, his origins are tied intimately to the transformation of London into a traction city in *Fever Crumb*. When alive, his name was Kit Solent and he was responsible for bringing to light the lost work of Auric Godshawk, which would eventually enable Quercus to conquer London and turn it into the first traction city; after death, his body is resurrected by the last surviving Scriven, Fever's mother Wavey Godshawk, using an ancient stalker brain taken from the very Scrivener Institute that created the Scriven race in the first place. From the very beginning, therefore, Grike is a hyrid not only of materials and forms, but also of eras: he is the literal embodiment of a cyclical human relationship with technology.

However, Grike is not a simple replacement of human body with machine parts. Graham (2014) argues that "much of the anxiety accompanying the invasive effects of technoscience focuses on the dismemberment or effacement of the body" (176); in Mortal Engines and Fever Crumb, however, the bonding of machine with body cannot be seen as straightforwardly erasing the human body. Throughout the many series, in fact, Reeves emphasizes not only his frighteningly inhuman body (such as bladed hands and glowing eyes), but also the distinctly mortal human body—such as the slimy preserved skin of his face—which is intimately entwined with the machine elements. The same is true of Anna Fang's resurrection as the Stalker Fang: when Fishcake finds the dismembered Stalker Fang at the end of *Infernal Devices*, for example, he discovers not only the "beautiful" bronze face mask (320), but also "the head, a skeletal gray face cupped in a metal skull" (321). In *Fever Crumb*, Fever herself becomes a similarly modified human/machine hybrid: "She is half-Scriven, part cyborg, and contains nanotechnology that repairs her wounds and illnesses" (Dean-Ruzicka 2014, 62). While the technology embedded within her makes her less vulnerable to the effects of mortality, however, it is Fever's human body that is emphasized as her mind skips back and forth through time—a body that is beautiful, vulnerable, and sexually oriented in a way that machine consciousness is shown not to be.

While Fever is inextricably entangled with machinery, she has emphatically not escaped embodiment.

Anna/Stalker Fang is resurrected twice in the series: once by Sathya to be the leader of the Green Storm, and then by Fishcake who yearns for someone to love him. Grike, even more extremely, will be resurrected many more times throughout the books: after his initial resurrection by Wavey in *Fever Crumb*, he will go on to be resurrected by Chrome and killed by Tom in *Mortal Engines*, then resurrected by Dr. Zero in *Infernal Devices*, surviving eventually beyond the end of the series in *A Darkling Plain*. Grike, like the Stalker Fang, will survive dismemberment and burial, as well as being run over by a traction city, falling from an airship down the side of a mountain, and a motionless, centuries-long "sleep mode." What is remarkable, however, is the fact that Reeve's insistence on the human bodily core within these Stalkers means it is not mere machine and human consciousness that endures, but an actual physical human shell. In fact, the eventual inability of the Stalker technology to eradicate the human memories and personalities embedded within those bodies suggests that it is the very fact of human physical embodiment that makes human consciousness possible. In a similar manner, Fever is shown to neither be consumed or effaced by her technological components, nor able to overcome or efface them; instead, these components expand and alter her conscious perspective.

At the same time, therefore, consciousness is shown through these posthuman characters to become increasingly less focused on the needs and desires of the individual, and more and more on those of the collective. The Stalker Fang, for instance, is able to temper the intense personal interests of Anna and the genocidal Stalker Fang, eventually "merging care for the planet and care for human beings" (Curry 2013, 98) for the good of both. Fever's personal yearning for love and family will likewise be superseded, thanks to the stalker brain embedded within her skull, by an awareness of the destructive potential of technology and a desire to protect the human/environment relationship from reliving the destruction of the ancients. Grike becomes less concerned with his own loneliness and confusion through his many resurrections, instead deciding finally that his purpose was to be a "remembering machine" (*A Darkling Plain* 531), feeding stories of the past to the future generations of humanity. Interestingly, Reeve does not pronounce on whether this function will prove helpful or harmful to the human race; by leaving this question open-ended and in light of the previous failures of historical knowledge and wisdom throughout the two series, this ending has the feel more of another turn of the circle than of a true resolution of the narrative, returning the reader to the beginning of the story by literally repeating the first line of *Mortal Engines*. This narrative, which literally has no end and no beginning, becomes embodied in the cyborg body that remains tied to the physical environment and embedded within it.

Grike's closing observations of the "simple people" living in a "wooded vale" supported by environmentally friendly "delicate airborn ships of wood and glass" and the "misty mirrors" of antigravity technology (*A Darkling Plain* 531) imply two things. Firstly, they imply that his overarching concern has become the placement of humans within sustainable relationships with the environment, for he is relieved to see that he has awoken to a world where his relationship to the world to which he is tied to is mutually supportive. As the opening description of him in this passage, as overgrown with wildlife, suggest, he is now as much a part of the land as he is an individual, and his constant regeneration has enabled him to see beyond (although not abandon) his sense of self, to a wider collective perspective. Secondly, they imply that humanity has neither evolved nor degenerated: this is neither a celebration of progress, nor a nostalgic primitivism. The people Grike sees and approves of live simply, and their society combines the primitive and rustic—stone building, goats taken to pasture—with the technologically sophisticated—antigravity technology and airships. They seem, at his arrival, to neither remember the past nor yearn for the future. If Reeve had ended with this vision, the narrative might indeed have been seen as having achieved a utopic end-of-time resolution in place of the many averted apocalypses of the different plot lines. Grike's presence, and his desire to relate the past, however, undermine this sense of closure: his stories, it is implied, are important and these people, therefore, may well find themselves drawn back into the endless cycle of progress, destruction, and regeneration. Equally, the lessons shared by Grike may well help avert a return to the cycle, which in *Mortal Engines* seemed inevitable—that of endless progress toward self-destruction. Critically, it is the posthuman body, firmly embedded within a vulnerable environment, which makes this cycle visible and undermines the myth of progress and linear time.

In an exposition for *The Guardian* about the seemingly endless appetite of teen readers for bleak dystopian fiction, including his own Mortal Engines series, Philip Reeve wrote that "by visiting such woes on teenagers like themselves, these stories may make it easier for young readers to think about them, and to imagine what it might be like to live in a police state or a shantytown" (2011b 34). Reeve argues that these dystopias not only allow young readers to imagine their role in hypothetical future scenarios, but also to empathize more fully with those who already live these dystopian experiences. Reeve's comments participate in an ongoing debate about the effectiveness of dystopia in motivating young readers to assume social responsibility. However, as can be seen in Mortal Engines and Fever Crumb, the engagement of dystopia with posthumanist philosophy opens up the possibility of a new kind of narrative, less constrained by the humanist imperatives of the bildungsroman. In a similar manner, posthumanist discourses allow a departure from the correlative of the bildungsroman—

the narrative of societal progress. By abandoning these "myths" of progress, YA dystopias achieve one of the triumphs associated by Zoe Jaques (2015) with the posthuman in children's fiction, offering "sophisticated interventions into debates about what it means to be human or non-human and offer ethical imaginings of a 'posthuman' world" (5). These dystopias explore the way in which posthuman technology changes the terms of embodiment, making sustainable relationships with place and environment imperative for both individuals and society as a whole. Elaine Ostry (2013) provides a stark assessment of the dilemma for young readers when faced with an apocalyptic bildungsroman narrative: "With the death of nature comes our death because we are nature, and its possible regeneration need not include us. No amount of personal growth can change that" (110). However, as Reeve demonstrates over the course of his two series, a posthuman engagement with technology debunks the certainty of an escape from nature, and makes it vital that human beings work toward sustainable relationships with the natural world. As Donna Haraway (2016) famously asserts, "Our machines are disturbingly lively, and we ourselves frighteningly inert" (11). By exploring this realization, YA dystopias ultimately promote a reconceptualization of identity as inherently entangled in wider environmental cycles of destruction and regeneration, exposing young readers to the inescapability of environmental accountability.

NOTES

1. Dinerstein (2006) defines the Adamic as "invested in recuperating an Edenic purity earned through virtuous work" (575), and discusses its origins as the medieval monastic belief that "the pre-Fallen Adam, immortal and created in the divine likeness, was *recoverable* through individual piety and work in the 'mechanical arts'" (575). He traces this belief through Euro-American culture, to show how it helped to inform a chronological myth of progress including the "discovery" of the Americas, the conquest of the Western frontier, space-age exploration, and finally the posthuman.

2. See also Onion (2008), who writes that steampunks can be viewed as "enamoured of technology, and convinced of its ability to endow man with a stronger sense of his own humanity and his interconnections with the material world" (143). As Forlini (2010) discusses, there is an inherent contradiction in this view between a humanist celebration of humanity's control over technology and nature, and a distinctly posthumanist recognition of and celebration of the nonhuman other; this contradiction is more or less prevalent depending on the expression of steampunk in question. While many steampunk cultural practices fall prey to this tendency, literary approaches have tended to be more critical of the humanist pitfalls of steampunk, adopting dystopian tropes which emphasize the need for more posthumanist approaches.

Chapter Six

Adam Rapp and Mike Cavallaro's *Decelerate Blue*

Solarpunk, Consumerism, and the Posthumanist Future

As touched on in previous chapters, the most prevalent theme in both the YA dystopian genre and in posthuman and ecocritical fiction is, beyond a doubt, the human relationship to technology. This relationship has always been complex, but in the current digital and media era, with technology and liberal humanist capitalism inextricably entwined like never before, that relationship has come under the spotlight in more extreme ways. As many researchers have pointed out (Rutsky 2017; Graham 2002; Vint 2007, to name but a few), the response to this relationship seems to veer between that of intense optimism and excitement, and that of fear, panic, and anxiety. Eskey (2017), reviewing the recently published YA dystopian graphic novel, *Decelerate Blue*, describes it as portraying what can be understood as "technofear": "What cuts truly deep about this story is that this where our society seems to be heading to now. We may not have chips imbedded in our arms, but we have cellphones that we check on average eighty-times a day. What's to say we won't be use [*sic*] to the idea of getting a tiny chip installed if it's advertised as 'timesavers' and 'effortless'" (Eskey 2017). In contrast, the Apple website (2018), in a section that proudly details Apple's commitment to protecting the environment, seems blind to "technofear." What is striking about this web page is the way in which it uses words and imagery together to reinforce the impression of sleek efficiency and hi-tech, futuristic solutions. The characteristic smooth, high-contrast white and black color scheme subtly suggests cleanliness and purity, and images dominated by sweeping lines, which draw the eye around the screen, as well as content portraying sleek metal fuel cells, solar panels, and even a humanoid recycling robot, evoke a future in which technology is fast, powerful, and exciting. The rhetoric of progress and innovation feature heavily in the quoted passage, and on the page as a whole; all in all, while this page may be ostensibly about Apple's corporate commitment to reducing the harm to the environment wreaked by the information technology industry, in reality it is nothing more than yet another desire-inducing advertisement for a future dominated by I-technology. It is no coincidence that the letter "I" features so prominently in Apple branding: these products are not only about information, but also about personal desire and the construction of subjecthood based around technological consumption.

The link between advertising and technology that Eskey identifies in his review harks back to my earlier exploration of Shusterman's *Unwind*, but in Adam Rapp and Mike Cavallaro's graphic novel *Decelerate Blue* (2017) there is a clear difference: rather than falling back on technology as the answer to humanity's environmental problems in contrast to consumer greed as the cause, *Decelerate Blue* emphasizes the entanglement of consumer desire with technological whitewashing of environmental problems. This chapter will explore the ways in which both the solarpunk content of this graphic novel, as well as its specific form and context, advocate for a posthumanist relationship with technology as an antidote to consumer-driven humanist environmental destruction.

TECHNOLOGY AND THE HOSTILE ENVIRONMENT

If there is one literary phenomenon that has engaged with the humanist assumption of a separate, hostile environment, it is cli-fi, or climate change fiction. This group of texts spans many genres, including science fiction and dystopia, and has seen a boom in recent years in film, television, and literature—including, and especially, those texts aimed at a YA audience. Cli-fi is typified by critical examination of the Anthropocene, or the specific impact of human beings upon what is seen as a rapidly degenerating environment. In discussing why this particular theme might have come to prominence in recent years, critics have had to look no further than current news and media. Tuhus-Dubrow (2013) for example, speculates that "[p]erhaps climate change had once seemed too largescale, or too abstract, for the minutely human landscape of fiction. But the threat seems to have become too pressing to ignore, and less abstract, thanks to a nonstop succession of megastorms and record-shattering temperatures" (59), while Leikam and Leyda (2017) point out that "[t]o date, the Trump administration's decidedly anti-environmentalist agenda, especially its stated intention to withdraw from the

Paris Climate Accord, is further fueling the production of cli-fi and intensifying the scholarly and public attention paid to these texts." As these comments suggest, it is the realization of the devastating consequences of a degraded environment for human populations that forms the cornerstone of conflict in cli-fi narratives: floods, hurricanes, global warming, and loss of biodiversity are prevalent tropes, and frequently feature in apocalyptic and postapocalyptic dystopian settings. While these texts, like others examined within this collection, view the natural world as hostile and threatening, they also make clear the culpability of human civilization in provoking that hostility.

Cli-Fi texts often have a distinctly pedagogical leaning, therefore, serving as cautionary tales for readers about the potential consequences of their actions. These texts can also be practical as well as cautionary: "some ecocritical analyses promote literary representations of climate change as providing lessons to their readers on how to cope with, adapt to, or mitigate against climate change" (Johns-Putra 2016, 274). With this in mind, it is easy to see why cli-fi literature has become so prevalent within children's and YA culture; as Hamilton (2015) explains "today's teenagers and young adults, as digitally connected as they are, know more than any other generation that the fiction they see in popular culture could well be the reality they inherit" (6). In others words, cli-fi raises awareness among young readers that the environment they do, and will, inhabit is hostile and threatening, but the genre also provides suggestions for how this hostility might be managed or mitigated by present or future action. Through the depiction of young protagonists, cli-fi also inevitably implicates young readers in both the problems and solutions to climate change. As such, it presents readers with the idea that the nature/culture binary is an illusion that cannot be sustained in the face of impending human-generated environmental destruction. When cli-fi meets dystopia (as it often does), "climate change is depicted not just as an internal or psychological problem but for its external effects, often as part of an overall collapse including technological over-reliance, economic instability, and increased social division" (Johns-Putra 2016, 269).

It is in this challenge to the nature/civilization binary divide that cli-fi meets posthumanism. Cli-fi texts depict environments that are threatening to the point of destroying this divide, encroaching on and fundamentally altering human civilization in ways that demand recognition of entanglement and reciprocity. This chapter is concerned specifically with the way in which solarpunk texts and graphic novels, as specific types of cli-fi text, achieve this challenge to humanist ideology through a specific engagement with the human relationship to technology. As explored in detail in the previous chapter, punk fictions often take technology as a starting point for radical reconceptualizations of the human relationship to the environment: in solarpunk and graphic novel cli-fi texts, both form and content contribute to this reconceptualization. The recently published *Decelerate Blue* is a solarpunk graphic novel in which individuals struggle to balance relationships to both technology and environment, and in which both technology and environment are shown to be equally threatening and enticing.

The novel tells the story of Angela, a young girl living in a world where mass consumption has been legislated as a mandatory part of life by an authoritarian government that tracks the commitment of individuals to fast-paced consumerism by means of surveillance technologies. Citizens comply happily in the name of securing their "guarantee"—a government-issued status whose sinister significance is never fully explained in the narrative, but which requires the modification of everything from speech to sleeping arrangements and even classic literature. Against this frenetic backdrop, Angela yearns for fulfillment that simply cannot be satisfied by the megamall, tracking chips, and cries of "go, Guarantee, go!" However, her whole life takes a new and exciting turn when she falls accidentally into an underground resistance movement dedicated to pursuing a slow lifestyle, free from the demands and surveillance of the Guarantee Committee. The dangers are high, however: the Guarantee Committee are ruthless in their insistence on conformity, and Angela and her new friends run the risk of not only censure, but state-authorized violence as well, if they are caught.

Significantly, both the above-ground and below-ground environments in *Decelerate Blue* can be seen as threatening. Above ground, the protagonist exists in an environment that epitomizes the Anthropocene: concrete, glass, and plastic have eradicated almost every glimpse of the "natural" world, leaving only a highly controlled human-oriented skin of development visible. Even in spaces where nature has been permitted to remain, such as the garden outside of Angela's window, or the park next to the Megamall, human influence prevails: the garden is tainted by hidden surveillance cameras, while the Megamall's shadow looms high above the trees in the park. These spaces are hostile in their sterility and infertility, signaled by Angela's unhappiness within them and reinforced by the dreary lack of color and organic line that typifies their depiction on the page. However, it is made clear in the novel that this hostility is a direct result of the violence inflicted by human civilization itself: this society seems to dread natural environments as a reminder of that which cannot be controlled and which has been cruelly exploited and destroyed. Technology in this above-ground environment is the source of power and control, and has been used to erase any sign of entanglement with the natural world.

This is made evident by the mirror-image environment that exists below ground. In this space, nature remains dominant. Thick rock and earth not only protect and conceal the rebels, but also limit their oxygen and their ability to produce food. The lake is a site for communal celebration, but also a site of danger and death: at least one individual has drowned in it, and it dominates many pages of the novel in a manner similar to the Megamall above ground. The individuals in this space, however, are careful not to fight against their environment, seeking to adapt to it rather than controlling it. Turning the traditional basis of the dystopia on its head, in *Decelerate Blue* the environment is shown to be hostile only to those who initiate violent conflict against it, and technology becomes a means of reconnecting with a natural world that is both dangerous and nurturing.

TECHNOLOGY AND THE SELF: DISSATISFIED SUBJECTIVITY

In *Decelerate Blue*, dissatisfaction is linked intimately to technology and the relationship to it that individuals and communities form—a relationship that is always fundamentally disembodied. R. L. Rutsky (2017) explains that images of the posthuman and posthumanism have historically been deeply implicated in fears about the human relationship to technology, with that relationship either viewed as a means of elevating the human beyond human limitations, or as the means whereby the human is supplanted, enslaved, and ultimately destroyed. The fear of technology is linked directly to humanist ideologies that seek to preserve a "pure" version of humanity; as Vint (2007) explains "technology is rapidly making the concept of the 'natural' human obsolete" (7), while in a comment that echoes the themes in *Unwind*, *The Giver*, and *Chaos Walking*, Davis (2014) writes that "[w]ith pills modifying personality, machines modifying bodies, and synthetic pleasures and networked minds engineering a more fluid and invented sense of self, the boundaries of our identities are mutating as well" (1). Technology, therefore, can be understood as a means of mitigating human dissatisfaction, and one which move the human being ever further away from the "natural" state that would provide contentment. More than anything else, *Decelerate Blue* is a narrative that explores dissatisfaction: both the dissatisfaction that spurs the consumer to ever greater consumption, and the dissatisfaction that arises from the empty attempt to construct subjectivity from such consumption.

Decelerate Blue opens with scenes that imply the demonization of technology through both word and imagery. In the opening scene, the protagonist, Angela's father, describes to his family a party celebrating his success in landing his technology firm a big contract. To accompany his retelling of the party, the reader is offered a series of panels zooming in more and more closely to first a flashback of the party itself, and then the family sitting around the dinner table. Both scenes emphasize the focus of the company—the production of Quicktop, described as "the *fastest* drying bonding agent in industrial history" (2, original italics). The panels, themselves spaced geometrically on the page like a stack of children's building bricks, reflect the geometric and angular nature of the imagery: faces (with the exception of

Angela's) are pointed and sharp, and the black-and-white coloring of the panels emphasizes the blocky architecture and straight lines that make up the scenery. An impression is formed very quickly of technology coupled with a fast-paced, consumer lifestyle in which sleek regulation of everything from language to buildings is the norm; furthermore, the pinched and hungry look on the angular faces of the company employees and Angela's parents, as well as Angela's gentle frown, suggest an unhappiness directly linked to this technologically constructed setting. As the narrative builds, the reader is offered a plethora of technological products to loathe and fear, from the Megamall, which seems to dominate both the landscape and the page (5, 43), to the "standing ergo beds" (15) that permit occupants to sleep standing upright. Spisak (2017), in a short review of the novel, writes that "the black and white illustrations bristle with sharp, jagged edges and lines that suit the harsh world" (278). These hyper-futuristic technological products are presented through both word and image as being not merely absurd, but also threatening: they are linked to harsh images that suggest discomfort, disorientation, and domination. However, posthumanism and the posthuman are not merely about fear of technology; as we saw in *Mortal Engines*, posthumanism requires a more complex and nuanced relationship with technology, and one which is—as Katherine Hayles (1999) advocates—fundamentally embodied. As Elaine L. Graham (2002) writes, "The 'end of the human' . . . may involve modes of post/humanity in which tools and environments are vehicles of, rather than impediments to, the formation of embodied identity" (199). It is this idea: that technology need not be antithetical to either embodiment nor to humanity, which is explored in the ensuing scenes of *Decelerate Blue*.

This shift from technology as threatening to technology as empowering occurs after Angela accidentally falls into, and is taken in by, the underground resistance movement. In a scene that mirrors Alice's iconic journey down the rabbit hole, Angela is introduced to a world dominated not by a lack of technology, but instead by a different way of viewing the world—one that is so radically antithetical to what both reader and Angela are used to that it is as disorienting as any Mad Hatter's tea party. From the moment Angela enters this new world, the harsh lines and angles of her old world begin to be replaced by more rounded, curving, organic shapes and forms, starting with the towering trees that mark the entrance to the cave, which rear up into the sky like giant arms, offering to protect Angela and—coincidentally—blocking the threatening view of the Megamall behind them. Music (53) is depicted as curving threads of sound—people are frequently shown surrounded by circular halos of light (53–54)—and the organic forms of rocks, water, ropes, and wood have replaced the restrictive lines and angles of concrete, metal, and plastic. In this new underground world, moreover, the technology that dominates life is communal and life-affirming. Angela encounters chip-removal medical technology (62–63), which counters the invasive chip implantations; air canisters (65), which help the "floaters" adjust to, rather than alter, their environment; and even a sunlamp powered by a peddle-bike (85) that is used to grow grass artificially. These technologies are figured as communal; they are not owned by or imposed upon individuals, but instead function to hold the community together. The bike and sunlamp are good examples: these alternative technologies work only because the community agrees to power them: relying on communal physical labor ("for every minute you stare at Lucy you have to ride the bike" [85]) in place of consumption of natural resources, they create a locus for shared pride and effort as well as a useable product. Technologies in the underground world are used to grow food, make music, and—most importantly—liberate individuals from the control of the mainstream authoritarian society: as such, the novel illustrates the ways in which technologies can function as solutions to social and environmental problems, rather than their catalysts. Importantly, these technologies are shown to support rather than erase embodiment. For example, in contrast to engineered foods that taste of nothing, and beds that hinder sleep, the resistance movement's technologies anchor people in their bodies: Angela learns to love the taste of slow-grown foods (94), to feel music as an emotive, embodied experience (108–9), and—critically—to accept the alteration of her body. The titular decelerate blue drug has been specially engineered to alter both mind and body: "The micropill lowers the heart rate and conserves oxygen in the body" but has also been "engineered to release the neurotranmitters that support the ability to envision things" (153). This is a different response to the biotechnologies demonized in *The Giver*: here, biotechnology has been repurposed as the means by which the individual can return to a truer experience of the body, free not from technology, but from authoritarian economies and governments. The form of the novel also supports this return to embodiment: As Baetens and Frey (2014) explain, in graphic novels "what we are confronted with from the very first until the very last panel is not the character's *thinking* . . . but the character's *body*" (174, original emphasis): panels in *Decelerate Blue* show, rather than tell, the effects of these liberating technologies on Angela's body, and the reader sees her frown disappear, color return to her features, and her expression relax. Importantly, a corresponding connection to the environment is also portrayed. Angela is seen in direct bodily contact with natural elements (water, rocks, and trees) and animals (the cows, goats, and sheep in the barnyard), and the scenes in which she finds love and sexual fulfillment are dominated by organic imagery: vines twine and leaves and flowers blossom (81, 110) as she learns to love with body and mind. That her lover is a woman, and that this is not made the explicit focus of the narrative, is a further indication of a new and more flexible mindset: here bodies are both vital and non-determinative. Hayles (1999) and Wolfe (2010) argue for a posthumanist ideology that embraces, rather than rejects, embodiment, seeing a focus on embodiment as a primary resource for the destabilization of humanist privilege. In *Decelerate Blue*, technology's power to embody and ground a subject in a communal and inclusive identity is foregrounded and celebrated.

SLOWING THINGS DOWN: VISUAL NARRATIVE AND SOLARPUNK

Like the steampunk fiction explored in chapter 5, solarpunk, too, offers serious engagement with posthumanist themes. Both steampunk and solarpunk offer visions of a future which, instead of embracing the humanist impulse to discard the past and pursue what is new and better, celebrates the posthumanist reuse and reimagining of the past and present as the most sustainable option for the human race.[1] In this sense, it is a version of what Goicoechea (2008) terms "technoromanticism," or "a mixture of technophilia, idealism and nostalgia for a utopian virtual future that will reproduce the pleasures of a lost Eden" (3). Solarpunk imagines this utopia as a future in which already existing technologies are reinvented not as products of capitalism and consumer desire, but as the catalysts for inclusive, communal, and entangled identities. Solarpunk shares its roots and ideology with steampunk, but takes a different approach to exploring the human relationship with the material world. One proponent of the movement describes the relationship between steampunk and solarpunk as follows:

> Solarpunk also conflates modern technology with older technology, but with a vital difference. In the case of steampunk, the focus on Victorian technology serves as a guideline for imagining an alternative world. In the case of solarpunk, the interest in older technologies is driven by modern world economics: if oil isn't a cheap source of energy anymore, then we sometimes do best to revive older technologies that are based on other sources of energy, such as solar power and wind power. (*Republic of the Bees* 2017)

Another explanation, offered by the fan site Solarpunk Anarchist, similarly explains that "While steampunk imagines a past that might have been, based on Victorian-age technology, solarpunk imagines a future that could be, based on current-age technology" (Owens 2016). Solarpunk, therefore, replaces the technologies of the past (such as steam power) used to reimagine the human/nonhuman relationship in steampunk with the technologies of the present, such as solar power, which might be used differently to fashion an alternative present or future. Adam Flynn (2014), writing as part of the Arizona State University Center for Science and the Imagination Hieroglyph

Project, offers what is currently the closest to an academic explanation of the movement:

> Solarpunk is about finding ways to make life more wonderful for us right now, and more importantly for the generations that follow us—i.e., extending human life at the species level, rather than individually. Our future must involve repurposing and creating new things from what we already have (instead of twentieth-century "destroy it all and build something completely different" modernism). Our futurism is not nihilistic like cyberpunk and it avoids steampunk's potentially quasi-reactionary tendencies: it is about ingenuity, generativity, independence, and community.

Solarpunk, therefore, presents a vision of an alternative reality in which the marginalized alternative technologies already available to the human race, such as solar- and wind-powered renewable energy, vertical gardens, organic farming, and so on, are mainstream and pervasive. Solarpunk proponents imagine a world in which, similarly to steampunk, individuals are able to interact personally with technology to find solutions that work for themselves and their communities, rather than for the interests of multinational corporations and exploitative capitalist organizations.

As many of those who write about solarpunk explain, this is a vision that is eutopic rather than utopic; it imagines a significantly better existence for humanity (and for nonhumans) without the drive for perfection and end-of-time impossibility implied by traditional visions of utopia. The implications for environmental studies are clear: solarpunk encourages individuals and communities to take charge of the future through a reappropriation of technology and a rejection of any technology that is environmentally or socially exploitative. In a review of cli-fi in both popular culture and literary studies, Johns-Putra (2016) summarizes some of the key tropes of the cli-fi literary movement. He notes, for example, that "[i]n some novels, usually those with contemporary or very near-future settings, climate change is a phenomenon that requires individuals' engagement as a political, ethical, or even psychological problem" (269). Markley (2012) argues that cli-fi literature "asks us to take seriously the potential of science . . . to foster new, expansive visions of humankind's co-implication in the natural world" (8), and Murphy (2014) suggests that climate change fiction encourages readers to move from denial to "recognition, acceptance, and the will to act" (149). Taken together, what these comments suggest is that solarpunk texts speak to the issues of adaptation and resilience as major issues in the wider context of climate change discourse. Solarpunk fiction can be understood as a specific brand of cli-fi, and one that seeks to teach readers how to live with the reality of climate change. As such, it meshes well with posthumanist ideologies in general. As Clarke and Rossini (2017) argue, "to practice posthumanism means to relinquish claims of spiritual absolution from natural contingencies" (xii); this includes a relinquishment of the drive for ever more technologically complex "progress" as the solution to the problems of the future.

What is significant—and radically posthumanist—about the technology in *Decelerate Blue* is that the rebels do not seek new technologies, nor do they reject technology altogether: instead, they rely on existing technologies and alter the humanist approach to those technologies that usually informs human/technology relationships. The underground community in *Decelerate Blue* uses both the technologies of their own society and the older technologies familiar to us from our own, and they use these technologies in support of community and sustainability, and in opposition to capitalist individualism and consumer-driven progress. A good example of this is the way in which the novel presents medical technology.

In the mainstream society, medical technology is streamlined, commercialized, and commodified: subjects are dehumanized as they consume health, and the body becomes another product for social control. For example, when Angela visits her grandfather (18–22) we see him strapped to a machine that monitors his heart rate and, the narrative implies, far more as well. Medical infographics—line charts and gridded screens—dominate the page, while a nurse in futuristic scrubs is rendered impersonal by the reflective visor that hides his eyes and most of his face. Medical equipment fills the rooms with tubes, monitors, and buttons, almost obscuring the more homely touches that mark this as a personal home—the decorative moldings around a door, or the cuckoo clock on the wall. Angela's grandfather, similarly, seems to disappear behind the tangle of wires attached to his skull and inserted into his nostrils: he explains that these are "putting something in my fluids" (20), designed to keep him both docile and functioning at a level deemed acceptable by the Guarantee Committee. Angela's grandfather has become a victim of medicine, which manipulates his mind and body to turn him into yet one more product to be manufactured and maintained (or discarded) in this fast-paced society. The visored nurse reappears at the end of the narrative, when Angela is herself placed in a rehabilitation center to monitor her recovery—both from the violence of the raid on the underground community, but also from her exposure to the radical deceleration ideologies. Similarly, the chips which have been inserted under the skin of those who carry a Guarantee are a medical insertion, but they guarantee not the health and well-being of the wearer, but instead that of the authoritarian society: by monitoring the whereabouts and movements of the chipped individual, they turn submission and surveillance into a product—a desirable feature of the Guarantee. Later in the narrative, Angela's girlfriend, Gladys, describes a mental rehabilitation center she had been sent to: the center sought to "cure" Gladys by making her sprint and recite "mantras about leanness and efficiency" (103); once again, social control is being dressed up as medical intervention (this time mental health care), as a means of coercing the individual into a mindset more compatible with extreme consumerism. For these individuals, medicine involves a radical alienation from both body and environment, equating sterile artificiality with health.

In contrast, the same medical technologies in the underground community are used to re-familiarize individuals to body and environment, and to build community. Critically, the medical removal of the medically inserted Guarantee chips is a locus for these ideas: removal of the chip is celebrated with a communal ceremony, willingness to undergo the risky procedure is considered a test of commitment to the ethos of the community, and those who have had their chips removed describe it as "the most important decision I have ever made" (101). The procedure, however, is neither clinical nor depersonalizing: images of the band singer Slowneck after his chip-removal procedure goes wrong show him lying in a normal bed, minimally hooked up to a drip, and surrounded by human touches: a carafe of water, a curtain, an extra pillow. The surgeon's face is clearly visible in a close-up shot, and it is suffused with sympathy and worry. Most important, however, is the fact that the procedure has gone badly: Slowneck has picked up an infection, and is dying. Here medicine is in the service of community, it is an embodied process, and it is fallible: the expectation that the patient is under the authority of the doctor has been removed, and the patient is more than just another product to be consumed by society.

Such relationships with technology are scattered throughout the novel: they use sunlamps and grow-tunnels, drip-feeds, oxygen cans, peddle-bikes, and even bioengineered drugs, but they use them not as consumable products, but as the means by which community is powered and a relationship to environment is formed. In the above-ground society, technology impedes access to the natural environment: hospitals imprison individuals in their own bodies; homes, schools, and offices cage people in concrete and glass; and the megamall blocks access to the few patches of forest and grass that remain. Artificial environments, which are easy to control and in which one can be controlled easily, are the norm, and nature is viewed with suspicion. Like the surveillance camera disguised as a bird-box in a tree (13), capitalism and consumerism are built into the artificial fabric of this society. In contrast, the underground community experiences the natural environment directly: farming technologies require a nuanced understanding of light, temperature, humidity, soil, and so on; the peddle-bike connects individual bodies to the labor of energy production; the waters of the lake are pervasively present, and the chip removals forge a direct connection between the people and the animals (also having their chips removed). These technologies, therefore, are solarpunk in their reimagining of the triangular relationship between individuals, technology, and environment.

Time is also a critical means in *Deceleration Blue* of exploring the way in which human subjectivity can be expanded and complicated through relationships with technology. This is particularly the case when one considers the formal elements of the narrative working alongside the solarpunk themes. Lisa Diedrich (2017) explains that graphic narratives share "a preoccupation with exploring how subjects come into being" and can therefore be understood as deploying various complex formal elements as a means of articulating "a concept of the subject as always in the process of becoming in relation to both human and non-human others," rendering "the posthuman subject not as something one *is,* but rather as something one *does*" (96–103). Like the technological relationships it espouses, therefore, the novel rejects a concept of the self as defined by linear time and progressive development. This emphasis on the fluidity and nonlinear nature of the development of the self is emphasized by the form of the narrative itself. Kukkonon (2013) describes nonlinearity as a key feature of graphic novels and comics in general: "Order, time, and rhythm are supplied by the reader and by the order and duration in which the panels are read" (54). In other words, the way in which readers control the development of meaning on the page mirrors the functions of experience and memory in real life: time speeds up, slows down, pauses, and is replayed just as the character, reader, or individual wishes it to, meaning that individual subjectivity develops in layers. While the traditional novel suggests the development of characters into "real" and "complete" individuals as a result of a steady progression of linear events, the graphic novel shows the same development as being something that occurs as a result of repetition, backtracking, circularity, and so on.

Angela, as the protagonist, is the classic example of this. When the novel opens, the reader is introduced to her parents who, in their excitement, naivety, and gullibility seem almost childlike; in contrast, Angela's cynicism, questioning nature, and sincerity show her to be more mature; she has progressed toward subjectivity and selfhood to a much greater extent. The double-page spread on which Angela and Gladys first kiss, is a good example. Although the panels detail a chronological sequence in which the two girls walk through the cave system, holding hands as they explore it, the eye of the reader is drawn first to the images at the bottom right of the spread: images that show a second kiss, and Angela's confused reaction in bright reds, pinks, and yellows—all the more startling in that these are the first colors to have appeared anywhere so far in the novel. In the bottom left, their intertwined hands form the bottom of a heart shape that fragments the chronological sequence imposed on top of it and implies the romance several panels before the kiss occurs, while the following page continues with their exploration of the cave community as if nothing had occurred. As the reader's eye moves in this nonlinear way about the page, Angela is shown not to be stable or progressive in her identity: she is neither straight nor gay, neither in love nor out of it, and she is not progressing toward a better understanding of her sexuality. Instead, she is having experiences that will not be processed by herself or the reader until later, but which may have had fruition much earlier. Angela's "process of becoming" takes place, significantly, in a natural space: the caves are enclosing, protective, and obscuring: safe from the scrutiny of the Guarantee Committee, Angela is free to develop at her own pace and in her own direction.

The graphic novel format, therefore, actively invites the reader to question—if not outwardly reject—the humanist myth of progress, both technological, and personal, and both intertwined. Baetens and Frey (2014) comment that "[g]raphic novels slow down time and make readers approach the page as a single picture, a space to meditate on the gaps between the images and heart-wrenching stories" (97). Narrative and medium, in other words, become dissociated, and the reader is given the opportunity to see them as separate, constructed, and—therefore—questionable. Rippl and Etter (2013) argue that for any narrative form, "[t]he medium as the carrier of the signs is never transparent or 'innocent'; its internal structural and medial laws define the ways in which the categories of time and space are used" (201). In the case of the graphic novel, space and time are defined as nonlinear and fluid, inviting a corresponding concept of self and body as fluid and mutable. This, in turn, supports a posthumanist reading of the narrative, inviting new ways of reading the body, society, and the environment in ways the reject the myth of the humanist subject. As Perry Nodelman (2012) observes of the comic/graphic novel format, "the extreme fragmentation and instability of the sequence seems revelatory of a deliberately unsettled world view inherently full of new possibilities" (440–41). In *Decelerate Blue*, these possibilities revolve around the body and the environment, with each becoming entangled with the other on the page. Diedrich (2017) argues that "in comics, time becomes spatialized" (98): we see this with the many dream scenes: when she dreams of Georgetta, for example, Angela's body is shown moving through the dreamscape dominated by water, which ripples and pools around her and defines the duration of the dream. Chute and DeKovan (2006) describe how this type of representation of embodiment in space offers posthumanist possibilities when they describe "[t]he form's fundamental syntactical operation" as "the representation of time as space on the page" which allows "hybridity as a challenge to the structure of binary classification that opposes a set of terms, privileging one" (769). As Angela learns to adapt her body, her subjectivity, and her relationship with technology to the needs and demands of a new environment, the humanist privileging of time over space is deconstructed, rendered visible, and ultimately rejected. *Decelerate Blue*, therefore, embodies a new way of considering the human relationship with technology, and with the environment. However, as we shall see in the next section, it is not merely in its textual and visual imagery that this graphic novel embodies posthumanist ideology; the graphic novel's form and production reflect the solarpunk ethos, offering an alternative to the dystopian novel as a mainstream consumer product reflecting the very capitalism it criticizes.

FORM AND PRODUCTION: THE POSTHUMANIST GRAPHIC NOVEL

As a subcategory of the wider comics genre, YA graphic novels are both radically different to text-only productions, and at the same time similar in their steady rise to mainstream popularity. Despite the growing interest of mainstream publishers and markets, however, graphic novels remain radical in their roots, and in this sense they are an ideal medium for the exploration of posthumanist themes. Clarke and Rossini (2017) argue that "there is a congruence between the posthuman and the 'post-literary'" (xix); it is possible that the graphic novel embodies the type of new and adaptive literature that they call for. Graphic novels can be understood as posthumanist in their construction; as discussed in the section above, the visual elements of the graphic novel defy the traditional delivery of humanist narratives. As Diedrich (2017) explains, "In their very form, comics thematize boundaries and their leakiness: panels are breached, borders dissolved, lines are drawn and undrawn, boundaries are played with, on, and beyond" (99). In other words, by drawing attention to themselves as embodied objects and unstable carriers of meaning, comics and graphic novels undermine the humanist equation of body with narrative with truth: each element in that humanist triangle is shown to be mutable, inviting a reimagination of not only the narrative on the page, but also the narrative of the self and of society. Furthermore, as Lefèvre (2011) explains, "Drawings in comics are static and strongly stylized, so the spectator becomes aware of their handmade quality" (73), while Baetens and Frey (2014) describe graphic novels and comics as "the almost biological expression of the author, whose body is made manifest through his or her personal style" (135). The graphic novel format, therefore, in inherently inimical to the ethos of capitalism and consumerism, in that it represents nonconformity, non-reproducibility, and quality over speed and distributability. Victoria Flanagan (2014) argues that "the thematic engagement of contemporary YA fiction with posthuman ideology is frequently accompanied by experimental narrative forms, so that the construction of posthuman subjectivity as multiple and fluid is correspondingly reflected in the construction of the text itself" (60). Not only does the graphic novel format present such posthuman subjectivity, but so does its production context which is equally multiple and fluid. As Baetens and Frey (2014) argue, graphic novels—unlike traditional narrative forms—resist the easy commodification of their content; their hand-drawn quality and the time they take to produce does not translate easily between different media (panels may become distorted, for example, when a graphic novels is digitized as an ebook), making them fundamentally embodied products. This is slow literature, inherently resistant to a consumer culture that exploits resources to push consumable and disposable products onto individuals desperately seeking subjectivity.

Decelerate Blue is a novel that demands this type of slow reading. As a one-shot graphic novel, it replaces the easily digestible serialized format of traditional comics with a dense and complexly plotted narrative that requires multiple readings to unpick the layers of meaning. The stark black-and-white images, moreover, are unfriendly to the scanning eye: to pick out detail, the reader must slow down and focus on an image (whether a single panel, multiple panels, or an entire page) for some time. Details providing context are minimal: we are never told who the Guarantee Committee are nor how they came to be in power, and the only hint that is provided about what they want is in the megamall: like consumer culture in our own world, the forces driving *Decelerate Blue* are unseen and yet disturbing. However, the novel's sparsity of contextualizing detail again encourages slow reading: the reader, in teasing the detail out of the text, learns to critically decode norms to get at the ideologies underlying them. An anonymous review in *Kirkus Reviews* (2016) criticizes the novel for being, itself, a fast-paced consumer product:

> [I]t suffers from its own acceleration, narrowing what could be a vast world. There's enough here for three or more books to give readers more time with Angela as she decelerates, learns, and finds love in resistance fighter Gladys and to introduce more than the singular obviously non-white character met here. (164)

However, I would argue that such a reading misses the main point: the novel makes the best that it can of an already accelerated production context; it cannot escape from the consumerism that has produced and distributed it. It can, however, work deliberately to expose the workings of consumerism in both form and content, encouraging a new concept of technology not as a consumable product, but as something that can be used to promote a future based on collectivity, inclusivity, embodiment, and sustainability.

As explored in the introduction to this volume, storytelling is one of the most powerful tools used in the dissemination and normalization of humanist ideologies. However, as Baetens and Frey (2014) explain, "storytelling cannot be separated from its inherent materiality: the form is critical" (164). The graphic novel's particular materiality, by resisting the illusion of transparency, resists the narrative as a vehicle for humanist ideologies. Chute and DeKovan (2006) argue that "Graphic narratives, on the whole, have the potential to be powerful precisely because they intervene against a culture of invisibility by taking the risk of representation" (772). If the exploitation of environment to fuel a consumer culture predicated on a false notion of humanist progress is that which is invisible, then graphics novels such as *Decelerate Blue* take us one step closer to a more varied and nuanced form of representation. In demonstrating to readers the value and usefulness of existing technologies as a solution to the problems created by new technologies, *Decelerate Blue* pushes for readers to adjust their perception of the human relationship to nature and technology: a call to action that is prevalent in cli-fi more widely. By illustrating—literally—the value of an adaptive mindset, *Decelerate Blue* provides just one example of how solarpunk fiction can enable young readers to imagine resilient futures as both embodied and technological beings.

NOTE

1. Portions of this chapter appeared first as an article on my blog; see: Harrison (2017).

Conclusion

Young Adult Dystopia and the Posthuman Perspective

An article in *The Wall Street Journal* complains that "[c]ontemporary fiction for teens is rife with explicit abuse, violence and depravity" (Gurdon 2011). This is not an uncommon viewpoint: with so many pressing issues facing young people in the world today, it can be tempting to see speculative fiction as at best frivolous and at worst harmful. Even for literary critics, the dystopian genre can be problematic; in their comprehensive examination of the tropes of dystopia in modern YA fiction, for example, Carrie Hintz, Balaka Basu, and Katherine R. Broad (2013), discussing the retention of the bildungsroman structure so traditional to the wider genre of children's literature, express concern that "the political potentials of YA dystopias have been foreclosed by this association with more traditional narrative structures" (7). However, as I hope the studies in this volume have suggested, such a complaint falls short of considering the complex agendas and ideologies that often emerge as these texts play out the tension between humanist realities and posthuman possibilites. Far from being exercises in escapism, YA dystopian fiction encourages young people to think critically about embodiment, social responsibility, and the consequences of their own and others' actions. These texts offer nuanced blueprints for how the future might be different: for better or for worse. As such, they may be just what is needed to empower young readers. Young people not only inhabit hostile environments today; they increasingly face the idea of a planet rendered hostile in the future through environmental decline and social upheaval. At the same time, a social framework predicated upon humanist ideologies and invested in technological solutions seems to be ill-equipping young people to thrive within such an environment. With bodies and subjectivities that are increasingly posthuman in nature, young people may well find that a shift to posthumanist thinking is the only viable option for a successful future, and speculative fiction, more than any other source, offers a model for such thinking to potentially develop from.

Young people in today's society inhabit increasingly hostile environments in which they are being forced to adapt to the environmental problems created by previous generations. Climate change caused by generations of forest clearance and fossil fuel use for industrial growth, for example, has made changes to the way young people experience the outdoors, natural spaces, and their own bodies: a good example might be the rise in 2018 of lyme-disease-carrying tick populations across North America in response to the warmer, wetter summer weather (Week Staff 2018). Industrialization has also contributed to a scarcity of all types of resource, from water to petroleum, making activities like recycling a part of the millennial generation's everyday life. A quick look at the *Young People's Trust for the Environment* website (YPTE 2018), for example, reveals rhetoric that paints a dismal picture of a planet with clogged waterways, dirty oceans, and rapidly expanding rubbish dumps—a miasma of filth and toxins that is growing every day. The rise of bacterial resistance and super-viruses have made increased medicalization a feature of most young people's existence: in December 2018, for example, the CDC reported record-breaking numbers of pediatric deaths due to new strains of the influenza virus (CDC 2018), exacerbated by a rising incidence in non-vaccination in the United States (Sun 2018). Environmental pressures have also created social problems that are becoming too pressing to ignore. Many young people, even in the developed world, occupy food deserts (Tulane University 2019), have regular contact with refugees (see, for example, the wealth of material available on the *Young People for Refugees* Facebook Page [YPR 2019], which chronicles the contacts of young Australians with refugees fleeing violence and deprivation), or suffer the health effects of urban pollution: according to the *World Health Organization* (WHO 2018), "more than 90% of children breathe toxic air."

The result of this plethora of alarming facts is that young people—at least according to the media (which they are reading, studying, watching, and having brought to their attention in school)—live in an environment that is increasingly hostile to their existence. They are hearing that the food, water, fuel, and other resources available to them are scarce, inadequate, or contaminated; the air they breathe is toxic; and the land is increasingly unable to support the lifestyles they have been brought up to expect. This is an environment in which unseen natural enemies lurk, deadly and waiting to infect them. It is also a shrinking environment: one in which even running away from danger is becoming increasingly difficult. These are not problems young people are unaware of. Increasingly, movements spearheaded by young people, such as the *Young People for Refugees* group and *Ryan's Recycling Company* (Hickman 2019), founded by eight-year-old Ryan Hickman in 2016, are demonstrating that young people are not only aware that they live in an increasingly hostile environment, but that they are motivated to find solutions. Of course, this motivation springs in part from the fact that the media is not only showing today's world as hostile, but is increasingly depicting to young audiences a future environment which is hostile to dystopian extremes.

A single search in Google, using the key words "environment future," yields results that make clear the timeliness of the dystopian genre. At the top of the list, an article in the *Guardian* features a quotation from the director of programs at UNICEF who warns that "As more extreme weather events increase the number of emergencies and humanitarian crises, it is children who will pay the highest price" (Harvey 2018). The third result, an article featured on the *Weather Channel* website, presents a warning from NOAA that "disruptive tidal flooding known as 'nuisance flooding' that now affects the US Gulf and Atlantic coastlines on 3 to 6 days per year will strike as often as 80 to 180 days a year by the 2040s" (Wright and Henson 2018). Further down this first page of results, an article in *The Independent* from February 2018 warns that no amount of high-tech technology will be sufficient to prevent the rise in atmospheric CO_2 (Gabbatiss 2018). Renowned dystopian novelist Margaret Atwood warns in another *Guardian* article that climate change will likely have the highest impact on vulnerable groups such as women and children, and that environmental pressures are likely to lead to increased violence and civil unrest in the future of today's children (Harvey 2018). Accompanied by dramatic imagery of flooded coasts, drowned cities, and towns wrecked by hurricanes, such media stories make clear that apocalypse is far from being a fantastic speculation.

It seems clear, therefore, that the speculative narratives young people are so drawn to—in dystopian best sellers like *The Hunger Games*, *The Giver*, and *Unwind*, but also in television series such as *The 100* and *Fifth Wave*, films such as *Farenheit 451* and *The Darkest Minds*, and video games like *Metro Exodus*—are not only possible but also likely future realities for today's young people. These media stories, with which the internet and popular media are flooded, depict a future that is just around the corner, and in which the humanist concept of a hostile environment over which civilization must exert control is taken to the extreme. Even more frightening, however, is the fact that unlike their popular culture counterparts, these nonfiction forays into dystopia provide no cohesive blueprint for a positive way forward. While one story laments industrial innovation as inadequate, another might hail it as the only viable solution to the problem of CO_2 emissions. Some stories about air pollution call on industry to make changes, while others heap the blame on individual consumers. The very democracy that supposedly makes the media valuable is also potentially confusing and discouraging: with so many different opinions all claiming to be verifiable fact, young people might well wonder how exactly workable solutions can be found.

While, as we saw previously, therefore, young people are clearly aware and motivated to act on the social and environmental problems of current and future dystopias, they may well lack a robust set of tools with which to approach solutions.

In the lives of most young people, the obvious places to turn for guidance on how to build a better future—assuming they turn away from the mixed messages in the media in search of more cohesive information—are fairly straightforward: young people can turn to education, to politics, and to technology. The problem for many, however, is that these avenues for action are firmly rooted in the same humanist ideologies which, as we have seen, lie at the root of many dystopian scenarios. In education and higher education, many critics have noted a turn away from critical thinking toward an emphasis on skills which commodify the student as a member of the workforce. To give just one indication of this trend, use of the National Assessment of Educational Progress's "Nation's Report Card" tool (NAEP 2018), when measuring for results at the national level on the most recent 2018 assessments, showed 42 percent of students at or above proficiency in economics and 43 percent at or above proficiency in technology and engineering literacy, but results as low as 12 percent in US history, 37 percent in reading, and no data collected at all for the arts. One educational expert commenting on 2016 PISA results, which showed the United States trailing behind other nations educationally, dismissed the findings as irrelevant, stating that "an economy, especially today, is driven by individual exceptionality. Entrepreneurship, entertainment, inventiveness, creativity—no tests can measure that" (Heim 2016). The current US education secretary, Betsy DeVos—herself from a wealthy entrepreneurial background—has been criticized for her support of an entrepreneurial approach to education, lending support to private charter school and for-profit higher education institutions at the expense of public education.

With such views—emphasizing the humanist bias toward individual success and gratification, and toward capitalist technological development—prevalent among many education experts and reflected in much of the present educational policy, students are ill-equipped to think beyond individual actions and economic motivations.

In politics, of course, young people lack rights across the board when it comes to decisions about their bodies, their education, their guardianship, their environments, and nearly all aspects of their lives. According to the European Youth Forum, for example, "There is a clear discrepancy between the rights young people have according to the law and the extent to which they are able to enjoy those rights in practice. This effectively means that young people's rights remain unrealized" and points out many violations in practice of the rights of young people, including the discrepancy in some developed nations between the legal voting age and the legal age at which a person can run for office (European Youth Forum 2017). In the United States, the National Youth Rights Association (NYRA 2018) details the rights infringements that young people commonly face, including the curtailment of freedom of speech within schools, and the inability to vote on issues directly affecting their lives and futures. Advocates for Youth (Advocates for Youth 2019) similarly documents the lack of rights young people can access in terms of their own bodies, including the right to confidential health care and the right to refuse certain medical interventions.

What these grim assessments suggest is that to compliment the dystopian outlook presented by popular media, young people are being denied the social tools that might equip them to implement social and ideological changes. Young people lack the ability, for example, to vote for legislation to control climate change, limit urban development, or regulate pharmaceutical development. They may even lack the educational resources that would enable them to see the necessity of doing so, where no economic or personal gain is involved. In a society that values individual profit, financial success, and economic and national growth, young people are actively discouraged from learning about and implementing collective and socially responsible actions outside of a liberal-humanist framework.

One area, of course, that modern developed societies do place value is in faith in science and the development of technology as a solution to social and environmental problems. Because the primary humanist response to the depicted hostile environment is to exert greater control, science and technology are lauded as the means of exerting that control. However, even in this area, young people are being poorly equipped to cope with the hostile environments the media insists they are surrounded by. Technology in the globalized twenty-first century is increasingly a matter of privilege, available for both use and development increasingly only by the wealthy. The use of technology by young people, furthermore, is primarily focused toward personal entertainment and corporate profit. Young people in the United States and Europe today, as the media frequently laments, seem permanently hooked to personal devices, consuming social media (Facebook, Titter, Snapchat, Instagram) and entertainment (Netflix, Hulu, YouTube) and limiting their ability to engage deeply with the material world around them: "mobile device and social media uses have an unfavorable relationship with attention, memory, impulse control, and academic performance" (Alaimo 2018). These technologies run the risk of perpetuating the disembodiment Katherine Hayles (1999) warns about in *How We Became Posthuman*, fostering the myth that the material world that is becoming so hostile is in fact irrelevant and unnecessary. For young people increasingly surrounded by environmental threat, technology can offer a convenient source of escapism. (It can also be used to facilitate activism denied through more traditional means, but that is a discussion for another project.)

As our earlier brief look at the Apple website in chapter 6 suggested, technology developers—most of them geared firmly toward entertainment and consumer gratification—make a show of applying their own highly developed technological innovations to mitigating their harm on society and the environment. Especially considering the pressure now being put upon young people to enter STEM fields and keep their nations at the forefront of technological development (US Department of Education 2019), technology is increasingly being lauded as the *only* tool available to and endorsed for young people to solve the problems of the future. Young people are encouraged to channel their effort and passion into, for example, the development of nanotechnologies for green manufacturing, biofuels, and tidal energy technologies, rather than thinking critically about the mindsets and ideologies that have created the problems in the first place. This emphasis on technology is, as has been discussed elsewhere in this collection, yet another iteration of the nature/civilization binary of humanist thought: the assumption that the nonhuman environment is hostile and needs to be controlled and dominated for humanity to survive and thrive. However, as we have already seen, the media makes clear the limited ability of technology to maintain this divide, as human technological ability increasingly falls short of matching the harm already generated. The drive for ever-more technological innovation, however flawed it may be in terms of solving social and environmental problems, is therefore a reality of life for many young people.

With these ideas in mind, it is perhaps not surprising that so many young people in the developed world today are dissatisfied and angry. Some studies point to rising issues with anxiety and depression among young people (Silverman 2018), and with the media continuously emphasizing a bleak and untenable future, this is not that surprising. An article in *The Guardian* in 2018 features young people speaking out about their dissatisfaction; individuals between the ages of sixteen and twenty-three cite the rising cost of education, scarcity of jobs, mental health issues, pressure at school, and loneliness as reasons why they are unhappy about their lives and futures, and in many of the commentaries, technology lurks as a common, uniting factor in bringing these pressures to the forefront (Obordo 2018). Perhaps what this reveals, however, is that just as the fictional dystopia might not be so dystopian after the humanist perspective is removed, so, too, these young people might be suffering from entrapment within a humanist framework that no longer meets their needs and expectations. For young people today, both their bodies and their experiences are increasingly posthuman. The issues highlighted on a daily basis by the media increasingly demonstrate the failure of humanist society to keep the nature/culture binary intact. The humanist insistence on humanity's dominance, separateness, and control over the nonhuman is being challenged on all sides by the problems it has created with marginalized groups, nonhuman others, and the environment. It is young people who are experiencing the effects of this challenge to humanism, as they grapple with an increasingly bleak outlook for the future.

It may well be, in this case, that posthumanism offers young people the most viable option out of dissatisfaction and depression, and toward a viable future. However, it seems clear that the exposure to posthumanist mindsets are unlikely to be offered through official channels: as we have seen, traditional media, education, and politics remain firmly rooted in humanist ideologies. It is for this reason that popular culture—and specifically speculative fiction—has an important role to play in enabling young people to envisage a successful and fulfilling future, and in equipping them with the tools they need to survive in a world in which humanist ideology is increasingly fragile. In a critique of what she terms the "informatics of domination" in modern Western education, Donna Haraway (2016) identifies a "growing industrial direction of education (especially higher education) by science-based multinationals (particularly in electronics- and biotechnology-dependent companies)" (48–49). In light of Elaine L. Graham's (2002) insightful insistence on the constructed nature of scientific truth as just one more narrative among narratives, the need for YA fiction that reveals the instability of these "truths" becomes apparent, as resistance to such forms of domination. Science and literature have drifted far apart as critical disciplines (76); falling on either side of the humanist dichotomy of mind/body, literature stakes its claim to the human mind and spirit, while science attempts to account for what is left over: human bodily ontology and the nonhuman world of matter, in all its myriad forms.

As posthumanist theory erodes the validity and practicability of this dichotomy, however, the age-old antagonism between science and arts is also beginning to erode. As Elaine L. Graham (2002) explains, "Science and popular culture may both be regarded as representations of the world, in that both deploy images and rhetorical conventions which do not simply report reality, but construct, mediate and constitute human experience" (14). Iconic children's and science fiction writer Ursula K. Le Guin (1996) makes a similar observation when she remarks that "A book holds words. Words hold things. They bear meanings. A novel is a medicine bundle, holding things in a particular, powerful relation to one another and to us" (153). Speculative fiction, in others words, offers to young people a means of seeing the world not as something to be fought against, conquered, and exploited, but rather as an environment peopled with living organisms, in which they are inextricably entangled and which are a source of both bounty and danger. By showing how the future might be, speculative fiction provides the blueprint for making it so in reality. It is a form of education, and a catalyst for activism, invention, and legislation. It is the stepping-stone on which young people can begin a new path into the future.

Bibliography

AbdelRahim, Layla. 2015. *Children's Literature, Domestication, and Social Foundation: Narratives of Civilization and Wilderness*. London: Routledge.
Advocates for Youth. 2019. "Our Bodies. Out Lives. Our Movement." *Advocates for Youth*, 2019. https://advocatesforyouth.org.
Alaimo, Stacy. 2014. "Oceanic Origins, Plastic Activism, and New Materialism at Sea." In *Material Ecocriticism*, edited by Serenella Iovino and Serpil Oppermann, 186–203. Bloomington: Indiana University Press.
Alaimo, Kara. 2018. "Cut back on screen time in 2019." *CNN*, December 29, 2018. https://www.cnn.com/2018/12/27/opinions/cut-back-on-screen-time-in-2019-alaimo/index.html.
Apple. 2018. "Environment." Apple website, 2018. https://www.apple.com/environment/.
Applebaum, Noga. 2010. *Representations of Technology in Science Fiction for Young People*. New York: Routledge.
Åsberg, Cecilia. 2017. "Feminist Posthumanities in the Anthropocene: Forays into the Postnatural." *Posthuman Studies*, 1(2): 185–204.
Badmington, Neil. 2000. "Introduction: Approaching Posthumanism." In *Readers in Cultural Criticism: Posthumanism*, edited by Neil Badmington, 1–10. London: Macmillan Press Ltd.
Balaji, Murali. 2013. "Thinking Dead: Our Obsession with the Undead and Its Implications." In *Thinking Dead: What the Zombie Apocalypse Means*, edited by Murali Balaji, ix–xviii. Lanham, MD: Lexington Books.
Baetens, Jan and Hugo Frey. 2014. *The Graphic Novel: An Introduction*. Cambridge: Cambridge University Press.
Bell, Alice R. 2009. "The Anachronistic Fantastic: Science, Progress and the Child in 'Post-Nostalgic Culture.'" *International Journal of Cultural Studies*, 12(1): 5–22.
Berger, James. 1999. *After the End: Representations of Post-Apocalypse*. Minneapolis, MN: University of Minnesota Press.
Bigger, Stephen, and Jean Webb. 2014. "Developing Environmental Agency and Engagement through Young People's Fiction." In *Experiencing Environment and Place through Children's Literature*, edited by Cutter-Mackenzie, Amy, Phillip Payne, and Alan Reid, 131–44. London: Routledge.
Boluk, Stephanie, and Wylie Lenz. 2011. "Introduction: Generation Z, the Age of Apocalypse." In *Generation Zombie: Essays on the Living Dead in Modern Culture*, 1–17. Jefferson, NC: McFarland and Co, Inc., Publishers.
Boyce, Frank Cottrell. 2009. "Tomorrow's Litter: Philip Reeve's Prequel to his Mortal Engines Series Impresses Frank Cottrell Boyce." *The Guardian*, June 27, 2009. https://www.theguardian.com/books/2009/jun/27/fever-crumb-philip-reeve.

Bradford, Clare. 2010. "'Everything Must Go!': Consumerism and Reader Positioning in M. T. Anderson's Feed." *Jeunesse: Young People, Texts, Cultures*, 2(2): 128–37.
Bradford, Clare, Kerry Mallan, John Stephens, and Robyn McCallum. 2008. *New World Orders in Contemporary Children's Literature: Utopian Transformations*. London: Palgrave.
Braidotti, Rosi. 2013. *The Posthuman*. Maldon, MA: Polity Press.
Broglio, R. 2017. "Romantic." In *The Cambridge Companion to Literature and the Posthuman*, edited by B. Clarke and M. Rossini, 29–40. Cambridge: Cambridge University Press.
Buckley, Catherine. 2013. "The Heart-Throb Zombie: Teen Movies and Summit Entertainment's Construction of *Warm Bodies*." In *Thinking Dead: What the Zombie Apocalypse Means*, edited by Murali Balaji, 215–26. Lanham, MD: Lexington Books.
Bugajska, Anna. 2016. "Of Neverland and Young Adult Spaces in Contemporary Dystopias." *The ESSE Messenger*, 25(1): 12–23.
Buell, Lawrence. 2001. *Writing for an Endangered World: Literature, Culture, and Environment in the US and Beyond*. Cambridge, MA: Belknap.
Bullen, Elizabeth, and Parsons, Elizabeth. 2007. "Dystopian Visions of Global Capitalism: Philip Reeve's *Mortal Engines* and M. T. Anderson's *Feed*." *Children's Literature in Education*, 38: 127–39.
Canavan, Gerry. 2010. "'We Are the Walking Dead': Race, Time, and Survival in Zombie Narrative." *Extrapolation*, 51(3): 431–53, 343.
Caradonna, Jeremy. 2014. "Is 'Progress' Good for Humanity?: Rethinking the Narrative of Economic Development, with Sustainability in Mind." *The Atlantic*, September 9, 2014. https://www.theatlantic.com/business/archive/2014/09/the-industrial-revolution-and-its-discontents/379781/.
CDC. 2018. "2018–2019 Flu Season: Flu Activity Elevated Nationally." *Centers for Disease Control and Prevention (CDC)*, December 21, 2018. https://www.cdc.gov/flu/spotlights/flu-activity-elevated.htm.
Cengiz, Oznur. 2017. "Inhuman Human Nature: Lois Lowry's The Giver." *Eurasian Journal of Social Sciences*, 5(2): 18–24.
Cheney, Jim. 1987. "Eco-Feminism and Deep Ecology." *Environmental Ethics*, 9: 115–45.
Chute, Hillary L. and Marianne DeKoven. 2006. "Introduction: Graphic Narrative." *Modern Fiction Studies*, 52(4): 767–82.
Clarke, B., and M. Rossini. 2017. "Preface." In *The Cambridge Companion to Literature and the Posthuman*, edited by B. Clarke and M. Rossini, xi–xxii. Cambridge: Cambridge University Press.
Curry, Alice. 2013. *Environmental Crisis in Young Adult Fiction: A Poetics of Earth*. New York: Palgrave Macmillan.
Curtis, Claire P. 2010. *Postapocalyptic Fiction and the Social Contract: "We'll Not Go Home Again."* New York: Lexington Books.
Davis, Rocío G. 2014. "Writing the Erasure of Emotions in Dystopian Young Adult Fiction: Reading Lois Lowry's The Giver and Lauren Oliver's Delirium." *Narrative Works*, 4(2): 48–63.
Dawson, Janis. 2006. "'Beneath their Cheerful Bunny Faces, His Slippers had Steel Toe Caps': Traction Cities, Postmodernisms, and Coming of Age in Philip Reeve's *Mortal Engines* and *Predator's Gold*." *Children's Literature in Education*, 38: 141–52.
Dean-Ruzicka. 2014. "Of Scrivens and Sparks: Girl Geniuses in Young Adult Dystopian Fiction." In *Female Rebellion in Young Adult Dystopian Fiction*, edited by Sara K. Day, Miranda A. Green-Barteet, and Amy L. Montz, 51–74. Burlington, VT: Ashgate.
Derrida, Jacques. (1997) 2008. *The Animal That Therefore I Am*. Translated by David Wills. New York: Fordham University Press.
Diedrich, Lisa. 2017. "Comics and Graphic Narratives." In *The Cambridge Companion to Literature and the Posthuman*, edited by Bruce Clarke and Manuela Rossini, 96–108. Cambridge: Cambridge University Press.
Dinerstein, Joel. 2006. "Technology and its Discontents: On the Verge of the Posthuman." *American Quarterly*, 58(3): 569–95.
Echterling, Clare. 2016. "How to Save the World and Other Lessons from Children's Environmental Literature." *Children's Literature in Education*, 47(4): 283–99.

The Economist. 2011. "The Anthropocene: A Man-Made World." *The Economist*, May 26, 2011. http://www.economist.com/node/18741749.
Ellis, Erle. 2018. *Anthropocene: A Very Short Introduction*. Oxford: Oxford University Press.
Eskey, Nicholas. 2017. "Review: Adam Rapp and Mike Cavallaro's 'Decelerate Blue' Speaks Truth for Today's 'Go-Go' World." *The Beat*, 27 February, 2017, http://www.comicsbeat.com/review-adam-rapp-and-mike-cavallaros-decelerate-blue-speaks-truth-for-todays-go-go-world/.
Estok, Simon C. 2009. "Theorizing in a Space of Ambivalent Openness: Ecocriticism and Ecophobia." *Interdisciplinary Studies in Literature and the Environment*, 16(2): 203–25.
———. 2014. "Painful Material Realities, Tragedy, Ecophobia." In *Material Ecocriticism*, edited by Serpil Oppermann and Serenella Iovino, 130–40. Bloomington: Indiana University Press.
European Youth Forum. 2017. "Promoting Youth Rights." *European Youth Forum*, 2017. https://tools.youthforum.org/youth-rights-info-tool/human-rights-and-young-people/.
Faull, Katherine M. 2014. "The Experience of the World as the Experience of the Self: Smooth Rocks in a River Archipelao." In *Re-Imagining Nature: Environmental Humanities and Ecosemiotics*, edited by Alfred Kentigern Siewers, 197–214. Lewisburg, PA: Bucknell University Press.
Federal Drug Administration (FDA). 2017. "Ritalin® and Ritalin-SR® Prescribing Information." Novartis Pharmaceuticals Corporation, last modified January 2017. https://www.accessdata.fda.gov/drugsatfda_docs/label/2017/018029s055lbl.pdf.
Featherstone, Mike. 1982. "The Body in Consumer Culture." *Theory, Culture and Society*, 1(2): 18-33.
Flanagan, Victoria. 2014. *Technology and Identity in Young Adult Fiction: The Posthuman Subject*. Houndsmills, Basingstoke: Palgrave Macmillan.
Flynn, Adam. 2014. "Solarpunk: Notes toward A Manifesto." Arizona State University Center for Science and the Imagination, September 4, 2014. http://hieroglyph.asu.edu/2014/09/solarpunk-notes-toward-a-manifesto/.
Forlini, Stefania. 2010. "Technology and Morality: The Stuff of Steampunk." *Neo-Victorian Studies*, (3)1: 72–98.
Foucault, M. 2008. *The Birth of Biopolitics: Lectures at the Collège de France 1978–1979*, translated by G. Burchell, edited by M. Senellart. New York: Palgrave Macmillan.
Fraustino, Lisa Rowe. 2011. "The Comfort of Darkness." *New York Times*, December 21, 2011. https://www.nytimes.com/roomfordebate/2010/12/26/the-dark-side-of-young-adult-fiction/the-comfort-of-darkness.
Fromm, Harold. 1996. "From Transcendence to Obsolescence: A Route Map." In *The Ecocriticism Reader: Landmarks in Literary Ecology*, edited by Cheryll Glotfelty and Harold Fromm, 30–39. Athens: University of Georgia Press.
Fukuyama, Francis. 2002. *Our Posthuman Future: Consequences of the Biotechnology Revolution*. New York: Picador.
Fuller, Steve. 2017. "The Posthuman and the Transhuman as Alternative Mappings of the Space of Political Possibility." *Posthuman Studies*, 1(2): 151–65.
Gabbatiss, Josh. 2018. "Future Technology 'Cannot Rescue' Mankind from Climate Change, Say Experts." *The Independent*, February 1, 2018. https://www.independent.co.uk/environment/future-technology-cannot-rescue-mankind-climate-change-global-warming-a8187806.html.
Garrard, G. 2012. *Ecocriticism*. London: Routledge.
de Geus, Marius. 1999. *Ecological Utopias: Envisioning the Sustainable Society*. Utrecht: International Books.
Goicoechea, María. 2008. "The Posthuman Ethos in Cyberpunk Science Fiction." *CLCWeb: Comparative Literature and Culture*, 10(4): 1–11.
Gooding, Richard. 2014. "Our Posthuman Adolescence: Dystopia, Information Technologies, and the Construction of Subjectivity in M. T. Anderson's *Feed*." In *Blast, Corrupt, Dismantle, Erase: Contemporary North American Dystopian Literature*, edited by Brett J. Grubisic, Gisele M. Baxter, and Tara Lee, 111–27. Waterloo: Wilfrid Laurier University Press.

Graham, Elaine E. 2002. *Representations of the Post/Human: Monsters, Aliens, and Others in Popular Culture*. New Brunswick, NJ: Rutgers University Press.
Graham, Ruth. 2014. "Against YA." *SLATE Book Review*, June 5, 2014. www.slate.com/articles/arts/books/2014/06/against_ya_adults_should_be_embarrassed_to_read_children_s_books.html.
Greely, Henry. 2017. "Human Reproduction in the Twenty-First Century." *Posthuman Studies*, 1(2): 205–23.
Griffin, Catherine. 2012. "Interview with Carrie Ryan, Author of the *Forest of Hands and Teeth* Series." *Pennsylvania Literary Journal*, 4(3): 33–40, 109.
Groves, Jason. 2009. "The Ecology of Invasions: Reflections from a Damaged Planet." *Global South*, 3(1): 30–41.
Gurdon, Meghan Cox. 2011. "Darkness Too Visible." *Wall Street Journal*, June 4, 2011. http://online.wsj.com/article/SB10001424052702303657404576357622592697038.html.
Halberstam, J. and I. Livingston. 1995. "Introduction." In *Posthuman Bodies*, edited by J. Halberstam and I. Livingston, 1–19. Bloomington: Indiana University Press.
Hamilton, Tyler. 2015. "Will the Rise of "Cli-Fi" Spur Youth into Climate Action?" *Corporate Knights*, 14(2): 6.
Haraway, Donna. 2016. *Manifestly Haraway*. Minneapolis: University of Minnesota Press.
Harrison, J. 2017. "Steampunk and Solarpunk: The Future Looks Familiar." *The Worrisome Words Blog*, December 7, 2017. https://theworrisomewordsblog.weebly.com/blog/steampunk-and-solarpunk-the-future-looks-familiar.
Harvey, Fiona. 2018. "Margaret Atwood: Women Will Bear Brunt of Dystopian Climate Future." *The Guardian*, May 31, 2018. https://www.theguardian.com/environment/2018/may/31/margaret-atwood-women-will-bear-brunt-of-dystopian-climate-future.
———. 2018. "Why the Next Three Months are Crucial for the Future of the Planet." *The Guardian*, October 5, 2018. https://www.theguardian.com/environment/2018/oct/05/why-the-next-four-months-are-crucial-for-future-of-planet-climate-change.
Hayles, Katherine N. 1999. *How We Became Posthuman*. Chicago: University of Chicago Press.
Heim, Joe. 2016. "On the World Stage, U.S. Students Fall Behind." *Washington Post*, December 6, 2016. https://www.washingtonpost.com/local/education/on-the-world-stage-us-students-fall-behind/2016/12/05/610e1e10-b740-11e6-a677-b608fbb3aaf6_story.html?utm_term=.87bb254ee2fc.
Hickman, Ryan. 2019. "About Ryan's Recycling Company." *Ryan's Recycling Company*, 2019. http://ryansrecycling.com/about/.
Hillard, Tom J. 2009. "'Deep into that Darkness Peering': An Essay on Gothic Nature." *Interdisciplinary Studies in Literature and Environment*, 16(4): 685–95.
Hintz, Carrie. 2002. "Monica Hughes, Lois Lowry, and Young Adult Dystopias." *The Lion and the Unicorn*, 26(2): 254–64.
Hintz, Carrie, Balaka Basu, and Katherine R. Broad. 2013. "Introduction." In *Contemporary Dystopian Fiction for Young Adults: Brave New Teenagers*, edited by Carrie Hintz, Balaka Basu, and Katherine R. Broad, 1–15. London: Routledge.
Hintz, Carrie and Ostry, Elaine. 2003. "Introduction." In *Utopian and Dystopian Writing for Children and Young Adults*, edited by Carrie Hintz and Elaine Ostry, 1–20. New York: Routledge.
Hubler, Angela. 2014. "Utopia and Anti-Utopia in Lois Lowry's and Suzanne Collins' Dystopian Fiction." In *Little Red Readings: Historical Materialist Perspectives on Children's Literature*, edited by Angela Hubler, 228–44. Jackson: University Press of Mississippi.
Huggan, Graham, and Helen Tiffin. 2010. *Postcolonial Ecocriticism: Literature, Animals, Environment*. New York: Routledge.
Hughes, James. 2017. "Algorithms and Posthuman Governance." *Posthuman Studies*, 1(2): 166–84.
Jagoda, Patrick. 2010. "Clacking Control Societies: Steampunk, History, and the Difference Engine of Escape." *Neo-Victorian Studies*, 3(1): 46–71.
Jaques, Zoe. 2015. *Children's Literature and the Posthuman*. London: Routledge.

Johns-Putra, Adeline. 2016. "Climate Change in Literature and Literary Studies: From Cli-Fi, Climate Change Theater and Ecopoetry to Ecocriticism and Climate Change Criticism." *Wiley Interdisciplinary Reviews: Climate Change*, 7(2): 266–82.
Jones, Steve. 2011. "Porn of the Dead: Necrophilia, Feminism, and Gendering the Undead." In *Zombies Are Us: Essays on the Humanity of the Walking Dead*, edited by Cory James Rushton and Christopher M. Moreman, 40–61. Jefferson, NC: McFarland and Co, Inc., Publishers.
———. 2013. "XXXombies: Economies of Desire and Disgust." In *Thinking Dead: What the Zombie Apocalypse Means*, edited by Murali Balaji, 197–214. Lanham, MD: Lexington Books.
JRRL. 2010. "What is Steampunk?" *Steampunk.com*, last modified October 13, 2010. http://www.steampunk.com/what-is-steampunk/.
Kennon, Patricia. 2017. "Monsters of Men: Masculinity and the Other in Patrick Ness's *Chaos Walking* Series." *Psychoanalytic Inquiry*, 37(1): 25–34.
Kirkus Reviews. 2016. "Decelerate Blue." *Kirkus Reviews*, December 15, 2016, 164.
Kertzer, Adrienne. 2012. "Pathways' End: The Space of Trauma in Patrick Ness's 'Chaos Walking.'" *Bookbird*, (50):1, 10–19.
Komsta, Marta. 2017. "'Men are Noisy Creachers': Dystopian Consciousness in Patrick Ness's *Chaos Walking* Trilogy." In *Explorations of Consciousness in Contemporary Fiction*, edited by Grzegorz Maziarczyk and Joanna Klara Teske, 38–55. Boston, MA: Brill Rodopi.
Kukkonen, Karin. 2013. "Space, Time, and Causality in Graphic Narratives: An Embodied Approach." In *From Comic Strips to Graphic Novels: Contributions to the Theory and History of Graphic Narrative*, edited by Daniel Stein and Jan-Noël Thon, 49–66. Berlin: De Gruyter.
Latham, Don. 2004. "Discipline and Its Discontents: A Foucauldian Reading of The Giver." *Children's Literature*, 32: 134–51.
Lauro, Sarah Juliet. 2011. "The Eco-Zombie: Environmental Critique in Zombie Fiction." In *Generation Zombie: Essays on the Living Dead in Modern Culture*, 54–66. Jefferson, NC: McFarland and Co, Inc., Publishers.
Lauro, Sarah Juliet and Karen Embry. 2008. "A Zombie Manifesto: The Non-Human Condition in the Era of Advanced Capitalism." *Boundary 2*, 35(1): 85–108.
Le Guin, Ursula K. 1996. "The Carrier Bag Theory of Fiction." In *The Ecocriticism Reader: Landmarks in Literary Ecology*, edited by Cheryll Glotfelty and Harold Fromm, 149–54. Athens: University of Georgia Press.
Lefèvre, Pascal. 2011. "Mise en Scène and Framing: Visual Storytelling in *Lone Wolf and Cub*." In *Critical Approaches to Comics: Theories and Methods*, edited by Matthew J. Smith and Randy Duncan, 71–83. New York: Routledge.
Leikam, Susanne, and Julia Leyda. 2017. "Cli-Fi in American Studies: A Research Bibliography." *American Studies Journal*, 62: DOI 10.18422/62-08.
Lenz, Millicent. 1994. "Am I My Planet's Keeper?: Dante, Ecosophy, and Children's Books." *Children's Literature Association Quarterly*, 19(4): 159–64.
Levy, Michael M. 1999. "The Young Adult Science Fiction Novel as *Bildungsroman*." In *Young Adult Science Fiction*, edited by C. W. Sullivan III, 99–118. Westport, CT: Greenwood Press.
Lowry, Lois. 1993. *The Giver*. New York: Houghton Mifflin Harcourt.
———. 2000. *Gathering Blue*. New York: Houghton Mifflin Harcourt.
———. 2004. *Messenger*. New York: Houghton Mifflin Harcourt.
———. 2012. *Son*. New York: Houghton Mifflin Harcourt.
Mączyńska, Magdalena. 2011. "History, Story, Lies: Patrick Ness's 'Chaos walking' Trilogy as a Search for Humanity, Independence and Individuality." *Kwartalnik Opolski: Organ Opolskiego Towarzystwa Przyjaciół Nauk*, 57(4): 73–84.
Markley R. 2012. "'How to go Forward': Catastrophe and Comedy in Kim Stanley Robinson's Science in the Capital Trilogy." *Configurations*, 20: 7–27.
Marx, Leo. 1967. *The Machine in the Garden: Technology and the Pastoral Ideal in America*. New York: Oxford University Press.

McCallum, Robyn. 1999. *Ideologies of Identity in Adolescent Fiction: The Dialogic Construction of Subjectivity*. New York: Garland.
———. 2009. "Ignorant Armies on a Darkling Plain: The New World Disorder of Global Economics, Environmentalism and Urbanisation in Philip Reeve's Hungry Cities." *International Research in Children's Literature*, (2)2: 210–27.
Mendlesohn, Farah. 2004. "Is There Any Such Thing as Children's Science Fiction?: A Position Piece." *Lion and the Unicorn*, 28(2): 284–313.
Morrissey, Thomas J. 2013. "Parables for the Postmodern, Post-9/11, and Posthuman World: Carrie Ryan's *Forest of Hands and Teeth* Books, M. T. Anderson's *Feed*, and Mary E. Pearson's *The Adoration of Jenna Fox*." In *Contemporary Dystopian Fiction for Young Adults: Brave New Teenagers*, edited by Carrie Hintz, Balaka Basu, and Katherine R. Broad, 189–201. New York: Routledge.
Murphy, P. D. 2014. "Pessimism, Optimism, Human Inertia, and Anthropogenic Climate Change." *Interdisciplinary Studies in Literature and the Environment*, 21: 149–63.
NAEP. 2018. "How Did U.S. Students Perform on the Most Recent Assessments?" *National Assessment of Educational Progress (NAEP)*, 2018. https://www.nationsreportcard.gov.
NASA. 2018. "NASA Strategic Plan, 2018." National Aeronautics and Space Administration (NASA), 2018. https://www.nasa.gov/sites/default/files/atoms/files/nasa_2018_strategic_plan.pdf.
Ness, Patrick. 2008. *The Knife of Never Letting Go*. Somerville, MA: Candlewick Press.
———. 2009. *The Ask and the Answer*. Somerville, MA: Candlewick Press.
———. 2010. *Monsters of Men*. Somerville, MA: Candlewick Press.
Nodelman, Perry. 1985. "Out There in Children's Science Fiction: Forward into the Past." *Science Fiction Studies*, 12: 285–95.
———. 2012. "Picture Book Guy Looks at Comics: Structural Differences in Two Kinds of Visual Narrative." *Children's Literature Association Quarterly*, 37(4): 436–44.
NYRA. 2018. "Voting Age Status Report." *National Youth Rights Association (NYRA)*, 2018. https://www.youthrights.org/issues/voting-age/voting-age-status-report/.
Obordo, Rachel. 2018. "'Social Media Has Poisoned Us': Young Britons on Why They Are Unhappy." *The Guardian*, April 9, 2018. https://www.theguardian.com/society/2018/apr/09/social-media-has-poisoned-us-young-brits-on-why-they-are-unhappy.
Onion, Rebecca. 2008. "Reclaiming the Machine: An Introductory Look at Steampunk in Everyday Practice." *Neo-Victorian Studies*, 1(1): 138–63.
Ostry, Elaine. 2004. "Is He Still Human? Are you?: Young Adult Science Fiction in the Posthuman Age." *The Lion and the Unicorn*, 28(2): 222–46.
———. 2013. "On the Brink: The Role of Young Adult Culture in Environmental Degradation." In *Contemporary Dystopian Fiction for Young Adults: Brave New Teenagers*, edited by Carrie Hintz, Balaka Basu, and Katherine R. Broad, 101–14. New York: Routledge.
Owens, Connor. 2016. "What is Solarpunk?" *Solarpunk Anarchist*, May 27, 2016. https://solarpunkanarchists.com/2016/05/27/what-is-solarpunk/.
Oxford English Dictionary Online. 2017. "Progress." Oxford English Dictionary Online, 2017. http://www.oed.com/view/Entry/152236?rskey=d0apmJ&result=1&isAdvanced=false#eid.
Oziewicz, Marek C. 2015. *Justice in Young Adult Speculative Fiction*: A Cognitive Reading. New York: Routledge.
Ozog, Cassie. 2013. "Zombies and the Modern American Family: Surviving the Destruction of Traditional Society in *Zombieland* (2009)." In *Thinking Dead: What the Zombie Apocalypse Means*, edited by Murali Balaji, 127–40. Lanham, MD: Lexington Books.
Parrinder, Patrick. 2001. *Learning from Other Worlds: Estrangement, Cognition, and the Politics of Science Fiction and Utopia*. Liverpool: Liverpool University Press.
Pettit, Michael. 2013. "Becoming Glandular: Endocrinology, Mass Culture, and Experimental Lives in the Interwar Age." *The American Historical Review*, 118(4): 1052–76.
Plumwood, Val. 2003. "Decolonizing Relationships with Nature." In *Decolonizing Nature: Strategies for Conservation in a Post-Colonial Era*, edited by William H. Adams and Martin Mulligan, 51–78. London: Earthscan.

Pollock, Greg. 2011. "Undead is the New Green: Zombies and Political Ecology." In *Zombies Are Us: Essays on the Humanity of the Walking Dead*, edited by Cory James Rushton and Christopher M. Moreman, 169–82. Jefferson, NC: McFarland and Co, Inc., Publishers.
Rapp, Adam, and Mike Cavallaro. 2017. *Decelerate Blue*. New York: First Second.
Reese, Sarah. 2014. "Call and Response: The Question of the Human/Non-Human Encounter." In *Re-Imagining Nature: Environmental Humanities and Ecosemiotics*, edited by Alfred Kentigern Siewers, 237–48. Lewisburg: Bucknell University Press.
Reeve, Philip. 2001. *Mortal Engines*. London: Scholastic Inc.
———. 2003. *Predator's Gold*. London: Scholastic Inc.
———. 2005. *Infernal Devices*. London: Scholastic Inc.
———. 2006. *A Darkling Plain*. London: Scholastic Inc.
———. 2009. *Fever Crumb*. London: Scholastic Inc.
———. 2010. *A Web of Air*. London: Scholastic Inc.
———. 2011a. *Scrivener's Moon*. London: Scholastic Inc.
———. 2011b. "The Worst is Yet to Come: Dystopias are Grim, Humorless, and Hopeless— and Incredibly Appealing to Today's Teens." *School Library Journal*, 57(8): 34–36.
Reid, Roddey. 1995. "'Death of the Family,' or, Keeping Human Beings Human." In *Posthuman Bodies*, edited by J. Halberstam and I. Livingston, 177–99. Bloomington: Indiana University Press.
Republic of the Bees. 2017. "From Steampunk to Solarpunk." *Republic of the Bees*, May 27, 2008. https://republicofthebees.wordpress.com/2008/05/27/from-steampunk-to-solarpunk/.
Rippl, Gabriele, and Lukas Etter. 2013. "Intermediality, Transmediality, and Graphic Narrative." In *From Comic Strips to Graphic Novels: Contributions to the Theory and History of Graphic Narrative*, edited by Daniel Stein and Jan-Noël Thon, 191–217. Berlin: De Gruyter.
Ross, Andrew. 1999. "The Social Claim on Urban Ecology." In *The Nature of Cities: Ecocriticism and Urban Environments*, edited by Michael Bennett and David W. Teague, 15–30. Tuscon: The University of Arizona Press.
Rushton, Cory James and Christopher M. Moreman. 2011. "Introduction: They're Us: Zombies, Humans / Humans, Zombies." In *Zombies Are Us: Essays on the Humanity of the Walking Dead*, edited by Cory James Rushton and Christopher M. Moreman, 1–10. Jefferson, NC: McFarland and Co, Inc., Publishers.
Rutherford, Jennifer. 2013. *Zombies*. New York: Routledge.
Rutsky, R. L. 2017. "Technology." In *The Cambridge Companion to Literature and the Posthuman*, edited by Bruce Clarke and Manuela Rossini, 182–95. Cambridge: Cambridge University Press.
Ryan, Carrie. 2009. *The Forest of Hands and Teeth*. New York: Random House.
———. 2010. *The Dead-Tossed Waves*. New York: Random House.
———. 2011. *The Dark and Hollow Places*. New York: Random House.
Sambell, Kay. 2004. "Carnivalizing the Future: A New Approach to Theorizing Childhood and Adulthood in Science Fiction for Young Readers." *The Lion and the Unicorn*, 28(2): 247–67.
Sawers, Naarah. 2009. "Capitalism's New Handmaiden: The Biotechnical World Negotiated Through Children's Fiction." *Children's Literature in Education*, 40: 169–79.
Seaman, Myra J. 2007. "Becoming More (than) Human: Affective Posthumanisms, Past and Future." *Journal of Narrative Theory*, 37: 246–75.
Shusterman, Neal. 2007. *Unwind*. New York: Simon and Schuster.
———. 2012. *Unwholly*. New York: Simon and Schuster.
———. 2013. *Unsouled*. New York: Simon and Schuster.
———. 2014. *Undivided*. New York: Simon and Schuster.
Siewers, Alfred Kentigern. 2014. "Introduction." In *Re-Imagining Nature: Environmental Humanities and Ecosemiotics*, edited by Alfred Kentigern Siewers, 1–41. Lewisburg, PA: Bucknell University Press.
Silverman, Rosa. 2018. "The Real Reason Today's Children are so Unhappy." *The Telegraph*, February 8, 2018. https://www.telegraph.co.uk/family/parenting/real-reason-todays-children-unhappy/.

Sisk, David W. 1997. *Transformations of Language in Modern Dystopias*. Westport, CT: Greenwood Press.
Snell, Heather. 2016. "Ready Made for the Market: Producing Charitable Subjects in Dystopian and Voluntourist Young Adult Novels." *Papers: Explorations into Children's Literature*, 24(2): 96–126.
Soper, Kate. 1995. *What is Nature?: Culture, Politics, and the Non-Human*. Oxford: Blackwell.
Sophia, Zoe. 1984. "Exterminating Fetuses: Abortion, Disarmament, and the Sexo-Semiotics of Extraterrestrialism." *Diacritics*, 14: 47–59.
Sorensen, Leif. 2014. "Against the Post-Apocalyptic: Narrative Closure in Colson Whitehead's *Zone One*." *Contemporary Literature*, 55(3): 559–92.
Spisak, A. 2017. "*Decelerate Blue* by Adam Rapp." *Bulletin of the Center for Children's Books*, 70(6): 278.
Stephens, John. 1992. *Language and Ideology in Children's Fiction*. London: Longman.
———. 2010. "Impartiality and Attachment: Ethics and Ecopoesis in Children's Narrative Texts." *International Research in Children's Literature*, 3(2): 205–16.
Stewart, Susan Louise. 2007. "A Return to Normal: Lois Lowry's The Giver." *The Lion and the Unicorn*, 31(1): 21–35.
Sturgeon, Noeil. 2009. *Environmentalism in Popular Culture: gender, Race, Sexuality, and the Politics of the Natural*. Tucson: University of Arizona Press.
Sun, Lena H. 2018. "Percentage of Young U.S. Children Who Don't Receive Any Vaccines Has Quadrupled Since 2001." *Washington Post*, October 11, 2018. https://www.washingtonpost.com/national/health-science/percentage-of-young-us-children-who-dont-receive-any-vaccines-has-quadrupled-since-2001/2018/10/11/4a9cca98-cd0d-11e8-920f-dd52e1ae4570_story.html?noredirect=on&utm_term=.7156927b32b0.
Tarr, Anita, and Donna R. White. 2018. "Introduction." In *Posthumanism in Young Adult Fiction: Finding Humanity in a Posthuman World*, edited by Anita Tarr and Donna R. White, ix–xxiv. Jackson: University Press of Mississippi.
Teleky, Richard. 2015. "The Cyborgs Next Door: Thinking about Posthuman Studies." *Queen's Quarterly*, 122(4): 506–17.
Trites, Roberta Seelinger. 1997. *Waking Sleeping Beauty: Feminist Voices in Children's Novels*. Iowa City: University of Iowa Press.
———. 2014. *Literary Conceptualizations of Growth: Metaphors and Cognition in Adolescent Literature*. Philadelphia: John Benjamins Publishing Company.
Tuhus-Dubrow, Rebecca. 2013. "Cli-Fi: Birth of a Genre." *Dissent*, 60(3): 58–61.
Tulane University. 2019. "Food Deserts in America (Infographic)." *Tulane University School of Social Work*, 2019, https://socialwork.tulane.edu/blog/food-deserts-in-america.
US Department of Education. 2019. "Science, Technology, Engineering and Math: Education for Global Leadership." *US Department of Education*, 2019. https://www.ed.gov/stem.
Vint, Sherryl. 2007. *Bodies of Tomorrow: Technology, Subjectivity, Science Fiction*. Toronto: University of Toronto Press.
Wasson, Sara. 2015. "Scalpel and Metaphor: The Ceremony of Organ Harvest in Gothic Science Fiction." *Gothic Studies*, 17(1): 104–23.
Webb, Jean. 2013. "Challenging Teenage and Young Adult Reading in the UK: The Novels of Philip Reeve." *Tema y Variaciones de Literatura*, 41: 155–71.
Week Staff. 2018. "Rise of the Ticks." *The Week*, May 19, 2018. https://theweek.com/articles/773703/rise-ticks.
Wheeler, Pat. 2013. "'Another Generation Cometh': Apocalyptic Endings and New Beginnings in Science Fictional New London(s)." *Critical Survey*, 25(2): 57–70.
White Jr., Lynn. 1996. "The Historical Roots of Our Ecological Crisis." In *The Ecocriticism Reader: Landmarks in Literary Ecology*, edited by Cheryll Glotfelty and Harold Fromm, 3–14. Athens: University of Georgia Press.
WHO. 2018. "How Air Pollution is Destroying our Health." *World Health Organization (WHO)*, October 29, 2018. https://www.who.int/air-pollution/news-and-events/how-air-pollution-is-destroying-our-health.

Wohlmann, Anita, and Ruth Steinberg. 2016. "Rewinding Frankenstein and the Body-Machine: Organ Transplantation in the Dystopian Young Adult Fiction Series Unwind." *Medical Humanities*, 42(4): e26–e30.

Wolfe, Cary. 2010. *What is Posthumanism?* Minneapolis: University of Minnesota Press.

———. 2014. "Learning from Temple Grandin, or, Animal Studies, Disability Studies, and Who Comes after the Subject." In *Re-Imagining Nature: Environmental Humanities and Ecosemiotics*, edited by Alfred Kentigern Siewers, 91–108. Lewisburg, PA: Bucknell University Press.

Wright, Pam and Bob Henson. 2018. "Earth Day 2018: The 10 Most Pressing Environmental Concerns Facing Our Planet—And Rays of Hope for Each." *The Weather Channel*, April 20, 2018. https://weather.com/science/environment/news/2018-04-18-earth-day-2018-10-concerning-things-future-of-planet.

YPR. 2019. "Young People for Refugees." *Facebook*, 2019. https://www.facebook.com/yprbendigo/.

YPTE. 2018. "Recycling." *Young People's Trust for the Environment (YPTE)*, 2018. https://ypte.org.uk/factsheets/recycling/rubbish#section.

Zipes, Jack. 2003. "Foreword: Utopia, Dystopia, and the Quest for Hope." In *Utopian and Dystopian Writing for Children and Young Adults*, edited by Carrie Hintz and Elaine Ostry, ix–xi. New York: Routledge.

Index

abortion, 53, 67–68
animals, 5, 30, 42, 44, 47, 54, 59–63, 68, 77, 89, 108–110, 113
animal studies, 13–14, 53–54, 59–60
Anthropocene, 3–5, 15, 104, 106
apocalypse, 3, 6, 12, 19–20, 28–31, 87–101, 121
The Ask and the Answer, 56, 62, 64

bildungsroman, 6, 9, 12, 14, 20–25, 36, 46, 69–74, 78–80, 91, 97–102, 119
biotechnology, 36, 37–39, 70, 72, 76, 78, 108–110, 125

capitalism, 14–15, 16, 44, 67–82, 84, 95, 103, 110, 113, 115–116
Cavallaro, Mike. *See Decelerate Blue*
Chaos Walking, 13–14, 51–66
children, 9–10, 24, 27–28, 37, 39, 40–41, 54, 67–68, 72–74, 75, 77, 120, 121. *See also* reproduction
civilization, 2, 4–5, 9, 12, 20, 25, 29–30, 31–33, 36, 39, 40, 41, 43–49, 55, 68, 84, 85, 89–90, 92, 105, 106, 121, 124
cli-fi, 104–105, 111
climate change, 4, 30–31, 75, 82, 104–105, 111, 120, 121, 123
consumerism, 67–69, 73, 74, 75, 77, 81, 82, 83, 87, 106, 107–110, 112, 113, 116, 117
cyclical time, 84–87, 93–101

The Dark and Hollow Place, 22, 24, 26, 28, 29–30, 31, 32
A Darkling Plain, 89, 95, 100–101
The Dead-Tossed Waves, 22, 23, 26, 28, 29–30, 31, 32
Decelerate Blue, 16, 103–118

ecophobia, 28, 30
ecosemiotics, 63
education, 71, 122–123, 124–125
environment, hostile, 2–3, 4, 12–16, 20, 27, 28–32, 36, 37–48, 52, 63–64, 66, 68–74, 84, 86, 87, 88, 89–90, 92, 95, 97, 104–106, 119–124
evolution, 3, 7, 8, 14–15, 30–31, 33, 38, 41–43, 47, 51–52, 54, 64, 65–66, 79, 83–98

family, 3, 12, 20, 21, 24–28, 43, 75, 81, 100. *See also* children; reproduction
Fever Crumb, 15–16, 83–102
The Forest of Hands and Teeth, 12, 19–33
frontier myth, 51–52, 65

Gathering Blue, 43, 45, 46
The Giver, 12–13, 35–49
graphic novel, 1, 16, 103, 105–106, 108–110, 114–117

humanism: definition of, 4–5, 9, 35, 69; humanist hero, 13, 24, 46–49, 58–59,

137

65, 67, 69–72, 78, 80, 97–98;
neoliberalism, 44, 51, 67–82; reason, 4, 5–7, 37, 41, 43, 52–53, 54, 59–60, 62, 65

infection, 19–28
Infernal Devices, 95, 99–100
information era, 5, 103
information technology, 8, 104

The Knife of Never Letting Go, 55–57, 60, 61–62, 63–64

language, 13, 51–66, 84
linear time, 84–87, 98
Lowry, Lois, 12–13, 35–49. *See also Gathering Blue*; *The Giver*; *Messenger*; *Son*

Messenger, 44–46, 48
Monsters of Men, 56, 57–58, 60, 62, 64, 65
Mortal Engines, 15–16, 83–102

Ness, Patrick, 13, 51–66. *See also The Ask and the Answer*; *Chaos Walking*; *The Knife of Never Letting Go*; *Monsters of Men*

organ transplantation, 71–72, 76, 81

political activism, 122–123
postcolonialism, 53–54
posthumanism: definition of, 2, 7; posthuman embodiment, 5, 7, 15, 20–28, 52, 78–80, 98, 124
Predator's Gold, 95, 97
progress, 4, 11, 12–13, 14–15, 51, 83–102, 104, 112, 115, 118

Rapp, Adam. *See Decelerate Blue*

recycling, 74–78
Reeve, Philip, 15, 83–102. *See also A Darkling Plain*; *Fever Crumb*; *Infernal Devices*; *Mortal Engines*; *Predator's Gold*; *Scrivener's Moon*; *A Web of Air*
reproduction, 6, 12, 21, 23, 24–25, 27, 40–41
Ryan, Carrie, 12, 19–33. *See also The Dead-Tossed Waves*; *The Dark and Hollow Place*; *Forest of Hands and Teeth*

Shusterman, Neal, 14, 67–82. *See also Undivided*; *Unsouled*; *Unwind*; *Unwholly*
science, credibility of, 12, 52, 125
Scrivener's Moon, 89–90
sex. *See* reproduction
solarpunk, 105–106, 110–116
Son, 40–42, 44–46, 48
space exploration, 51–52, 63
steampunk, 93–97, 98, 102n2, 110–111

technology, 67, 68, 69–70, 79, 81, 83–102, 103–118, 123–124

Undivided, 77, 79
Unsouled, 76, 77, 79, 80
Unwholly, 72–73, 75–76, 79
Unwind, 13–14, 67–82
urban development, 86–87, 90
utopia, 3–4, 5–6, 9, 11, 12, 39, 66, 67, 83, 110

visual narrative, 110–116

A Web of Air, 95, 95–97

zombies, 19–33

About the Author

Jennifer Harrison is an instructor of English at East Stroudsburg University, where she teaches English literature, composition, and creative writing. She earned her PhD in children's literature from the University of Wales, Aberystwyth. Jen's research focuses on three primary areas in the field of children's and YA literature: environmental studies, posthumanism, and materialism; she is particularly interested in children's nonfiction, children's publishing, and the intersections between fiction and social media. She is an editor for the peer-reviewed journal *Jeunesse*, as well as a long-time reviewer for the review website *The Children's Book Review*. She also produces an academic blog on the subject of children's literature, entitled *The Worrisome Words Blog*.

www.ingramcontent.com/pod-product-compliance
Lightning Source LLC
Chambersburg PA
CBHW050910300426
44111CB00010B/1455